THE DARLINGTONS

THE

DARLINGTONS

by Sylvia Brooke

SEARS READERS CLUB · CHICAGO

*This is a special edition published exclu-
sively for the members of SEARS READERS
CLUB, P. O. Box 6570A, Chicago 80, Illi-
nois. It was originally published by Farrar,
Straus and Company.*

I took from the chimney shelf a detached and ancient Diary.
It was my Diary.
Brushing the cobwebs from the rambling pages I began to read.
It was a Diary of true and false virtues,
Of selfishness and unselfishness,
Cruelty and pleasure.
The value of love was there
And the futility of hate.
When I had finished reading it
I was ashamed of what I had written
And desolate of the secrets I had laid bare.
Hastily I put it back where I had found it
And left it amongst the cobwebs and the dust.
But after many moons here it is.

SYLVIA BROOKE

THE DARLINGTONS

I

I was sitting on the window ledge weeping and rocking myself to and fro so that the tears sprinkled down my cheeks and past my trembling mouth onto the doll that lay stretched across my knees. As they ran down my face I caught some of them with the edge of my tongue and wondered why tears were so salt.

I had good reason to be miserable for all gladness had been taken from me. My head was sick and my heart faint with fear of the world.

The world seemed to have no foundation. I did not seem to belong to any part of it. It was an evil world and there was nothing to be gained from it but tears. It was evil and ugly as a toad, so Henrietta said, and I half believed her.

Henrietta said a lot of things; she liked the sound of her own voice, admonishing and laying down the law. She liked the sound of herself saying, "Life is like this," and "Life is like that." She had a lust for preaching and was enthralled by the sense of her own power.

Papa said the world was made out of the hearts of men and women and that their life stories were on God's record. He said that if you went through your span of years and left no story then God was tempted to place you upon earth once more to try again. For the world was a pageant, so Papa said, for God to look at. He had kings and clowns, noblemen and dustmen

3

who all had a part to play. If you came upon a man who had lingering recollections, that man had most assuredly lived before and died and been driven back to live again. I did not want to live again. I wanted to die and go to Heaven and remain there.

Even Mamma said the world was full of iniquity and that it had a garden of weeds spread across its loveliness with corrupted roots, and the evil of its doings lay upon people as a load.

But Papa laughed in his carefree way and declared that he himself was one of the corrupted roots Mamma was referring to and that it was his deeds that lay heavily upon her.

They would not leave the world alone, neither Papa nor Mamma nor Henrietta; they tore at it like dogs picking the best meat from a bone. They growled and snarled over it and destroyed it.

You could not argue with either Papa or Mamma; they were so sure of themselves and they left no chain of reasoning. You could not argue with Henrietta either, for she would not tolerate any other opinion than her own.

It was mostly because of Henrietta I had made up my mind to die. It was because of my dear sister that at the age of twelve I had made a covenant with death and an agreement with God.

Henrietta would play little pranks upon me in the daytime, but it was worse in the evenings when she concealed herself in dark corners and bounced upon me with a ghostly scream, or moaned from behind some heavy curtain. She loved to watch me tremble and quake with fear; my fluttering trepidation nourished the latent cruelty which lies so often in a child.

It was as much my fault as hers, for I played into her hands. If only I had been violent and bold and defied her appetite for harrowing my soul; laughed at her and paid her back, tear for tear, torture for torture.

"If I commit suicide," I said to God, "that will be my story and Your record of my life, so there will be no need for You to send me back to live again."

"If I commit suicide," I said to myself, "Henrietta will be sorry."

The tainted secrets Henrietta had poured into my ears and the things she had told me had given me an excess of fear that never left me. I wanted this to be my last evening upon earth, and already I could feel the grave falling upon my small thin shoulders and wrapping me round in its dust.

Nobody in our large house knew I was going to die; how could they know? For it must be distinctly understood it was a solution of my own making and no one else's. What I was about about to do belonged privately and exclusively to me and was the outcome of prolonged thought and meditation.

Papa and Mamma would be sorry.

Henrietta might even shed a tear and the servants grieve and wish they had been kinder to me.

This was the very thing I craved for, this playing upon human sympathy.

Then there was our bailiff, Mr. Bemrose. What would he think and how would he feel? Would he remember and regret what he had done? Would Henrietta remember and regret that she had told Papa and Mamma about us?

If only there had been someone besides Henrietta for me to ask, "What do Mr. Bemrose's fondling and caressing and

5

broad free handling of me mean? Why do his kisses bruise and scorch my mouth?" But there was only Henrietta, and I was obliged to tell her because of the terror and distaste I nursed within me.

Of course she made it worse; I might have known she would. She always wanted to make things worse for me. She made the world go round in my head. She sent it leaping and flying like a ball of fire in my brain. It broke my slumbers, this mad inhuman world of hers, there was so much violence in wickedness.

Mr. Bemrose was wicked and his kisses were a sin. I did not want to live after what my sister told me, there was no reason for living if all men were like that.

With both Papa and Mamma the most approved person round and about White Orchard Manor was their bailiff, for in their unseeing eyes he could do no wrong. He knew so well how to creep into everyone's good graces—he was a honey-mouthed parasite clinging to our home. I thought him wonderful, for he was tall and slim and there was gold in his hair and in the little whiskers that framed his pallid face. I would watch him go moping through the house and want to help him, and sometimes when he looked up from his work and smiled at me in his wan pathetic way, the tears would fill my eyes. I used to follow him about the garden like a little dog, or sit beside him with adoring homage.

It did not offend me when Mr. Bemrose called me a thick-skulled hoddy doddy and sometimes pulled my hair. He was the only human being who had ever taken notice of me, outside the family, and he did not seem to mind me running at his heels. Sometimes he would go with me and let me feed the chickens or collect the brown eggs out of the nests.

"How does a cow make its milk?" I asked him once.

Mr. Bemrose gazed at me with his melancholy blue eyes. "By eating grass I suppose," he replied.

"If I eat grass then will I have milk?"

"Miss Susan, why do you ask such silly questions?"

"But it is not silly, Mr. Bemrose, I want to know."

"Well, I am not telling you," replied the bailiff.

Then another day I would say to him, "Does a cloud weigh anything, Mr. Bemrose, and is there really a man in the moon?"

"Of course not, Miss Susan, it is only an old saying."

I picked one of the brown eggs from the basket and gazed at it carefully.

"Can you lay an egg, Mr. Bemrose?"

"How could I, you ninny."

"Why not?"

"Because I am a man and men do not lay eggs."

"But if you had been a woman could you have laid one then? Can I lay an egg when I am grown up?"

This was a question even Mr. Bemrose did not care to answer.

"You ask the silliest things, Miss Susan," he said petulantly, "and you are getting on my nerves."

"But, dear Mr. Bemrose, be patient with me, tell me this one thing—where do babies come from if not from an egg?"

"Oh, they just come," replied Mr. Bemrose evasively and left it at that. I wondered what I would do if a baby "just came" to me.

And all the time Mr. Bemrose was becoming more and more important to himself and feeling his feet; and the more confident he became the more cunning he was, knowing and acquainting himself with all the things that drew me to him. He was artful and contriving and sly as an insidious fox. Moreover, he had now acquired a small and awkward moustache which looked as if it had been thrown onto his face from a long distance, there to balance precariously upon his upper lip. It was unbelievable the difference this slight growth made to his character; he began to assume a certain insolence and flippant bearing that exasperated the whole household. Yet I still thought him wonderful and took his effrontery for manliness. He was my knight in shining armour, a paragon to dream about.

Once, after I had been gazing at him for a while in solemn admiration, he said to me: "You like me, do you not, Miss Susan?"

"Oh yes, Mr. Bemrose, yes indeed I do."

"And I like you in spite of your childish ways; you have been kind to me since I have been here. I wonder why."

"Kind! When I ask you all those questions?"

"My fireside is a bare one, Miss Susan, and I am not happy there. My home is not precious to me for I feel my parents do not want me."

"Poor, poor Mr. Bemrose."

"What would you do if I was to go away?"

"You mean leave White Orchard Manor?"

"Yes."

I clasped my hands passionately, my eyes brimming over with tears.

"I think I would die," I murmured.

He leaned back stroking his moustache and smiling; he really had a most ingratiating smile.

8

"I did not know you cared for me so much," he said.

"I hope you will live with us always and always, Mr. Bemrose, and for ever."

"Thank you, Miss Susan, that is very good of you I am sure."

"Now you are making fun of me."

"Indeed I am not. I am most serious, I assure you."

"Do you like being a bailiff, Mr. Bemrose, I mean do you like being here working for Papa and Mamma?"

"I am well situated, Miss Susan, and it suits my purpose."

"What is your purpose? What would you like to be most in all the world?"

"I would like his Lordship's riches and his house and all his worldly goods."

"Including us?"

"Including you."

"Do you like my sister, Mr. Bemrose?"

"I am not paid to either like or dislike. I am not hired to have an opinion."

"But you are my friend, you can say anything to me."

"I am proud to hear you say so, Miss Susan, extremely proud."

How little I knew what lay beneath that smooth and plausible manner.

There was a wood behind our orchard, a piece of the forest sliced off and isolated and forced into the garden. A thin path threaded through it made of cinders. I was afraid of this wood because it was there that Mr. Bemrose had concealed himself, and from its thick undergrowth had leapt at me, clutching me in a violent embrace. It was there he had kissed me and I had felt the new hairs on his chin tearing my face.

Ever since then the wood had assumed monstrous propor-

9

tions, and there were weird shadows in it and the noise of wings flapping through the trees. It was a wicked wood trying to close in on me as Mr. Bemrose had. The smell of the damp grass and tall ferns would stifle me. With my heart panting and pounding I would think, "Suppose I fall, then Mr. Bemrose will find me and if he touches me again I shall die."

That was how much I exaggerated the facts of life. All this foolishness in the heart of a child who knew a little about everything but not enough.

And so it had gone on until the fateful evening when I had told Henrietta about Mr. Bemrose and his kisses, and she had gone straight to Papa and Mamma and repeated all that I had said to her so that Mr. Bemrose had been sent out of the house and I up to my room. I could not forget his face as he passed me on the stairs and the look of hatred that glared out of his eyes.

Henrietta said it was all my fault and that I must have encouraged Mr. Bemrose in some way. "A man will go wenching if you give him so much as a look, I know," she said. "And you with your calf's eyes never leaving his face—what else was the poor creature to do?"

"But he was my friend, Henrietta."

"Fiddlesticks," she retorted. "Even you must know better than that, Susan. There is no such thing as friendship between a maid and a man."

"What is there then?"

How I wished afterwards I had not asked her that.

Outside my window it was stars and snow. It was as if God had spread a white carpet so that the ghosts of His dead could walk unseen. It was as if He had commanded the skies to lay a bed for me to die upon.

Pressing my diminutive nose against the window pane I could just see the turn of the road. I could hear the sound of a horse trotting and the rumble of a chaise from a long way off. Sometimes the lamps of the chaise were visible like scant red coals in the dark night.

I looked at the leafless trees with their forsaken boughs like naked arms stretched out for pity. The little uppermost branches glistened like diamonds and shivered in the frozen air. I looked at the turret outside my bedroom window where in the summer I grew flowers. I loved most the hasty flowers, the foolish ones that blossomed in the snow instead of waiting within the warm bosom of the earth.

I sat and thought and thought, and the more I deliberated the more aware I became of confused voices in my head and incoherent whisperings.

First Papa, "What do you want to die for when life is so good to you?"

Then Mamma, "Foolish child, do you not know when you are well off?"

Henrietta's curling lips saying, "Poor Susan, she made so much of everything, especially the bad. She did not know there was plenty of good in the world; poor Susan, it is better after all that she is dead."

And last of all Mr. Bemrose, "I have been misled by your attentions, Miss Susan; was that my fault or yours?"

The turret was to be my bier. It was there I was to lie with my small bare body wrapped in snow. I would sleep there all through the night. I would die there outside on the turret.

The servants would find me in the morning and stoop over me peering and prying. They would scoop the snow from my closed eyelids and smooth it from my hair. They would murmur and whisper and say, "Whatever made the child do such a thing?" And Mrs. Trouncer would wipe the drip from her long nose with the back of her hand, for Mrs. Trouncer always had a perpetual drip on the end of her nose like the tap in the kitchen sink.

God would say, "It is all well with you now, little girl, for you have made a story." God would be pleased with me and let me stay in peace.

Henrietta would be forbidden to see me after I was dead and I wanted her to see me; I wanted her to know what she had done.

Both Papa and Mamma would be bowed down with remorse; they would ask one another questions as to whose fault it had been. It would never occur to either of them that it was their darling Henrietta's fault, and how much Mr. Bemrose had to do with it as well.

Mamma would blame Papa, but Papa would say, "Susan made the sad mistake of taking herself too seriously; she was never out of her own thoughts; there was always too much 'I am this' and 'I am that' about Susan."

And Mamma would say, "She was always very ignorant and backward for her age."

And all the time I would be lying there dead and yet in some strange way able to hear their argument.

I was in that stage of childish confusion when the passionate desire for a bedside scene and the weeping remorse of relations had become an obsession, that stage between infancy and adolescence when I was for ever taking life uneasily instead of submitting to its natural sequence. I did not go out enough in the fresh air, neglecting my body for the tending of my mind. I was thin and white and there were spots under my skin and a strange tenderness about my little breasts. I read books of an unfortunate selection, cruel, embittering and unsavoury. Of course I did not understand the purport of what I was reading, but the words and sentences clamoured in my brain.

Henrietta and I lived too much alone, at least I lived too much alone with Henrietta. Papa and Mamma believed in the strictest isolation during their daughter's infancy lest too much liberty should corrupt them. The irony of this did not escape me, considering what Henrietta knew and taught me about old and evil things; considering how I travelled with Dante and sank into the depths of Zola, fearfully creeping along those raw experienced pages, unable to tear myself away from gloom and terror.

Our parents were wholly ignorant of our characters and they were at that time almost strangers to us. We were together with them and yet ununited. We were like trees in a little forest that had been planted wide apart so that their branches should not touch when they grew old.

Our rooms were on the top floor of this large and lovely house, and I was too terrified to venture after dark along the ill-lit corridors because of Henrietta. We had little attics close up to the gabled roof, mean and shabby chambers they were with scant plain furniture. The beds of well-worn mahogany creaked and set our teeth on edge as we turned in them. The latticed windows were small and confining, but fortunately there were

13

skylights so that from our beds we could see the stars flickering like jewels in the velvet of the night.

A strange odour like dying leaves pervaded the dusty draperies, and there was no possible manner of warming the rooms or drying the damp in them. Round the sloping walls were long cupboards built between beams, and both Henrietta and I had wooden caskets wherein we kept our meagre clothing. They were not exactly gloomy, these two rooms, but neither were they gay. The furniture was too low to crawl under, and the closet too narrow to stand up in. At least that was a comfort to me when darkness fell, for there was no hunting beneath the bed and opening and closing of doors, and no fearful peerings into twisted corners. There was nothing that could make weird shapes when the shadows got full possession of my room, and yet it always seemed strange to me how ceilings changed at night. In the daytime they were smooth and white with the plaster laid on as even as a sheet; but at night forbidding- and evil-favoured shapes emerged out of the crevices and beams. If there was a streak of light under the door the ceiling would be sure to catch it and it would become monstrously proportioned. The oak beams would be like crooked ghostly arms holding the ceiling carelessly as if at any moment they might drop it. If there was a moon the furniture threw shadows across and upward, and the smooth ceiling became a broken sky of lumps and rounds and squares I could not account for. It became a map of ugliness, uncanny and repellent, so that I lay there wondering if Henrietta had played some trick upon me and planted some gruesome demon in my room.

When the woodwork cracked I would always make sure that it made the same sound in the same place; had there been any other sound I would have cowered under the bedclothes with my knees knocking together, praying to God it was no bogey. For Henrietta said there were indeed such things as bogeys and fiendish elves who only visited little girls with long black hair and frightened faces. To prevent these spectral intrusions it was necessary, she said, to have rich red hair like she had and a bold face like she had and to be free of fear. But how could I be free of fear when she did all she could to raise in me the most deadly apprehension, and to harrow my soul and chill my spine with her tales of astounding horror and malevolence.

Henrietta said that the roar of thunder was in reality the rumble of the wheels of Satan's wagons taking frightened little girls and boys who had not loved their sisters to hell, so that whenever there was a storm I imagined this procession of wagons crossing the sky full to the brim with blenched and trembling children. Whenever I saw the clouds gathering I would go to Henrietta and tell her how fond I was of her, and I would do little things for her all day until the storm was over.

It was Mamma's idea that we should sleep in these lonely attics, for she believed in rigorous simplicity. "It is a mortal sin to mis-spend," she would say, "and waste is an evil in the sight of the Lord and the Queen. The Lord gives in order that we should have plenty, but not to cast it neglectfully and without thought upon ourselves."

Mamma considered that the greatest care should be entertained in the fulfilment of this duty. Pity the poor by all means but with reasonable discretion. It should always be remembered there was a time for saving and a time for spending and she believed in parochial relief. Money, poured out of dissipating hands such as Papa's, was something to beware of, but Papa said considering it was his own money he could not see why the devil Mamma should keep the purse strings so resolutely closed.

Snobbery was Mamma's besetting sin and she always referred to God and the Queen in the same breath. What the Queen might think and what she might say concerned her deeply. She wore Royalty like a crown upon her head, and, when the Prince Consort died, she took upon herself part of the Queen's sorrow and went into retirement for so long a period that she was suspected of being pregnant.

There were so many things moving back and forth within my mind. My own uncomeliness against Henrietta's beauty, Mamma's sarcastic scolding tongue and Papa's rollicking indifference; and always there at the back of my mind was Mr. Bemrose.

I stirred when I thought of the bailiff, and the doll slipped from my knees. I was remembering so many unimportant things. My confused thoughts flew across my mind and only a few hung there, like bats upon a rafter, enabling me to trace backwards.

The clock on the Tower House opposite struck nine. It was a sad sound, like the clang of a church bell tolling for the dead.

It reminded me that it was time for me to go.

Papa and Mamma would be leaving the dining room; I could picture them retiring to the green and gold boudoir where they always sat after a meal. Mamma would be in her tight-fitting bodice and bustle, and Papa in his black velvet coat. Mamma would be discoursing upon the shortcomings of mankind, especially Papa's, the iniquity of youth and the curse of loose living. Papa would be proclaiming with brazen audacity that it was the only way to live.

How well I knew Papa and Mamma. She, so controlled and

patronizing, and he with his vague smile half listening to her, half dreaming, miles away.

I stretched myself and picked up the doll from off the floor. I had made up my mind to take Amelia with me; it would be more heart-rending and draw more tears to be found with this wax doll in my arms. Besides, Amelia was my friend, the only person I could safely tell my secrets to. She was an irritating doll with a perpetual smirk upon her face that could not be washed off. What had she to smile about, I wondered. Was it because she did not know the world? Henrietta would be asleep by now, lying with her arms spread out as if to embrace the universe, and her red hair like a flame across the pillows. Dear sweet Henrietta, lucky Henrietta without a care, sleeping the night away.

I was wearing a plain white bedgown that was far too short for me so that my feet were exposed and my arms, crimson with cold, bare to the elbow. I wondered if my blood was as frigid as my body and if I cut my finger it would force its way out like scarlet icicles.

Amelia was wrapped up in a shawl with her silly smirking face peering out of it. I wondered if she knew she was going to die out there in the snow with me.

Carefully I opened the latticed window and painfully squeezed out onto the ledge.

The earth and the skies were silent; there was not a sound from anywhere and my breath froze as it left my mouth.

I lowered myself onto the turret and almost screamed with pain as my feet first touched the snow. Then, slipping my bedgown from me, I stood naked with Amelia close against my tender bosom.

Scooping a space in the snow with my toes, I lowered myself

17

into it and lay flat upon my back gazing up at the twinkling, dancing stars.

At first the agony was almost more than I could bear, but after a while the snow felt warm and friendly, and my eyes began to droop in sleep. It seemed as if I was floating midway between the heavens and the earth.

So this was death?

It was not nearly so fearsome as life with Henrietta. This drowsy rapture, this sensation of being in a swing enthralled me. My unhappiness was falling from me, slipping from my mind as easily as the bedgown had slipped below my feet. My mind was free from the jumble and confusion of Mr. Bemrose and his passionate embrace, and Henrietta and her cruel enlightenment.

I thought I could hear music. I thought I could hear voices whispering and calling me. First Papa and then Mamma, then Henrietta and then God.

Just as I was believing that I was indeed dead and my soul on its journey through the frozen spaces to Eternity, I distinctly heard someone say:

"For mercy's sake, Miss Susan, whatever are you doing out there in the snow? Come in at once, you naughty child, or you will catch your death of cold."

And there, leaning out of the latticed window, was Mrs. Trouncer wiping the drip from her long and beaky nose.

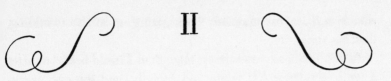

II

Springfield Town was a community of genteel and respectable people, mostly well born and with long family histories of distinction.

Some of the houses were lined along the cobble-stoned street so that everyone could see into everybody's windows; but a few of the better houses stood in semi-detachment on patches of grassland with gardens in front and back.

The poorer cottages had shops below and little coloured buildings hanging to the edge of them that looked gay and careless from without, but were sordid and dark within.

The town itself suffered from prying mischief-makers and the insistent plague of wagging tongues; for many of the inhabitants were elderly busybodies who had nothing better to do than slander, and whose charity went no further than their inquisitive noses. They were indeed experts in the noble art of destroying reputations and could smell out the weaknesses and folly of their neighbours as easily as a hound will sniff out a fox.

White Orchard Manor, our home, was a gracious residence and stood windward from the town by the side of the forest. A wide green path called Wingmeadow Lane led to the town.

It was an imposing building with tall gables and a kind of castle tower, and it had high hedges and fine iron gates to close it in. Immense trees stood like sentinels protecting the manor from the road, and long stretches of garden reached to the farm beyond.

White Orchard Estate was a place of great beauty and its garden was just the kind of garden every country home should possess. It had been designed by Papa and Mamma and created from an expanse of grassland and scattered forest trees. In summer it became a riot of roses swinging upon iron chains and wide herbaceous borders lining the brick paths. There was a large weeping willow in the middle of the lawn that looked for all the world like a little old lady in a crinoline gown. Papa christened the tree Victoria, because it looked so much like the good Queen. Mamma was shocked by this and pursed up her lips whenever she went past it.

A red brick terrace ran on one side of the garden and beyond the terrace was the farm. A high wall surrounded the whole estate and upon this grew peaches and apricots and golden plums. It would have seemed, at first glance, to be an enviable place to live.

Papa and Mamma had first come to White Orchard Manor from their honeymoon, and a year after that Henrietta and I were born. Mrs. Trouncer would often tell us that after Henrietta was delivered Doctor Wiffin left to climb into his chaise when—pop goes the weasel—out I came into the world.

Doctor Wiffin was the family physician. He wore tortoise-shell spectacles which gave an air of wisdom to his otherwise purposeless countenance. A bewildered and perplexed little man he was who, if he had had his life to live over again, would surely never have contemplated being a doctor. His favourite recreation was reading the morning paper and seeing how many people had died during the week, for it gave him a feeling of intense satisfaction to know that there were other physicians besides himself whose patients got out of hand.

Doctor Wiffin affirmed that I had only been born by hook or by crook. What he meant exactly by this he never explained, but Mrs. Trouncer told me that, whatever Doctor Wiffin might say, he should have known I was there and waited for me.

"You and your sister lay in the cradle," she said, "one dark and one fair. An angel and a scorpion side by side. You as pale as a waxen image, and Miss Henrietta fat and rosy-cheeked. It seemed as if that sister of yours had already sapped the very blood out of you, as if even then she wanted everything for herself. Lovely she was with her dimples and disarming ways, and you, Miss Susan, as desolate as a blighted child with a curse upon its head. Both your Papa and Mamma loved their wholesome lusty infant, but they had no patience for a weakling. His Lordship said the very sight of you unmanned him, and her Ladyship could never so much as glance in your direction. 'What did I conceive,' she moaned, 'what have I done? How did I beget a weed so closely woven to a flower?' And Doctor Wiffin's dog, you know, Miss Susan, the spaniel with a terrier's tail, was sick under the bed when it caught sight of you."

After that there were no more children and no heir was born to the noble name of Darlington. This failure of fulfilment preyed upon Papa's mind because he had been so certain he would have a son.

"I wish to God there was a pair of trousers in the nursery," he sighed ruefully, "for I swear by all that is holy I am frustrated by these family petticoats."

"Dear Edward, I did not know you could be."

"Femininity in one's own house, Lucy, has not the flavour of a next-door neighbour's wench."

"I heard the other day, Edward, that you could make love in almost any language; is that true?"

"A compliment, my dear, of which I am unworthy. Nevertheless, it has an element of truth. Making love in any language has an effervescence unlike anything else in the world, do you not agree?"

"I! My dear Edward, you should know me better. There are other things I find far more diverting."

"Such as?"

"It is hardly worth my while explaining, for you would not understand me."

"I find there is as much satisfaction in courting other people's wives as appropriating someone else's umbrella."

"I suppose you know you are being talked about?"

"My dearest Lucy, of course I am; without men like me there would be no conversation. I am a blessing to society."

"You do not mind then?"

"Mind! Good God, I like it, Lucy. I like to feel that our neighbours, our dear good neighbours, have something to warm their hands against on winter evenings, and something to strew the air with on these scented summer mornings. I am a benefactor, my dear Lucy; without me this little town would have no colour. You should be grateful that I am so notorious."

It was useless Mamma upbraiding Papa for his misdoings; she could not anger him however much she scolded. He was both an idler and a flirt, and instead of being ashamed he gloried in it. He would rise late and, descending to the dining room, breakfast upon a glass of ale. Then a few letters to be written

22

to his ladies, masterpieces of deception he delighted in. There was his wardrobe to be selected—every suit a mood and every mood some clandestine affair. His flower shop had to be visited, not so much to send his dear wife a bouquet, but because the wench who sold them to him had such delicious legs. Then a stimulant or two at the club and a bawdy story to be told with shouts of laughter, a small repast perhaps with one of his "angels" who could be persuaded to dally with a goose liver and roast, after which relaxation, a return to the club for a few hours of contemplating nature. Papa never admitted that he dozed as others did. With him it was always contemplating nature.

"What else would you have me do, Lucy?" he would ask Mamma.

"I suggest a little work, Edward, if it would not be too much exertion."

"My dearest Lucy, are you ill? Work is the ugliest word in the English language. It is a word, my love, which makes teeth go on edge and hair stand on end. Moreover, do I look the kind of man who could indulge in such strenuous activity?"

"You look to me just like other men, Edward, and they can work. If everyone felt as you do, what kind of a world would it be? There would be no light, no water, no food. Trains would not run and ships would not sail."

"Dearest Lucy, do not try to be operative; it ill becomes you. The people who run trains and sail ships are born to do so. They are set aside at birth for such a purpose. I was not. Oh, I know quite well what you are thinking, my love; you are wondering what confounded good I am to you."

"Indeed, Edward, I am not; men like you have not been put into women's lives for any excellent benefit."

23

And so they quarrelled, continuing with their differences, Mamma questioning and being given most deceptive answers, and Papa wriggling himself out of many an escapade by the skin of his teeth. I would listen to them and wonder if all marriages ended in such discord, and if all husbands and wives fell out in conflict such as this.

Mamma had a dignified and well-controlled scheme of things; her house was beautifully in order. She had ruled it by years of stern assertion, her only failure her inability to control our wild and raffish Papa. He refused to be uplifted by her culture. Had she been the muling puling perfumed kind, he might have ceded to her softness. But she remained the rigid ruler in corset and bustle, determined whatever else happened to have her own way about the house.

The first thing I could remember clearly about our childhood was the nurse we had and the deep hatred both Henrietta and I felt for her. Mrs. Lovegrove was short, ample-figured and unrelentingly severe. With her we were made to repeat the catechism three or four times over whilst she sat, her fat hands folded across her rounded body and a look of complacency upon her obese face. Her tempers were frequent, her punishments inflexibly carried out. In inflicting them she showed her passion visibly and Henrietta declared she was sadistic. I did not ask what she meant by this because I was afraid of what she would tell me, and a thrashing was better, I sensed, than what Henrietta had in mind.

When Mrs. Lovegrove left, Mamma endeavoured to take care of us alone and every day would teach us simple lessons and the capitals of countries. I dreaded those lessons. They beat against my brain like little hammers. Lists and lists of things I could not memorize would haunt me and keep me wakeful through the night. It was easy for Henrietta, who was quick and eager and not fearful of Mamma, whereas I was smock-faced and trembling the moment I opened her door. I hated the way her lips would curl as I stammered through my spelling, and how she would turn my timidity into ridicule so that she and her darling Henrietta could laugh at me. I hated the way she took Henrietta's part against me and made slighting remarks, rebuking and criticising me for every trifling defect.

Every morning we would go into Mamma's room whilst she was dressing and repeat our lessons to her, and an hour later I would be sure to retire in tears with Henrietta following me saying, "What a poor creature you are, Susan. Will you never learn to stand up for yourself? Confront Mamma as I do and she will never say a word to you; look how she is with me and how I can twist her and turn her any way I want to."

Eventually I found a way to beguile Mamma by copying out my answers onto a scrap of paper I held screwed up in my hand. Mrs. Trouncer, who always helped Mamma to dress, felt sorry for me with my eyes brimming over with tears and my face so white, and she begged Mamma to be more lenient, but Mamma replied, "Nonsense, woman, the child has to be taught. You would not have a lack-brain round the house, now would you?"

Whilst Mrs. Trouncer was brushing Mamma's long hair she would spread herself between me and the mirror so that I could not be seen reflected in it reading my answers from the scrap of paper, and then she would say to Mamma, "Miss Susan is improving. Do you not think so, my Lady?" and wink at me.

Only Henrietta knew the trick I was playing with my lessons

and was quick to take advantage of it, threatening to tell Mamma unless I paid her well to hold her tongue.

"You can have Amelia if you like, Henrietta," I pleaded, tearing out my heart, for she was, after all, my favourite doll.

"But I do not want Amelia. I have plenty of dolls of my own."

"Would you like my little pearl necklace then?"

"No, I do not want that either. The pearls are too small and it has too delicate a string."

"Would you like the money in my purse? I have saved a few coins from Papa."

Whenever we saw Papa in the town with one of his ladies he would send for us when we reached home and give us each a silver coin so that we should not tell Mama. I had a little purse full of these savings, for it was remarkable what it cost Papa to keep Mamma in ignorance. Very soon all that I had was transferred to Henrietta so that for a few days at least I could breathe freely.

Mamma indulged in every kind of fancy work and once a year there was a sale in Springfield Town so that the poor old souls round and about could benefit. Mamma believed in being charitable to those less fortunate than she; it always pleased her immensely to act the lady bountiful.

Papa was, without doubt, the best-dressed man in Springfield, moreover the handsomest, with great breadth of shoulder and blue eyes in a sun-tanned face. We did not see much of him when we were little but used to be brought down to the drawing room by Mrs. Trouncer for an hour after tea, very clean and starched and well behaved. Papa would frolic with Henrietta for a while and Mamma would sit beside me and instruct me in the art of sewing. "Since you have no looks, dear Susan," she would say, "I think it advisable that you should have ability."

Papa would smile proudly when he gazed at Henrietta, but when he looked at me he would raise his eyebrows and pucker up his face and say something in a low voice to Mamma. He nicknamed me "Go by the Ground" because I was so small in stature, and sometimes he patted my head and sighed and said, "What you lack in prettiness, Susan, my purse will be obliged to supply in riches."

Papa knew everything, at least so it seemed to me; he knew what made the sea salt, why it was dark at night, where the sun went when the moon came out and how life came into the world. I would ply him with questions because I loved to hear him answer them. He made little stories about everything on earth.

Once I said to him:

"Why is your head larger than mine, Papa?"

"Because I am wiser than you are, my child."

"Is your brain much much fuller than mine?"

"Pray God it is so; it could not be much emptier."

"But how do things get into our brains, Papa?"

"Through your ears and your eyes, Susan, that is if you know how to listen and where to look."

And then another time I would say:

"How deep is the sea, Papa? How far does the sky go? Why are shadows longer at the end of the day and yet I stay the same size, and why have I a shadow on one side of me and not on the other? What makes your eyes blue, Papa, and mine brown? Why do boys' voices break and girls' do not? And. . ."

But Papa, mopping his brow, would implore me to go back to my room and call wildly to the domestics for a glass of port.

When Mamma was feeling particularly gracious we would be

27

permitted to watch her attire herself for some concert or reception. There was a clock on the mantelpiece of her room that had a shining halo swinging round the face of it, and when the lights were lowered I used to think this glittering clock the most beautiful thing in the world.

"It is like dancing water," I said to Henrietta, "and gives me a funny feeling; does it give you a funny feeling also?"

But Henrietta replied witheringly that the clock did nothing to her except to tell her what time it was.

Sometimes Papa would sit at the little piano and play to us, for amongst his many accomplishments he was quite a musician and could play with both ease and grace. But the moment Mamma heard the music she would be sure to rush into the room and sing in a high querulous voice. When Mamma sang it was as if she was unloading her grievances and disburdening herself of all acrimony, and the evening would be spoiled.

Papa was not penny-wise where Mamma was concerned. He purchased her wondrous clothes and adorned her well. He gave her jewellery and fallals and furbelows to atone, so he said, for his sins. But to tell the truth, Papa liked to hear people say, "That dear and generous Lord Darlington; see how liberally he gowns his lady and lavishes his favours." Such remarks warmed him and seemed to satisfy his ego.

Mamma did not permit us any of the attractions of her wardrobe and there was no charm or allurement in our dress. Even the redness of Henrietta's curls was an affront so that they would be plaited and drawn into a net. Mamma would pat down our plain attire and assure us that simplicity was akin to God and to the Queen; and she would avert her eyes from my sister's perfect form as if it was a sin to see her rounding bosoms and the wondrous graces of her body.

Henrietta and I had a little hut we frequented which was on the top of a hill off Wingmeadow Lane, and there we would play most of the mornings. No one quite knew how the hut ever got there and some said it had once been the hiding place of poachers and thieves. It had a table and a bench and a fireplace; we pretended it was our home and took turns to sweep and clean it out. For hours we would sit there whilst Henrietta enlightened me and told me things.

I learned in that hut the things no child need ever know, and it was there Henrietta destroyed the loveliness of life. She made monsters out of human beings and filled the wooden cabin with fear. Men were "this" and "that," she said, and no one could escape from them. I learned what rape was and the full meaning of the Sixth Commandment.

I could never rightly understand why it was that Henrietta seemed to know so much more than I did, considering it was only a matter of hours between our age; but it was not so much quantity of knowledge as quality, and I used to think that the ghost of whoever had once owned the hut must be blushing at the things it heard and covering its eyes in shame.

And so it had gone on until that evening when at nine o'clock at night I had stepped out of my window in the snow to die.

For many days I had thought of different ways of dying. There was a little pond, for instance, concealed close to the farmyard for the cows to drink from, which I could have slipped into and drowned; I thought of poison or starvation, but none of these measures pleased me half so much as the venture through my window. That stupid latticed window was responsible for luring Mrs. Trouncer to my room. The cold wind driving through it had attracted and roused her from the warmth and sent her scuttling through the corridor to see what I was up to. If it had not been for that window I would be lying dead with a flower clasped in my quiet hands. My troubles would have been ended, my tortured mind at rest. It was all the fault of that telltale wall-eyed window letting in the draught, and I regarded it balefully, screening myself from it as from a mean and ugly visage.

Of course the following morning I was in great disgrace and told to remain in my room. The snow had done me no harm and I had not even been taken with a chill. There was no heart-rending scene with my body lying cold and still, but a bustle of angry domestics delivering me gruel and flouncing in and out of my room in quick succession.

Mamma of course came up to see me; this was an opportunity to admonish me which she could not miss.

"What was the matter with you, Susan?"

"Nothing, Mamma."

"There must have been something to make you do this terrible thing."

"Nothing particular . . . nothing really particular."

"But why did you do it, Susan, were you unhappy?"

"I am unhappy, Mamma."

"Unhappy about what? Have we not lavished our love upon you and given you our care? The trouble with you, Susan, is that you are too serious for your age."

I looked down at my hands twisting and turning in the bed-clothes, wondering how much she knew and what exactly Henrietta had told her regarding Mr. Bemrose. How could I explain to this cold and carping lady my agony, the pain in my mind and the shame of my body when Mr. Bemrose had placed his sleek white hand upon my heart?

"Why are you so serious, Susan?" repeated Mamma, a look of scorn upon her proud and handsome face. "And why are you unhappy? I have a right to know, do you not think so?"

"I cannot tell you, Mamma."

"You cannot tell me! My dear child, that is absurd. You creep out onto the balcony in the thick snow, clad only in your bedgown, and . . ."

"I was not in my bedgown, Mamma."

"More shame to you then. Have you lost all sense of decency? I am very angry with you, Susan. I do not remember ever having been so enraged before. You have committed a flagrant breach of etiquette of which our neighbours will most assuredly hear, and it may even reach the ears of our dear Queen herself. Have you no pity for our reputation? Have you no thought for others than yourself? To deprive yourself of life, to make away with what God has given you, is a most deadly sin for which you must ask forgiveness. I believe that we should punish you severely, but Papa is not inclined to take this serious view and says that retribution will fall naturally upon you. Therefore I suggest that you spend the rest of the day in prayer, and in the evening I will see that you have a sedative to rid you of these fancies."

Then, as she reached the door with an indignant rustle of her gown, she turned and gave me the strangest look.

"You may as well know," she said, pronouncing each word most carefully, "that Mr. Bemrose has been dismissed. He was a most excellent young man but hardly mature enough for the position which he held. I shall miss him greatly and I wish you

31

to fully understand, Susan, that we do not consider it entirely his fault that we have been obliged to adopt this measure with him."

She swept from the room and down the cedar-scented stairway to Papa, and I followed her softly, leaning over the side of it to hear what she would say to him and see what she would do.

Papa was reading, between the intervals of sipping his customary port.

"I wish you would speak to Susan," I heard her say.

"About what, my love?"

"I feel now that she is growing up there are certain things she should know concerning it."

"Such as?"

"Such as this affair with Mr. Bemrose; nothing in itself, I have no doubt, but the exaggeration of a puzzled mind. Nevertheless, it has greatly disturbed me and I am of the opinion that the child's thoughts are not wholesome and her appetite for knowledge distorted and unclean. I think perhaps it is time she was told the truth, Edward, so that she will know the difference between right and wrong."

"You mean you wish her to be told the facts of life?"

"Yes, Edward, that is precisely what I mean."

"And who do you think will take upon themselves this delicate task, my dear?"

"You will, Edward."

"I will! Great God, you amaze me, Lucy. Surely that is your department, my dear, rather than mine."

"I do not feel capable of confronting Susan, Edward. She is a strange child and just looks and looks until you feel you have sunk into her eyes. I feel sure you could enlighten her with the

32

utmost dexterity, and she would take it from you better than she would from me."

"But, Lucy, have pity on me. What in God's name will you have me tell her? Do you wish me to reveal to her the origin of sex and tell her in as calm a manner as I can the development of woman?"

"I think in view of what has happened it would be expedient, Edward; the child has received a shock, she has imagination and she is not nearly so advanced as Henrietta."

"You realize, do you not, my dear Lucy, that after my second glass of port I have a tendency to feel a little muddled."

"You have your lucid moments, Edward."

"Thank you, my dear."

"And I have no intention of permitting you to speak to Susan in befuddled insobriety."

So as they discussed and argued over this thing Papa was to tell me, I went back to my room. Had Henrietta omitted something, and was there still a torturing fact which had to be revealed? I crept back to bed and for no reason at all began to weep, and after a while I was lulled into a doze, counting my tears.

When I awoke I was told that as soon as the sun went down Papa would be waiting for me in his room.

"Stand up to them, Miss Susan," said Mrs. Trouncer as she helped me dress. "Don't let them put any silly notions into your little head. More scoldings, more clamour and correction; small wonder you wanted to put an end to it all, you unhappy child."

Grumbling to herself she carefully brushed my hair and put on my best frock. "There's a mortal satisfaction in knowing that you are spruce," she said.

33

"Am I spruce, Mrs. Trouncer?"

"You look all right but for that doleful expression. I've seen men hanged more cheerfully than you look at this moment; why do you take on so?"

When I stood before Papa with my hands meekly folded in front of me, he made out that he had not even noticed I was there and continued taking his snuff with a great deal of nose blowing and fluttering of his handkerchief. Then, clearing his throat, he leaned back in his chair to examine me.

"So this is the little creature who has caused all this ado," he said lightly. "My, my! Whoever would have believed it? What the devil was the matter with you, Miss?"

"Nothing that I know of, Papa," I replied almost inaudibly.

"Nothing, you say! Then why this unwholesome display of drama? This . . . this unwarrantable lack of self-control? What were you trying to do out there in the snow?"

"I wanted to die, Papa."

"You wanted to die! After all the trouble Mamma experienced in bringing you to life, ungrateful child!"

"I did not ask to be born, Papa."

"Neither did your Mama or I supplicate that you should be. But having been blessed or cursed with this exceptional event, do you think you had any right to depreciate it?"

"No, Papa."

"Are you not afraid of dying?"

"I am more afraid of life, Papa."

"Merciful God! For what reason?"

"I could name many."

"Then name them, child, for Heaven's sake name them. You should be ashamed of yourself for last night's escapade. Do you not know how wicked and sinful it is to sign your own death warrant and launch into Eternity without sanction."

"Yes, Papa."

"Yes, Papa . . . No, Papa; for the Lord's sake, child, have you nothing better to say than that? What are these whims and vapours, what is the meaning of this hysterical nonsense? Do you not feel well, Susan?"

"I feel very well, thank you, Papa."

"Was it because our bailiff kissed you? Did you think because of that you had suddenly grown a woman?"

"No, Papa, I am fully aware of my age."

"Well, what then?"

"I cannot tell you, Papa; you would not understand."

"So, I am a dolt am I, an imbecile, a moon calf?"

"No, no, dearest Papa, I did not mean that."

"Then what else, if I may ask?"

I did not answer. Tears filled my eyes and began coursing down my face. Papa thrust his hand into his hair and sighed. He seemed embarrassed and coughed several times which was unlike him as he was not of a rule put out.

"Confound it," he said, "I have never yet found an answer to tears. I hate the sight of them. They are a female subterfuge, a screen behind which they play upon our sympathy. You cannot weaken me, Susan. I asked you to come here for a purpose not only to upbraid you but to speak to you upon a subject that is, in our opinion, of the utmost importance. Why I should be the one to disillusion you, God knows. It is your mother's business more than it is a man's. You would have known it soon enough, no doubt, without my help."

"Known what, Papa?"

"The ways of the flesh and the devil, my dear child."

"I know them now, Papa."

"You do, eh? And may I ask who it is who has opened those innocent eyes of yours?"

"Books, Papa. Your books and Henrietta's tongue."

"Henrietta! What in the name of Jehovah has she to do with it?"

"I live in the library as you know. I spend most of my days reading. When I am not reading, dear Henrietta lays hold of me and does what she calls enlightens me. Believe me, Papa, she is no saint."

Papa sat aghast. I had never seen him look so utterly dumbfounded, for he had not thought of his beloved daughter in any other terms but beauty.

"God bless my soul," he said, "you do astound me, Susan."

"You look upon Henrietta as a lovable girl, do you not, Papa? Both you and Mamma think she is the very pink and pattern of perfection?"

"And you, I take it, do not think so?"

"I know her for what she is. May I tell you, Papa? I have wanted to tell someone for so long. Henrietta pursues me to my room. Thoughts horrible and wild pour from her mouth. Monsters are conjured up, hideous imperfect creatures of her imagination. She describes them to me before I go to sleep, 'so that you will be sure to dream, dear Susan,' she says to me and laughs at me cowering beneath the sheets. The dread and terror of those nights when I know she will come to me, the horror of being hemmed in by her as she closes the door and tiptoes to my side. 'Spare me this time,' I beg of her, 'spare me and let me sleep in peace.' The nights are so long when I lie awake,

36

Papa, when all the things Henrietta has told me are crowding round my bed."

Papa drank down a glass of port at one gulp; his face was red and his eyes were troubled.

"Are you asking me to believe this of my own child, Susan, that she is a tormentor and a bully?"

"I do not expect you to believe it, but I wanted you to know why I considered death was better than this persecution. For years I have listened to Henrietta and no one has rescued me from her terrifying training. I was obliged to let things go on as they were. I could not appeal to either of you. Henrietta is the very apple of your eyes; you dote on her, Papa, and idolize her beauty."

Papa blew his nose violently, looking everywhere and anywhere rather than at me.

"Dear, dear," he muttered at last, "this is really most distressing, most distressing indeed. I sent for you for quite another purpose. I did not dream that anything like this was occurring in my house. I wished to speak to you about the peak of blessedness, and here I find myself in a place of torment where Henrietta figures as a female Belial. I will speak to her, Susan, I assure you, child, I will go into this matter now that you have brought it to my notice. There is no real harm in Henrietta, there cannot be. She is a little wayward, that is all; you have more potential virtue, my dear, but you are as yet a phantom with no pith, no backbone to defend yourself. But it is you at this moment who are of importance more than Henrietta, and I beg that you will allow me to deal with one thing at a time. Mamma has called upon me to explain to you the mysteries of the way of life."

37

"Yes, Papa."

"You are at this moment close upon the period when a bud bursts into blossom; do you know what I mean, child?"

"No, Papa, I do not."

"That is correct, Susan, and why in God's name should you? I am afraid I have not made myself quite clear. What I am trying to say is concerning the . . . the opening, so to speak, of womanhood; has not Henrietta told you about that? It is of the utmost importance, Susan, and should be given thought to. Do you know the difference between good and evil, girl?"

"I do, Papa. I know what Henrietta calls it."

"To hell with Henrietta!"

"Yes, Papa."

"Do you know what it is?"

"I know what the Bible says."

"The Bible says a lot of things, my child, I feel sure even God did not mean and is apt to be a most confusing volume. Do you by any chance understand the origin of birth?"

"No, Papa."

"You do not know how the nuptial knot is tied?"

"I have read the marriage service in my prayer book."

Papa swilled some more port and once more mopped his brow.

"Growing from childhood to womanhood is a serious affair," he said, "during which time you may suffer a . . . a disturbed feeling, an afflicting emotion, a . . . a derangement as it were of your whole body."

"Do you mean I am going to be sick, Papa?"

Papa seemed to be becoming more and more uncomfortable.

"I suppose you might call it a kind of sickness," he replied, "and yet being natural it is not counted as such. You are most

38

prodigiously dull of understanding, Susan, which does not make it easy for me. I am no doubt a dolt at explanation, but it is not easy to expound the meaning of life. Do you think the moon is green cheese?"

"Of course not, Papa."

"Do you think the world is rosy?"

"What has the moon or the world got to do with my being sick?"

"Well, nothing, Susan, nothing at all, but I was wondering how young you were and how credulous a creature."

"I think the world is hateful, Papa. That is why I wanted to leave it. It is black and overburdened with evil, so Mamma says, and Henrietta says . . ."

"Your Mamma takes an exceedingly sombre view of life, child, and she has very little levity. As for Henrietta and her twiddle twaddle, we need take no notice of that. I personally like the world. It is a rare and agreeable place and good to live in if you know how. It is point of view which counts, Susan, and your Mamma, I regret to say, has no point of view further than her own surroundings. There are two ways of going out into the world, my dear one, richly and joyfully with a fortune in your pocket and a head full of hopes and a body full of well being; and the other way, towards a sea of trouble, comfortless and with an empty belly and an empty purse. Each of us travels his or her journey according to their station."

"But, Papa, whatever way you look at things you cannot make beauty out of ugliness."

"A man may have a crippled body, Susan, and still be a saint. How many people have you met? Have you encountered fools

39

and wise men, idlers and workers, human threads running through the towns, good, bad, strong and fragile?"

"No, Papa, I have not met many people."

"Well then, let me tell you this, Susan. A man on the road, a humble man, can be an ornament of grace, and what he has inside of him can shine brighter than the sun itself. As you say you have read your Bible you are doubtless cognizant of the story of Adam and Eve?"

"Why did he swallow the apple, Papa?"

"What apple, child?"

"The apple that stuck in his throat, that all men have."

"An allegory, my dear Susan, and all nonsense; what I mean is the story of the Garden of Eden."

"Oh yes, Papa, I know it all by heart."

"Do you . . . do you indeed, child? That is very creditable, very worthy indeed, and I wish I could say the same. But do you understand from it the difference between purity and lust, virtue and wrongdoing? A virtuous woman is held in high esteem however dull she may appear. You would not wish to become a fallen woman, would you now?"

"I do not wish to become a woman at all, Papa."

"And might I be permitted to enquire why?"

"Mrs. Trouncer says there is a great deal of nonsense talked about modesty and virtue; she says they are nothing but lost opportunities, that is all. She says that most women at heart are strumpets. 'What do you mean by strumpets?' I asked her, and she said, 'Ask his Lordship, he can answer that more readily than I can!'"

"God damn the woman! What did she mean by that?" roared Papa. "This really is an outrage. First my wife paints so gloomy a picture of the world you do not want to live in it; then Henrietta with her puny obscenity keeping you awake at night, and now Mrs. Trouncer, laughing at me behind my back. Have we an establishment of imbeciles and do I pay these domestics to babble impropriety against me? What else has Mrs. Trouncer told you, what else has she to say about my friends?"

"She did not tell me anything else, Papa."

"No! You astonish me. Are you sure she did not say that I was a loose fish and a libertine; are you quite certain she did not expound upon my shameless habits? It is a nice thing that we are none of us free from the wagging tongues of the servants' hall."

Papa's handsome face was suffused with red, his eyes were blazing. Afraid of the storm I had raised, I tried to soothe him.

"I am sure she did not mean to offend you, Papa," I stammered. "You know how fond the servants are of you."

"Are they . . . are they indeed? That is exceedingly good of them and I should perhaps increase their wages and remember them in my Will; but understand this once and for all, Susan, I will not have you discussing the problems of life with my domestics. If there is anything you want to know, why do you not come to me?"

"I will in future, Papa, I promise you I will."

"What can a creature like Mrs. Trouncer know about human beings, what mercy would she have? Even the lowest have two sides to them. No one is perfect. Never forget, Susan, that God made every beast of the field and every fowl of the air before he created woman; remind Mrs. Trouncer of this; it will put her in her place."

"Do men ever tire of the pursuit of women, Papa?"

"Why in Heaven's name should they when it is the finest of all sport?"

"I do not like men. I do not think I shall ever like them, Papa."

"Pish and tush, in the name of the Prophet, did you ever hear such nonsense. She does not like men, she does not think she will ever like them. . . . What is the matter with you, Susan, are you thinking still of Mr. Bemrose, that chuff, that bumpkin with no manners? Are you going to permit a chawbacon like Mr. Bemrose to represent mankind? Because one fellow tries to kiss you, are we all to be damned into eternity? Come, come, my dear, it is inconceivable that you should be so green."

He was silent for a moment, for the port had finally mellowed him, and he gazed upon the ground in sad reflection. Then suddenly he looked up and smiled at me.

"All this nonsense has completely taken out of my head what I was going to say to you, Susan," he said. "Can you remember?"

"It was about my being sick, Papa."

"Yes, yes, to be sure it was."

He put out his hand and drew me against his knees, looking me up and down from the top of my head to my heels, but his eyes were kind and his temper gone. Then he began to speak very quietly. I did not remember Papa ever having been so serious before. Of course I could not understand the purport of his talk, for he filled my ears with long-sounding words that held no meaning. It was something that the flesh was heir to, something that happened in the course of growing up, something that would happen to Henrietta and to me and could not be avoided. It made me tremble with fear and yet I did not know what I was afraid of; I dreaded its uncertainty of time, this change in my body to which he gave no name.

Then Papa cupped my small flat breasts in his hands and said that they would develop into pinnacles of beauty.

"There is nothing in this world more lovely than a well-formed woman," he explained. "There is nothing to be ashamed of in these, for they are God's masterpiece in the eyes of every man."

I reddened beneath his touch, feeling my face burn at the sound of his voice. In my ignorance I was filled with a sense of indecency. I remembered Mr. Bemrose and the way he had held me in his arms.

I moved away from Papa, farther and farther to the door, and well-nigh fell into Mamma who had just entered. She looked into my face and took me by the arm; she would not let me go.

"What have you done to Susan?" she asked shrilly of Papa. "Surely there was some way of telling her without frightening the child to death?"

That was all Papa needed to set him in a fury.

"Is that all the thanks I get," he shouted, "for doing other people's dirty work? Is it my fault that we have a looby for a daughter? In future see that you deal with your own progeny when it comes to telling them the facts of life!"

"I asked you to do it, Edward, because I thought you would keep sober; it seems I was wrong."

"God keep me from all women if they are as unreasonable as this," said Papa and crashed his glass upon the polished floor.

I went back to my attic and gazed at my figure in the mirror. Something was going to happen to me, but when would it happen and how would I ever know?

III

THE FOLLOWING AFTERNOON when we were all sitting in the drawing room having our tea Papa suddenly said:

"Henrietta, why do you torture Susan?"

"I do not torture her, Papa."

"Why do you fill her with terrifying tales and stuff her with nonsense the like of which I have never heard before?"

Mamma looked coldly at Papa and fondly at her darling.

"I am sure Henrietta does no such thing, Edward," she declared. "Henrietta is not like that. It is Susan who exaggerates so wildly, who makes so much out of so little."

"Kindly leave this to me, Lucy," replied Papa. "Well, Henrietta, what have you to say?"

"Susan is a ninny, Papa. She snivels and whines and is contemptibly afraid. I know her well and how her whole life is shadowed by fear. There is no strength in her character, Papa, and she carries so heavy a heart it is like living with a boggart. I like to see her gobble and gape and gulp down everything I tell her. Can you blame me when she is so credulous, when I can make her teeth chatter and her eyes start out of her head; the poor child has no sense."

"And you have no heart, Henrietta."

"Indeed, Papa? I am sorry if I have in any way displeased you."

"I am exceedingly disappointed in you, Henrietta, and you

44

will oblige me if in the future you do not go to Susan's room after it is dark. Do you understand me? Leave Susan alone and for God's sake let her sleep in peace."

"Very well, Papa."

That evening as we made our way upstairs Henrietta pinched my arm so viciously I could but cry out.

"Telltale tit, you are a clapperclaw, Susan."

"I am not a clapperclaw."

"Yes, you are; you are a scurvy pettifogging chitchat. First Mr. Bemrose and now me. What did you say about me? What did you tell Papa?"

"I only said you frightened me, Henrietta."

"Frightened you with what?"

"Does it matter now?"

"It matters considerably to me. Papa has never spoken to me like that before and I tell you I do not like it. What have you said to him, what lies did you conjure to make him so enraged? Unfortunately he cannot send me away as Mr. Bemrose was dismissed—that is a pity is it not, Susan, that your malice has been wasted?"

But I would not answer her and she dared not go with me farther than the door.

And so quarrelling and discontented and pulling many a long face, my sister and I began to grow up, and as the years went by Mr. Bemrose's husky kiss became nothing but a vague memory, and I discovered that what Papa had been trying to elucidate was not so disquieting after all, but merely God's way with women.

Henrietta and I did not seem to belong to Papa's generation and we looked upon his life, at that time, as being over and

45

in another age from ours, an old-fashioned age against which we imagined we stood out with the boldness of sudden bits of newly patched colour in a well-worn tapestry.

Papa spoke wise and true words; I was aware of that, and I knew that experience like his was the key to the meaning of life. But I could never imagine Papa and Mamma encountering momentous problems. I could not see how they could ever have become affianced; Mamma, bereft of her bustle and shorn of her petticoats, within the passionate embrace of Papa seemed to me beyond the bounds of possibility.

"Surely these two were never young as we are," I said to myself. "Their path was smooth and even; there was no Mr. Bemrose for Mamma to beat her heart against, no Henrietta to pollute her mind."

Once I asked Mamma if she had ever been indiscreet.

"Never," she replied firmly, "but your Papa has frequently been accused of loitering in Hyde Park."

"For what purpose, Mamma?"

"He said he had only stopped to wind his watch," and then she closed her lips firmly and would not tell me any more.

We were young ladies now and our skirts were flounced and we wore fashionable garments of the day. I still spent a great deal of my time in vitiated study and was deeply versed in books, reading undesirable things and steeping my mind in immodest and broad, free literature.

"You are a small queer girl, Miss Susan," said Mrs. Trouncer, disapproving of me, "and there's no understanding you at all. You are a terrible child for reading and no mistake about it. What do you find in those books that is better than fresh air?"

I loved the little homely library with its bookcased walls and

46

dark-blue tapestries, especially in winter when the fire was crackling in the grate. I would come down from my frozen attic and stretch and warm and dream in the blaze of the red flames. The smell of half-burned logs, the stinging smoke, if there was peat, hung about my eyes. It meant all of White Orchard Manor, this room where I could be alone, and in spite of the ugliness in life which rose out of the pages I was reading, I was happy there.

Henrietta had returned to favour and once more was Papa and Mamma's coddling. She bewitched them with her feline smile. Sweet and insidious, she was a very tender hypocrite. I hated her 'Yes, Papa . . . No, Mamma . . . Dear Papa,' knowing full well the dust she was throwing in their doting eyes. Vanity was her plaything and frequently she would cry, "Watch me and see how well I beguile and dupe and play a trick. Take a lesson from me, Susan." And she would laugh at Papa and Mamma behind their backs, preening herself.

There was, it had to be admitted, an elegant air about Henrietta, an unembarrassed grace. She imagined high-flown, pretentious things about herself, tossing her red hair about her shoulders, adoring herself. Her hair was an ornament of beauty, like burnished gold, tip-tinged with red.

She refused to be led by Mamma's "You cannot do that, my darling," or "See that you do this." She imagined the universe was her playground and that she could pick and choose her toys at will. She believed that everything God had ever made was crowded together upon earth for her amusement. Her vanity was overwhelming—round and round her mirror she would flutter as a moth round a flame.

I do not think there could have been twins so utterly unlike

47

as we were. My looks were a constant humiliation to Mamma who declared I favoured some throwback of the Darlingtons. Over and over again I kept saying to myself that if it had not been for Henrietta I might not have seemed so homely. Living with Henrietta was a constant self-abasement, with her flaunting loveliness and fearless mien for ever in my way.

It was "Henrietta this" and "Henrietta that"; I was sick and tired of her praises. How good she was, how comely, and what a happy family we should be because she graced it. Henrietta could do no wrong; she was the little angel; everyone admired Henrietta.

Mamma took great pains to have us both educated in delicate deportment so that we should be a credit to her when we went out into the world. My sister of course was highly accomplished and could play with great skill upon the harpsichord; whilst I could sing, though timidly, as if I was ashamed of the sound of my own voice.

We had a daily governess by the name of Miss Flint who came all the way from Springfield Town just to instruct us in the elegances and graces of the times. Miss Flint always wore mittens and a plain gold ring like a wedding ring, and attired herself in nothing but black. People said there was a sad story behind her life. Miss Flint had once been betrothed to an impecunious town clerk, a delicate gentleman who stooped when he walked as if always on the look out for something on the roadway. He coughed and wheezed considerably and suffered from violent spasms, and it was just this frailty, it was said, which appealed to Miss Flint. But about the time they were to be wed, in fact after the banns had been published, the town clerk was found sitting dead in his chair with a half-written letter to Miss Flint on his knees. She always carried this letter within the folds of her black dress, and it was told by those who lived near her that at night they could hear her weeping. In the daytime, however, when she was with us, she went about with the set expression of one who has closed a book with a snap and locked it. I felt sorry for Miss Flint and would do little things to try and entertain her. I would pick flowers and put them on her table. Henrietta said there was no need for this and that I was only wasting my time. She said Miss Flint was not the type to handle and hold a husband, and that the impecunious clerk was much happier dead than he ever would have been married to Miss Flint.

Although we were older now we hardly ever met anyone of our own age, yet the house was continually filled with famous people and we were obliged to listen to conversation of such a brilliant order that I became more and more despondent. What could I say that would be of interest to these needle-wits? My little chatterings on this and that seemed suddenly meaningless and thin. How could I be entertaining upon the maxims of Napoleon, the Roman Empire, Religion and Philosophy and Music? What did I know of such things except a few copy-book instructions gleaned from Miss Flint's timid lessons? Henrietta said she did not care and that if they could not listen to her they could at least look at her, "Which is more than can be said of you, unhappy Susan."

Papa monopolized the talk at table, where he was always in his element. It was not easy to get his voice out of our ears. Not that it was an unduly loud voice, but it had such a wish to be heard above the clatter of dishes and plates that whenever he spoke the domestics automatically stood still with whatever they had in their hands, and everyone in the dining room would seem to pause and look up from what they were eating to listen to Papa's oration. It must be confessed that he sometimes bored his audience with long and pointless windings into the past, but his exquisite sense of humour and ready wit usually saved him from monotony. Everything about these gatherings was orderly except Papa. The meal was chosen with the utmost care by Mamma, and was exceedingly well served. Mamma asserted that we entertained too frequently and she was for ever upbraiding Papa for his ceaseless invitations. But he would only laugh and shrug his shoulders and say, "You cannot call our lives together gay or hilarious or in any way illuminating; is it my fault, therefore, that we should be obliged to rely upon our guests to entertain us?"

We never travelled; the farthest I had ever been by carriage was to Springfield Town. Never once had I looked upon the sea or the mountains. Everything I knew of the world seemed to be confined to the small area of gardens, fields and giant forest trees that lay within the iron gates of White Orchard Manor.

I loved the wintry wind as it came hurtling round the corner, flinging the snow into people's eyes. I loved to see the snow being shaken from the branches and come clattering from the housetops. It seemed to me the wind had far more fun than I, blue-tinting children's noses and spraying their faces with snow. The wind laid snow on people's doorsteps; raised drifts and flung them into the recesses of the streets and glued white sheets upon the windows. The wind whistled in people's ears and tore hats from their heads and tossed flounces from slim ankles. It played pranks in chimneys and scared infants in their cots. It had no heart for the old folk with chattering teeth and knees knocking together.

I loved the rains and the wild patches of open grass where I could walk with no one to disturb me; and there, alone in the fields, I could forget Henrietta and Papa and Mamma and my vexation, and live in a dream world of my own. In those dreams of mine I would traverse many countries, let my thoughts play in the sands of faraway beaches and build castles there. But, as soon as I entered the manor, there was Mamma . . . Mamma with her austerity and Henrietta with her conceit, sweeping away my illusions and leaving the sands sifting . . . sifting with no trace of either my castles or my dreams.

It was wonderful how in the summer the sun filled White Orchard Manor. Not a nook or cranny escaped it. As it poured in at the latticed windows and crept along the papered walls, the whole building seemed lit up from the outside. The very gables were outlined with sunshine, the tall chimneys scorched with it.

Yet the corridors were cool because long shadows enclosed them and there were no windows through which the sun could force its way. But, once out of the corridors, you came upon the cedarwood stairs where splashes of light lay upon the scented woodwork. From then on to the sitting rooms, with their long french windows to the ground, was a riot of coloured carpets; and in the summer, when these windows were wide open, the smell of sweet roses pervaded the whole place. Sometimes I used to think our home must be like God's Heaven.

The late autumn was the only time when White Orchard Manor was not beautiful. Then it was clothed and wound round in fog, for the house rested upon clay soil and a yellow mantle spread itself across the fields and lay over the garden like a shroud. It was then that the big house shivered and icicles hung in pointed needle shapes from the roof. From out of the chimneys came little threads of smoke which the fog lapped up, and the lights from our windows were like watering eyes, blinking and winking in the vaporous haze.

I did not go out much in dirty weather such as this but remained bent over my books in the library, which was companionable and warm, and it was there I could always be found if anybody wanted me.

Mamma disapproved of my reading so much and said it was most uncommendable at my tender age, and Papa would counsel me not to be foolish and shut myself up against the world.

"Preserve yourself in discretion and modesty whilst you are young," he would say. "That is the whole of it, child, to keep young as long as ever you can, for youth, my dear, is the greatest gift and has the shortest span and not one hour of it should be wasted."

I often wondered about Mamma. Was she indeed of so delicate and refined a nature, or was she assuming the manners and modes of her beloved Queen? Nobody could possibly have called this era "once upon a good time"; there was nothing grand about it, not even anything to brag about. The Queen's retirement had constrained and lowered the tone of her reign; it had also helped to confine Mamma to her room. Society was sobered down to please the Queen, and Mamma had quietened with it. How I wished I could have been more like Papa and less like her: for it was from her, I came to believe, that I had inherited this darkness in my soul, this nameless dread.

From our earliest childhood we had been taught that little

girls were menials brought into the world only to wait upon men's pleasure. Men were the highest living creatures and should be exalted as such. Henrietta could feel nothing but contempt for such a view. "Men shall serve me," she said with a toss of her red hair. "You see how I will make them run."

Papa was quite happy within himself and was to himself a god in miniature. "I am only sorry for those who are not acquainted with me," he would say with his blue eyes twinkling. "I regret all the things they will miss in never knowing me."

He would spend hours painting this picture of himself in most gorgeous colours. It amused him, so he said, to lie awake at night and think how wonderful he was. "Live well, in the hopes that you may die with your boots on," was his motto, and when the day should come when his eyes were too dim to see a pretty face, and his limbs too old to chase after a wench, he would have no desire to remain upon this earth.

Mamma was exceedingly proud of her family tree, and it distressed her beyond all words to see one of its branches bend and fall. She believed fervently in inheritance and ancestors and family vaults. Deservedly respected, no breath of scandal had ever fanned or shaken her frigid piety. Papa, on the other hand, was a man of moonshine, a shameless profligate who preferred the world outside convention, the exciting world, as he called it, filled with the flotsam and jetsam of humanity.

"You cannot prejudice me, Lucy," he would say, "you cannot possibly prejudice me into believing that high society is the be-all and end-all of existence. I have seen too much of the world. I know it intimately. The ways and means of it and its insane acts and moments of great beauty. You have missed a lot, my dear, by closing yourself in from it. To be a good citizen

53

you must roam the city and meet every man and woman who walks the streets, the streets that are little threads of knowledge which pull at your heart strings and tear into your brain and make you think. Have you ever thought about people, Lucy, masses of people, not individuals? Have you ever paid attention to other people's lives? Flunkeyism, my dear, such as yours, I do not agree with. A human being is a human being whether in rags or in a quilted waistcoat. A gay cravat, believe me, will not conceal his make-up, or worn-out shoes display more than a naked foot. Rich frames, my love, do not make excellent pictures; it is the canvas within the frame and the way it has been handled which either makes it a masterpiece or a thing of little value."

Mamma was often both mortified and embarrassed by Papa's strange moralizing and told him so in no uncertain voice.

"Good blood like ours should not be wasted, Edward. It should be preserved and kept within the social compass; otherwise who knows where your blood may be if you once let it loose amongst the masses."

There were times when Papa would be in one of his country moods and when, metaphorically of course, he would explore England. There never was anything more gloriously imagined than Papa's mental excursions from his armchair to the country.

"Give me God's good air and freedom," he would shout from the depths of his comfortable cushions, and he would draw a long breath as if indeed he was inhaling a stomach full of weather. Of course Papa had every right to love the great outdoors, but I could not help feeling that an armchair and a few glasses of port wine would make him love almost anything. He knew that he often neglected us and, although at times he was

54

contrite and sad at heart, he had no zest for a decorous family life. Domesticity was the death of all genius, he maintained, and a man's personality was lost within the folds of a silk petticoat.

"Nothing means much to me except myself," he would say sometimes to Mamma.

"But what about the children, Edward, do they not mean anything to you?"

"No more and no less, my dearest Lucy, than a few moments of inadvertent rapture."

"Really, Edward, why must you shock me so?"

"The trouble with you, my dear Lucy, is that you are too deucedly straight-laced. Why do you perpetually refuse to face reality in any form or shape? There is nothing unbecoming in conception. It is a perfectly normal act of nature, either agreeable or completely senseless, that even the Queen herself has indulged in. Poets have made their fortunes because of it, musicians have filled our ears with music to express it. Volumes have been written eulogising its sensuous diversity, and yet, in spite of all this, sex is an immodesty from which you turn your chaste and virtuous eyes. It is women like you, Lucy, who make men like me deplore the dullness of a married life. Give me the wantons and the waywards, I say, for theirs is the life that all men wish to live."

Our cold and carping Mamma was often filled with discomfiture at Papa's outspokenness, and indeed, as we grew older, she was afraid that his way of living might corrupt us. I often wished she could have heard Henrietta telling me things, things that her darling daughter was acquainted with, but which she herself had not even heard of.

55

We had lately acquired a new domestic, a chambermaid called Rosaline. She was dark and buxom and, moreover, her roguish eyes looked frequently with approval upon Papa. Henrietta and I would often overhear conversations between them issuing from the dining room.

"Well, Rosaline, and how are we getting on? You are quite happy here, are you not?"

"Oh yes, my Lord."

"Let me know if there is any little thing you want; her Ladyship is always very busy."

"Thank you, my Lord."

"Not at all, my dear, not at all. I like to feel that everyone is happy. I reflect other people's moods; do you reflect, Rosaline?"

"I am sure I don't know, my Lord."

"Think it over, my dear, and see what you can make of it."

"Very well, my Lord, I will."

It was so evident to us, by the sound of her voice, that she had not the slightest idea what he was talking about. Then one day Mamma caught a glimpse of her giggling and tittering high upon Papa's knee, and the storm that rose upon this lashed White Orchard Manor for many a day. Needless to say, Rosaline was instantly dismissed, and Mamma engaged a maid of so fearsome a countenance Papa declared he well-nigh sputtered each time he found her in his way. "That is exactly how I planned it," said Mamma with a wry smile. "Here is a young person you will have no desire to include amongst your 'Angels' and I shall have no reason to see this excellent domestic descending on wings to dust the drawing room."

And so, whilst White Orchard Manor basked in the warmth

Papa's conversations, Mrs. Trouncer put ear to keyhole and ored up what she had heard for the benefit of the servants. "His Lordship is a one for the women," she told her wide-eyed teners. "The poor gentleman is so tangled in petticoats he can ot free himself. But he bears his imprisonment uncommon well; e likes the sound of them and the smell of them and the wink g of a baggage as she passes him by. Not that it surprises me, e way he goes on, with that spouse of his who could not tickle e palate of a saint; but mark my words, these romps of his ordship's and the way he drinks will be the death of him one y."

Papa used to tell Henrietta about his gallantries, boasting out them with his chest well out and his head high, but after s brief encounter with me upon the facts of life, he had spaired of my sagacity and did not think it worth his while to lighten me much further. The only times he would take notice me would be to reprimand me for my lack of confidence, and swear that his guests took umbrage at my dullness.

"Silence can be interesting, Susan," he said, "if it is accompa ed by intelligence of thought; but long spaces of inarticulation o not add to the gaiety of things. Conversation implies reci ocity, but whisperings and undertones do not increase the eneral flow of talk. I know you try, alas, most ineffectually to itertain. If you cannot wag a merry tongue of your own, my ar, for the Lord's sake steal other people's thoughts and make e most of them."

"But, Papa . . ."

"Do you know what constitutes a nuisance, Susan? There are vo kinds. The public nuisance who bellows and roars too udly and too long, and the dumb nuisance who is a drone about

57

the house. Fond as I am of you, my dear, I regret to inform you
I am obliged to look upon you as my most secluded source of
irritation."

"I am sorry, Papa."

"And so you should be, so you should be, child, considering
the care that was lavished upon your education. When I die you
will be extremely opulent and wealthy in all things. Pray do not
say anything suitable about hoping my demise will not be for a
long long time to come, when it is only natural you should wish
for me to break my unworthy neck. It is what a man of my
income is obliged to put up with; somebody is always wishing
he was dead."

"Papa . . . dearest Papa, I have no such thoughts; how can
you say such things?"

"I say them because they are true, Susan, but you are a good
wench and I have no doubt you wish me well. But, my dear,
exert yourself a little, sparkle and scintillate, have a run and be
run after. I do not desire, mark you, that you should set the table
in continuous mirth, but I do lament your pointless melancholy
which turns my guests yawning from their meal. A little more
levity, like Henrietta has, would well become you."

"You mean you would like me to be more like Henrietta?"

"She is no wit-snapper, God knows, but she is an excellent
listener. There is nothing men appreciate more than being well
listened to, Susan, and damn it, there are several ways of being
attentive. You can listen with half an ear, or you can give the
gentleman your full attention. You can be engaging or wool
gathering. The bend of a gracious neck, the thoughtful glance,
the smile of appreciation; these things are important, child, if
you wish to make a conquest."

58

"And Henrietta has these qualities, Papa?"

"To a certain measure she has them well enough."

"Well, she can keep them then," I replied bitterly, "for I do not want anything of hers," and, turning my back upon Papa, I swept out of the room.

Then, quite suddenly, the wheels of fate started to turn in Springfield Town and a piece of news spread light of heel through the cobbled street.

Wingmeadow Lodge had been sold.

The news unfolded as such things will in various forms; table talk in the rich houses and tittle tattle at the inn, for no one imagined anything could possibly happen to the house which had stood empty for so long.

Wingmeadow Lodge had a little estate that lay stretched across the highest ground in the district, and although the villagers were obliged to look up at it with their eyes, they looked down upon it in their minds.

It had been empty for as long as we could remember. It was a lean, mean-looking building with hardly a tree to be seen. The walls were grey and the windows had wooden shutters like dusty eyebrows hanging over them. The garden had wound itself into the lane with weeds clinging to the flowers like vampires sucking the colour and the strength from them. There was an unkept cruelty about the place, a feeling as you went in at the gate that this house did not want you.

There it stood with its back against the sky, a grim recluse, a grey-walled hermit caring for nobody and uncared for.

Dotted about were barns and granaries so familiar in country such as this, but somehow Wingmeadow Lodge did not seem to belong to them, and the barns and granaries kept well away from it, and the farms turned their doors from it; yet, there was no perceptible reason why this home should be so shunned; it was just one of those houses nobody liked.

Wingmeadow Lodge had been sold to a certain Mrs. Lynton Abigail, a lady dis-espoused, we learned, and with seven sons.

Tongues wagged in Springfield Town, and the cronies got together and nodded and nudged and drank cups of newly brewed tea as they talked. Who was Mrs. Abigail and where did she come from, and was it not a fact that there was much ado on account of some court scandal attaching to her? Mrs. Trouncer, who knew everybody's business better than she knew how to mind her own, went about tale-bearing and whispering that Mrs. Lynton Abigail was no better than she should be and was of so perverse a nature that even her own sons were afraid of her. She was an adventuress, Mrs. Trouncer affirmed, with more money than she knew what to do with, a painted, spirited baggage who had the attire of a harlot and wore so many jewels at a time they were enough to set the town ablaze.

Mamma accepted the gossip about these newcomers with extreme repugnance although she spent many an hour closeted with Mrs. Trouncer and questioned her closely. She charged us to keep away from Wingmeadow Lodge as she did not consider the family desirable or fit for our acquaintance. "It is best we should stand apart," she said. "Mrs. Abigail is, I have no doubt, a most worthy woman in spite of what they say, but she is not exactly one of us and is not in the front window of the fashionable world. Besides which, she has too large a family. Certainly that in itself denotes a lack of modesty and self-restraint."

"Pish and tush, my dear," replied Papa. "There is nothing

nore inspiring than a fruitful woman if she can be afforded
nd afford herself. I am told on the very best authority that
Mrs. Abigail is the finest breeder who has ever come this way
nd that she hardly had time to suckle one infant before another
was well upon the way; they came tumbling from her lovely
oody as easily as the leaves fall from a tree. God bless my soul,
even sons is a masterly achievement which I must confess I do
greatly envy."

"This conversation is most unseemly, Edward, and hardly
necessary before the children."

"Children be damned, Lucy, do you think of them still in
waddling clothes? Can it be that you still wish our darlings
o believe that babes are found in bullrushes, or that we ring a
oell and, heigh presto, a whelp is on the doorstep?"

"Certainly not, Edward; nevertheless, I see no necessity for
calling a spade a spade."

"You estimate your prudery too highly, my dear Lucy; there
s no shame in being brought to bed in childbirth. On the con-
rary, there is beauty in it. A mighty fire crackling in the hearth
and the swaddling clothes billowing in the warmth. The mid-
wife creeping about on tiptoe like a merciful ghost, and then,
of a sudden, the tearing agony like a violent storm passing across
he room and leaving behind it exquisite repose."

"Such eloquence, my dear Edward, could only come from
one who has never suffered childbirth. It does not, however,
alter my opinion that Mrs. Abigail's extensive family savours of
provincial homeliness, and that she flaunts her fruitfulness too
openly."

"In what way, Lucy, is she conscious of her glory?"

"They say she takes her seven sons with her no matter where

she goes, and that the streets are strewn with Abigails. They say she is never without them by her side, never alone, so that no one can converse with her without seven pairs of ears and seven pairs of eyes glued upon their words."

"Who says these things?"

"Everyone, Edward; it is the common talk."

Papa frowned and looked amazingly displeased. His eyes wandered up and down Mamma as if she were some strange phenomenon.

"I have never slapped your face, Lucy," he said, "but, by gad, I feel inclined to do so now. If there is one thing in this world I do detest it is malicious and promiscuous gossip. Here is a lady you have never met, you have not even seen her, and yet you have the audacity to make up your mind, and the effrontery to affirm that she flourishes and parades her brood. Can it not be that she is fond of them, and can it not also be that my dear wife is perhaps a little envious because she herself could never raise a son? Upon my soul, Lucy, I am surprised that you can so abase yourself as to listen to this gibble gabble."

"The Queen has been provoked by this lady's disrepute and she has been banished from court circles, and Lady Garmington says . . ."

"Lady Garmington . . . I might have guessed. That trussed-up old feline should have retired to a cats' home a century ago. By the Lord, Lucy, it amazes me that you, who are presumably a sensible woman, can behave so like a fool."

The storm ended in the usual way with Mamma sailing from the room and Papa stamping the floor and mulling port, and Henrietta having a few things to say about the folly of two grown-up people quarrelling like fire eaters over next to nothing.

Before the arrival of the Abigails there began the renovations to the lodge and preparations within doors, with workmen hurrying to and fro along Wingmeadow Lane. The shutters were repainted and gaily coloured curtains fluttered from the windows. The garden was disentangled from its weeds and the soil turned so that the smell of good earth pervaded everywhere. Richly tinted carpets were carried into the house and large-covered carts went by with pieces of furniture and beds and draperies bulging from them.

Henrietta and I could watch all this from the top of a gate at the far end of the lane, and we could just see the servants hurry back and forth until the last cart had been emptied of its load.

On the Sunday when the Abigails arrived, Wingmeadow Lane looked like some mysterious corridor of wild rose hedges. It was so quiet that every little bird could be distinguished by its song, and high up in the half-blue sky a lark twisted in its flight to soar for a moment over a bright patch of wild clover. Then a church bell tolled from across the village, and far away another bell from Springfield Town. In a field, close by, some children were playing and tearing up handfuls of buttercups, leaving a wound in the sweltering meadow like a scar in the center of a lovely face.

It was one of those fierce and burning days in June. All the streets and walls and roofs of the cottages were tinged with sunlight. Only the trees were cool with their leaves slightly curled like supplicating hands waiting to be rain filled. Small clouds softened the sky, making their way leisurely towards the horizon. Everything idled in the fevered heat, and only now and again the noise of a cricket bat and the shout of a child could be heard.

It appeared fitting, somehow, that the Abigails should "move in" in a blaze of summer, for Mrs. Abigail and her seven sons belonged so much to sunshine and warmth and the blue sky overhead.

Some of the townsfolk were grouped at the corner of Wingmeadow Lane like a cluster of crows cackling and cawing and sifting up dung. Both Papa and Mamma would have nothing to do with the arrival, although Papa declared very loudly in favour of giving this good lady the benefit of being seen, and that in a day or two he himself would like to have a look at the hussy to see what it was she had that so many women envied.

Mrs. Trouncer had taken us down to the town on a pretext of visiting some poor relation of hers; but in reality it was for nothing better than to peer and pry into every hole and corner to see what was going on.

Never in Springfield had so many people been seen at their doors, never had there been so many windows to polish and so much reason for lingering in the street. How energetic and solicitous the townsfolk had become for their houses, and how many ladders were raised to tie back refractory creepers on their walls. You would have thought that they cared for nothing better in this world than the houses that were facing the street. Nobody went to their back gardens or tended their kitchen doors, for they could not see round the corner from there or hear what was going on.

Mrs. Trouncer was in her element and flitted from one to the other.

"I've an extraordinary partiality for knowing about my next-door neighbours," she said, "and the fumes of a morsel of gossip are as good to me as the smell of a roasting pig."

It was not long before she had discovered how many servants had been hired at Wingmeadow Lodge and what were their duties, but I could not for the life of me see what business it was of hers, or of anyone else's, who Mrs. Abigail employed.

It was towards the late afternoon when we heard the rumble of wheels and the horses clattering on the cobble stones; a sound I was to remember always and one that would for ever strike a chord in my heart.

Very soon the great coach turned into the town and came towards us. The top was filled to the brim with trunks and bandboxes, with a man servant hanging onto them and onto his hat at the same time. There was a youth with a white peaked face, who was dressed as a groom, seated behind him and covered with dust, and the horses were stumbling and stretching with their load.

Then an amazing thing happened so suddenly and so swiftly we hardly had time to draw breath before it was over.

Just as the coach was about to swing past us, Henrietta, whom we had not been observing, stepped out from the pavement, as it seemed, right under the wheels of it.

The coachman stood up and dragged at the reins with such frightful oaths pouring from his lips that some of the townsfolk quivered and covered their ears. The maddened horses plunged and reared and fell back upon their haunches with the foam dripping from their steaming bodies and splashing from their mouths as the great coach came to a standstill.

Out of the window leaned a young man well favoured and with a strong clean beauty which at the moment was marred by the fury of his face. He looked at us standing motionless with terror, and then at the horses with their reeking sides, and last of all at Henrietta smiling and smirking and twisting her parasol round in her hands. Then he rapped out an oath and called down curses upon the girl who stood there so cool and complacent as if she had done nothing at all to disturb us.

"Damn and confound you," he roared, "do you want to get yourself killed, you red-headed nonny, or are you bereft of all reason and possessed of a devil? Do you think that we care to have our horses' mouths bleeding and the risk of them breaking a leg, just because a slip of a girl has not the sense to look which way she is going?"

Before she had time to reply he had said something to the coachman and, with a great deal of rattling of harness and grinding of wheels, the post chaise was put into motion. We had a swift vision of three small boys standing on the hinder seats with their noses hard pressed against the windows, and as they passed Henrietta they all three of them put out their little red tongues at her.

"Angels and ministers of grace, what underbred skipjacks!" screamed Mrs. Trouncer, shaking her parasol after the coach. "Did you ever in your life see such manners as that?"

But I had my eyes on Henrietta and was watching the look on her face.

"What made you do it?" I asked her. "Whatever made you do such a thing?"

"It was well timed," replied Henrietta, straining to look after the coach.

"Well timed for what, Henrietta?"

But she did not answer. She merely smiled to herself in a manner I did not like.

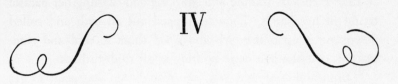

IV

THE ARRIVAL of the Abigails filled in a space of vague visions and happenings in which we played and worked and learned deportment. We seldom met the newcomers, as Mamma still refused to accept them. Why had they moved in, she grumbled, disturbing the peace with their colourful array? Wingmeadow Lodge had been better empty than filled with these clamorous jackanapes. She forbade us to roam in the lane or to go without a chaperon, and whenever we did come face to face with this family, Mrs. Trouncer would draw us to one side as if the very air they breathed would injure us.

The young man who had raged at Henrietta, and whose name we had discovered was Kelvin, would ride along the road and gravely raise his hat to us, but there was never so much as a smile on his face or a kindly look in our direction. Henrietta would stamp her foot and bite her lips with vexation and say what an arrogant unlicked cub he was to be sure and how she would teach him a lesson one day he would not be likely ever to forget.

Sometimes we met them on their way to church. Mrs. Abigail was tall and a little on the plump side which was not surprising considering she had given birth so freely. Vague and easy-going, she had allowed nature to do what it willed with her and, but for the mercy of God and the blessed event of Mr. Abigail's elopement with a hussy from out of town, she might have been the mother of several more sons.

Mrs. Trouncer informed us that Mr. Abigail had been a good-looking good-for-nothing who had left his wife for no better reason than that he found her too prolific and fruit bearing; for strange to say, he had never particularly wanted any children and had a strong and fearful dislike of them.

"Though what I say is," said Mrs. Trouncer emphatically, "a small man with a large family is a better man, and a braver and altogether a more satisfactory man than an impotent earl; not that I am throwing aspersions at his Lordship's present inutility, I can assure you."

Infants alarmed Mr. Abigail, so it was said, and Mrs. Trouncer, who was by now completely cognizant of their entire history, avowed it was true; their bubbling gurgling innocence had given Mr. Abigail a sense of guilt. How could he face his seven sons when they grew to man's estate and asked him to inform them about wenching? How could he face them when he himself had held many a fancy courtesan in his arms? "Not only that," said Mrs. Trouncer, "that was not the whole of it; the truth was that this litter of boys made him feel old and established and very much over-domesticated. So what does he do but up and skedaddle with his strumpet and that was the end of that."

Mrs. Abigail had a kind and sensible face which was far more attractive to the eye than actual beauty, and it was easy to see why men were so entranced by her and women so envenomed. She had dancing dark eyes and a large provocative mouth and she was most colourfully dressed and lavishly perfumed. Her arms were hung with trinkets which tinkled when she moved, and she seemed always to be laughing as if she had not a single care in the world.

68

Beside her were her seven sons, Kelvin, Henry, Phillip, Geoffrey, Shelly, Roger and Silvain; and as she sat in church with these seven Master Abigails all in a row, beginning with the little Silvain and stretching as far as the tall and handsome Kelvin, she was a sight the villagers could not take their eyes from. When they knelt to pray the three youngest would disappear from view so that there was a gap in the congregation like the space in the mouth of a man who has lost three teeth.

The church we went to was pretty enough with its simple spire and ivy clad walls. A little gate opened wide to receive us, and two ancient doors stood between the sunshine and the dark cold shadows of the aisle. As soon as we entered those doors I had the feeling we had left God outside in the warmth and were herded together for no better purpose than to pick each other to pieces. All desire to pray seemed frozen within me, and instead of thinking about God and the Gospel, as I had been taught, and indeed as I most fervently wished to do, I found myself thinking only of Henrietta and of the score I held against her.

When I asked Mrs. Trouncer the reason for this she replied:

"We don't belong to the church, that's why; none of us do excepting her Ladyship and it's been no help to her, poor soul. We ought not to go before God feeling the way we do about it, it isn't righteous."

"Are you a religious woman, Mrs. Trouncer?"

"Well I am and I ain't, as the saying is," she replied with her hand on her beak of a nose. "If Heaven was to send down a decent creature to preach, maybe I might consider it. But I ask you, what do we get? The fool of the family, most likely, with his witless prattlings and nonsensical prayers. I've better things to do at the manor, Miss Susan, than listen to him; things that, in spite of being Sunday, have to be done. Clean wholesome

69

things such as ironing and sweeping and tidying, even God Himself couldn't object to."

The Reverend Harper Barklett was prim faced and short sighted. As he preached his little eyes snapped from the pulpit at his parishioners, and his high-pitched voice came to them like the cracking of a whip across their conscience. He tossed his lean body from side to side as if determined to trounce and rebuke his assembled sinners, especially Papa, who behaved outrageously, repeating his responses in as loud a voice as he could muster in the hopes that Mrs. Abigail would look round at him. But Mrs. Abigail was an excellent Christian and never turned her head; only the three little boys peered over the back of the pew with their eyes as round as saucers.

"I wish you would listen more to the sermon, Edward," said Mamma petulantly as soon as it was over. "The poor man was extremely upset at the boldness of your manner."

"The church is all very well to be married in," replied Papa, "and the churchyard has its uses to be buried in, but this wail of woe, this whining incantation, chokes in my throat with its lamentable uselessness. I cannot be expected to implore the Deity to let bygones be bygones when I have not the slightest intention of reforming. As for you, my dear Lucy, you are already so absolved and so far on your way to Heaven you need no supplications from me or from the Reverend Barklett to improve your gracious passage."

Our procession from White Orchard Manor on Sundays was indeed impressive. First Henrietta and I with our hair drawn neatly into nets, our demurest petticoats and trim straw hats. Then Mamma with her backward flounces, embellished in her best, carrying a small prayer book in one hand and a diminutive parasol in the other; and Papa by her side, annoyed and elegant, protesting loudly against being forced from his armchair. Behind us the servants, with Mrs. Trouncer at the head of them, resplendent in her tight silk bodice, and behind her the uncomely chambermaids walking sadly with their hands folded before them.

I loved these gentle ambles to the church and the slow chiming of the bells, especially in autumn when the leaves were rotting in the clay soil, red and gold buried in black mire. I loved to see them lying in a pool of colour by the edges of the road, and to smell them and stir their fetid fragrance of fungus and wet brushwood. Then, in the winter days, all of us walking with our heads lowered and our skirts raised over our boots; the wind tossing the trees so that their lean drenched branches thrashed against the ground. I loved the smell of wet raincoats and dripping umbrellas laid on the benches close to the church door, and to see the people's faces in the dimly lit aisle looking like red apples shining between dark poke bonnets and small straw hats.

I tried to picture Wingmeadow Lodge and the Abigails preparing themselves for the morning Service, Mrs. Abigail selecting her most seductive gown and Kelvin his best coat. I imagined the little boys scrambling to have their hair brushed, and Geoffrey, the untidy one, mooning in the garden and forgetting what day it was. I could see them all in my mind's eye, always merry, always laughing together and at play. A happy home in spite of its hard-featured exterior so different from ours.

It was Mrs. Trouncer who first informed us how intrigued she believed Papa to be with the notorious Mrs. Abigail.

"He's at his tricks again, the old reprobate," she said in the familiar way she spoke of Papa, having been with us so long. "You would think he was tired of attachments by now, and nods and becks, and of kissing and bussing and sweet honeyed words.

But not a bit of it. A petticoat's a petticoat to most of us, but to his Lordship it's what's under it which counts. A slim pair of legs and a trim pair of ankles he's never lost an eye to. Maybe it's the contrast of his incompatibility with her Ladyship that's the cause of it, but what we say below stairs is he should have more respect for all of you."

"But, Mrs. Trouncer, how do you know all this, about Papa I mean?"

"I'm as fond of speculating as I am of spinach, Miss Susan," replied Mrs. Trouncer, "and spinach as you know is my favourite dish. There's something about groping and feeling and fumbling for information I never seem to tire of. I'm an imaginative woman, my dear, with a nose for ferreting that never fails me."

I do not think Mrs. Abigail was at first aware of Papa's admiration for her and how strong a hold her presence had upon him. He took to meandering through Wingmeadow Lane in the hopes of meeting her, and he hung about Springfield Town on any pretext whatsoever on the chance that she might be there shopping. But, to do him justice, he would always return with some nonsensical gift for Mama, which she received with a curl of her lip and a shrug of her shoulders because she knew full well the reason.

One day both Papa and Mamma were out walking with us when we met Mrs. Abigail and her sons as they were returning from the village. It may or may not have been a coincidence that Mamma was so intent upon the closing of her parasol; but the fact remained that she was unable to raise her eyes and therefore made out not to see the group before us. Papa drew to the side of the road and swept off his hat with a bow that would have done honour to a duchess.

"By gad, she is a gorgeous creature!" he said, his blue eyes

72

bulging at this wondrous sight. "The most enticing piece of femininity it has ever been my fortune to behold; she is like Dresden china in this dusty store of a town."

"I do not know to whom you are referring," replied Mamma, still playing with the fastenings of her parasol.

"Had you had the courtesy to look up, my love, it might have been more gracious."

"I am sorry, Edward, I was otherwise engaged."

"Was your parasol of such importance that you quite forgot your manners?"

"It was to me, Edward; it was a most expensive parasol and I do not care to misuse it. I am sorry indeed if I appeared discourteous."

"You appeared only as you intended to, my dear, extremely impolite. Mrs. Abigail is at this moment fully aware that you do not wish to meet her or her family."

"Is there any reason why I should, Edward? There are not many who receive her. Are you forgetting she is disespoused and . . ."

This was all Papa needed to set his temper flying.

"Disespoused say you," he roared. "And what if she is, what if she is, I ask you? Was it her fault that she was married to a rakehell of a husband, and would you have her take him back to bed? God protect me from a virtuous woman if she is filled with such hypocrisy as this. Let me tell you, Madam, you are more wrong than Mrs. Abigail since you tolerate my misbehaviour only because of what you think people might say. Mrs. Abigail has a fine character, she has a noble conception of what God ordained by marriage. God commanded that there should be no adultery did He not, but society says condone your sin-

73

ners, conceal them in your arms, champion your evildoers and preserve them from court scandal and the Queen."

"Really, Edward, I see no reason for this outburst."

"I am sorry, Lucy, but you have touched upon a subject which concerns me deeply. There is something wrong in the condemnation of divorce, something most confoundedly wrong in the exclusion of those who believe in freedom from the bond that has long ceased to be decent."

"The Queen says . . ."

"God damn it, the Queen is unaccountable! And for that matter who can measure what is in the heart of that poor lady?"

"Then I take it you wish me to destroy my prejudice and become acquainted with this chiffonier?"

"I go even further; I demand it, Lucy. It is my desire that you invite Mrs. Abigail and her family to tea, and see to it that you make a favourable impression, my dear, in the hopes that she will forgive your impoliteness."

Accordingly, a few days later Mrs. Abigail arrived at White Orchard Manor, and she presented not without humour each one of her sons by name.

"My first-born Kelvin, Lady Darlington, my second Henry. Phillip, Geoffrey, Shelly, Roger and Silvain," and Mamma received them frigidly upright behind the tea table.

Mrs. Abigail appeared to be brilliantly gifted and had a great variety of topics and news of general interest; whatever it was she touched upon she did so lightly and with such a wit it was a pleasure listening to her. Her voice was softly modulated, and as she spoke her hands were never still so that her profusion of bracelets set up a chime each time she moved them. She seemed possessed with a strange unearthly power from within, and as she swept into our drawing room there was a perfume round her more fragrant than the flowers.

It was not an outstandingly successful affair, this tea party of ours, for Mamma refused to unbend and made forced unnatural conversation, whilst Papa flirted outrageously with our lovely guest.

The three little boys, Shelly, Roger and Silvain, were freshly coloured with round bright eyes like beads. They sat stiffly upon high-backed chairs with their small hands folded on their knees. First they looked at Papa and then at Mamma and then at Henrietta. It was evident they had not forgotten how she had held up the coach, for when they looked at her I could see the tips of their little red tongues protruding between their lips. When they became aware that I was watching them they turned away their heads, wriggling uncomfortably.

Shelly was pale and flabby and had a hurried way of speaking as if his thoughts were running along a platform catching a train. The reason for this, I found afterwards, was that his brothers never gave him time to finish a sentence but always caught up with him and finished it for him.

Geoffrey was a tall and awkward lad who seemed to be stretching out of his clothes. He had a thick crop of tow-coloured hair which rose all over his head like a kitchen mop. He wished to become an artist and so fashioned himself upon their negligence of dress. He even held a pencil behind his ear as if at any moment he would oblige us with a drawing.

Phillip was tall and sturdy with a kind of outdoor freshness and down-to-earth way of thinking; he looked honest and merry and soon enveloped the room with the warmth of his good-heartedness. He was, Papa said, more like his mother than the rest of them, and had the same attractive manners.

75

It was easy to see that Henrietta's desire was Kelvin. This was a new Henrietta I did not know, this humble supplicating creature begging for attention. Never had I seen her so simpering and sweet, or heard her voice more honeyed. As Kelvin bent his head appraising her I longed to cry out to him, "Master Abigail . . . Master Abigail, keep watch, take warning, for this is but a trap being laid for you."

And so as I was watching them I had time to observe what kind of a man this was.

He seemed handsomer with the frown gone from his face, and was tall and dark, towering above his brothers. His eyes were wide apart, his brow noble and the fine shape of his head denoted a go-to-the-devil pride. Colourful he was and exciting as he brought new life into that room. There seemed to be magic in his every movement. I was drawn to him and yet repelled, as if beneath his beauty there was something to be feared. Afterwards I found out that his passions were deep rooted and his tempers like a violent storm.

My interest and curiosity so absorbed me that I found myself staring at him with my lips apart, and so deep was I in this contemplation of him I did not notice he was well aware of my close scrutiny until he suddenly turned to me and said:

"A penny for your thoughts, Miss Susan. We are an eyeful, are we not? Are we pleasant or unpleasant, well favoured or uncouth?"

For a moment it seemed as if the room was twisting and turning and that I was about to swoon. I could feel the colour first burning and then draining from my face, and I was trembling so I was obliged to cling to the edges of my chair. Then he laughed, such a pleasurable sound it went straight into my heart.

76

"There, there," he said, "I was but teasing. Please do not take it so amiss. It is not surprising anyone should stare at us, and if there were seven of you, Miss Susan, I would doubtless never take my eyes from you."

That night Henrietta raged into my room, her face contorted and her eyes ablaze.

"How could you," she cried shrilly, "how could you make yourself so cheap? What behaviour was that to stare the poor man out of countenance?"

"I was only looking, Henrietta."

"Looking at what, may I ask; he is a man just as other men and does not expect to be gazed at in that bumpkin fashion?"

"He is the handsomest man I have ever seen. Do you not think so too, Henrietta?"

"What I think is my own concern and has no bearing on your manners. What will he think of us, what will he say of us? That we are but country clods and imbeciles and unworthy of his notice."

And so she raged at me until my attic room was filled with the clamour of her tongue, and when she had gone I sank back into the comfort of my pillows and thought of Kelvin. I remembered the quick way he had of turning, the force of his movements and the power of his hands, and then I remembered Henrietta and the way that she had fawned upon him, and the frown on her face when he had turned to me.

"Henrietta is jealous," I said to myself, "and I do believe for the first time in my life I have disturbed her."

And with this engaging thought I fell asleep.

V

We were grown-up young ladies now, tolerably accomplished and well versed in manners. Papa was in his sixties, a man advanced in life and touched as it were by time with little flecks of grey. His countenance had become greatly softened by the influence of port, but he still looked remarkably youthful and when complimented upon his sprightly appearance would say with a chuckle:

"There is a mighty difference between a young blood and an old buck, especially in the calves of the legs, and believe it or not I am finding it increasingly difficult to rise from my armchair."

Mamma had not appreciably altered, her hours and days still spent by rule. She would even now rise regularly and go to bed at a specific time and I do not remember her ever having been late for a meal or behind in her duties. Papa, as we well knew, had no idea of time and conducted his life entirely by his moods. He rarely kept an appointment, unless with a petticoat, and was invariably late for every repast he attended. There never had been any law or order in anything he did; method of mind, he said, dulled every enterprise and took all the spice away from the meat. When he opened a door he had not the slightest idea where he was going or why in God's name he had put on his hat. There was no pretence about this. Papa's uncertainty of purpose had made him the idler that he was. No desire to do anything or to be anybody had ever entered his mind. To know how to live was his profession, and to find entertainment his life's work.

"This punctuality, my love, alarms me," he would say to Mamma when he found her sitting severely before him at the table. "You see I am endowed or cursed, whichever it may be, with what you might describe as an untidy mind. If I plan to eat at a certain hour it puts me off my appetite. The chime of a clock chokes an engagement. It is only the spur of the moment that gives zest to an adventure, the thrill of not knowing what is on the other side of the street."

Mamma's temperament went less and less well with Papa's; age had not mellowed her and they were still a most discordant pair. Mamma was more aware perhaps than he was of this incompleteness in their married life. Their continuous quarrels held the gossip below stairs. And yet there never was any question of their leaving one another. Mamma would not have tolerated divorce, firstly because of the disapproval of the Queen, and secondly because she considered anyone who had made their own bed as willingly as she had, should lie upon it until God determined otherwise. Mamma quite genuinely believed that union at the altar was inviolate; she had fallen in love with this rollicking blue-eyed man, she had seen him and wanted him and imagined her own rigid purity would tame him. And as for Papa, he found his good wife too excellent a background, too respectable a cloak for his iniquities, to wish ever to discard her.

Consider then the conditions under which we lived and the influences that were certain to react upon us.

Our parents had laid no definite foundation for us beyond our admirable education. We did not even share their pleasures, such as they were. The actions of Papa, the spectacle of his daily life and self-indulgent habits, had pervaded the whole of our child lives. Why did they quarrel? Why was there so little laughter between these two? Why were they so seldom together, even in the house? Those were the questions that we asked ourselves. Henrietta said it was because all men were born evil and most women were fools. But I thought it went deeper than that, much deeper. I thought it was what made books and poems and music often sad; it was what made tragedies and suicides and a host of broken hearts. Without it, poets and painters and writers and composers would have a pretty poor time touching the minds and consciences of their audience.

When we sat down to a meal I would find myself praying that at least they would avoid the subjects which upset them. Religion, political arguments and gossip from Whitehall evoked a storm that was so distressing to me I would stoop over the table with quickly swallowed mouthfuls so that I could make a hasty retirement to my room.

"My dearest Lucy," Papa would say, "part of your charm no doubt is your free interchange of opinion however variant it may be; but I feel obliged to inform you, my love, that if I were not a tolerant man, a very tolerant man indeed, I would be exasperated by your whimsical reasonings veering from side to side like wind-blown weathercocks."

"You mean you find me illogical, Edward?"

"A woman's privilege, my dear, is to change her mind, but not quite so frequently as you do. I am bound to confess I find your little quibbles extremely disconcerting. If only you would keep to the point, Lucy, it would make conversation so much pleasanter."

"The point being yours, I presume, and I must agree with your opinion?"

"On the whole, I believe you will find that I know best and that I am usually aware of what I am talking about."

"And I am not, is that it, is that what you suggest?"

"At times you are, and then there are occasions when you allow your thoughts to get the better of you and our argument depends upon what is on your mind and how much imprecation lies there."

And so in this strain between plentiful glasses of port, Papa would mortify and vex her and grate upon her feelings. Poor Mamma, she had indeed much to contend with as he practised on her patience, and it was not surprising that she spent most of her life with a brooding sense of wrong.

And what of Henrietta? Had she improved with age, had she and I drawn any closer throughout the years?

Imperious and impatient, Henrietta did not shift the scene nor stem the tide. She was still possessed of a strange unworldly cruelty, and it was not so much that I was afraid of her as it was of the effect she had upon me. What she had done to me I could not even cry over, for it seemed to me beyond all tears. Her system had been so subtle, my destruction so complete. It was not only that I had no force of character, but I had no qualities at all, no frame of mind, no fond illusions. Henrietta had taken most of my heart and left me with nothing but an empty shell.

"You have no notion of life, poor Susan," she said, "no spirit for it; therefore you should become a nun. Far better to retire and mope within some cloister, for you will never like the world. It is not for you, this savage routine of sex. What is there for you but disillusion, heartbreaking disappointment and tears? If the world was a bed of roses I would say go out in it, my dear sister, and garland yourself with its fragrance. But it is not, Susan. The devil has got hold of it and it is no longer in God's hands."

"You would like to be rid of me, Henrietta," I replied. "You would like me to be out of your way, is that it? Is the world not large enough for us both, or must you have it all and leave me none?"

"A child like you could never be in my way," said Henrietta. "We do not think the same thoughts or speak the same language in ideas. Even you, Susan, must have noticed that."

"I know that we are twin sisters."

"Does that bring us any closer?"

"I think it does."

"There is not one single thing alike in us. Can you name one? We are completely different, even in our thoughts."

"How do you know what I am thinking, Henrietta?"

"It is easy, dear Susan, because you have no reasoning of your own. Everything in that little head of yours has been placed there by the books you read and by me. You see I know the books you read, Susan, and your many excursions to the library. I remember all that I myself have told you. You are my creation, remember that, my dear, you are nothing else but my creation."

No, Henrietta had not softened in these years of time. There was the same bold look about her, the curling lips, the red rebellious hair. If she had changed at all it was for the worse, because with the hardness of her thoughts her face had assumed an overwhelming arrogance. Magnificent she was now in her full beauty, but gloating in her conquests.

Yes, truly, Henrietta was unalterable, and what she wanted she took without regret. There was no rescue from her and I could see myself walking through the years beside her, she always a little ahead of me, as if those few hours she had preceded me into life had given her the right to this importance.

She was, at this time, slender and supple with an air of proud and spiteful defiance towards mankind. The slight play of her features did not lighten her look or ease her manner of indomitable purpose. She remained cold and scornful, her great dark eyes a veritable temptation to anyone who sought a vixen for a mate.

Was Kelvin Abigail, with his moody perverseness and wild waves of temper, the man to be persuaded by such gerrymander?

Would Kelvin Abigail give way, weaken at her beauty and be overwhelmed by her seduction?

Over and over again I asked myself these questions and could find no answer.

Most of us recall the difficulty we had in childhood to express ourselves, how to begin an explanation to our feelings and how to end it. As I grew older the task of talking intimately was still upon me and, for the most part, I was tongue-tied socially and usually to be found sitting in retired corners praying to God no one would address me.

Papa with his gay volubility and easy flow of conversation could not understand me, and one day when I passed his room he called me to him.

"Well, little 'Go by the Ground'," he said in excellent humour, "and how is my dove today?"

"I am well, thank you, Papa."

"No quips and qualms, no probing into the 'why and wherefore' of existence?"

83

"No, Papa, I have been out for a walk."

"A walk, eh, and where did those timorous legs of yours carry you, might I ask?"

"I went cottage visiting, Papa, to see Mrs. Muffet's new baby."

"God bless my soul, another baby. How prolific these peasant people are! I did not even know that she was carrying."

"And yet, Papa, you must have noticed she had grown into a great magnitude of size?"

Papa leaned back his head and laughed that happy joyous laugh of his I loved so much to hear.

"My dear girl," he cried, "my very dear child, whatever do you take me for! Do you think I waste my time parading the village for corpulent women whose bouncing enormity pronounces them pregnant. Indeed, dear Susan, I have better things to do I can assure you. What species of infant is it this time that Mrs. Muffet has presented to her long-enduring spouse?"

"It is a girl, Papa, so dainty a thing I hardly dare go near it. Do you not think it a great pity that one cannot have a child without a man being involved in the making of it?"

"Merciful powers, what do you mean by that, Susan?"

"I mean, Papa, that I do not like men but I would very much like to have a baby."

Papa looked at me curiously for a moment and then we both laughed.

"By all the gods, you are a queer one," he said. "But unfortunately, Susan, or perhaps fortunately, science has not yet provided such an issue? In the meantime, my dear, do you not think it would be more rational not to undertake any improvement upon nature?"

84

Then of a sudden he grew serious again and drawing me to him made me stand against his knee.

"What is all this about not liking men?" he asked me. "Is this another of your vagaries, Susan, or can it be that Henrietta has so fooled you into believing all males are reptiles and should not be approached? Surely you feel some emotion, Susan? Some desire to go out and get affianced? Surely it cannot be that any child of mine is sexless?"

"I am all right, Papa. It is just that I do not care for men."

"But, my dear child, this is absurd. What is to become of you? The duty of parents as you know is to maintain their children, but, merciful Heaven, there is a limit to that duty and the day comes when it is up to the children to find some poor misguided imbecile who will take these parents' liabilities from them. You understand that, do you not?"

"You mean it is my duty to get married?"

"That is the natural conclusion, child."

"But I do not want to wed, Papa."

"Very few people perhaps would marry, Susan, if they could afford to live luxuriously in sin. Unfortunately it is only the very few whose incomes allow them this Elysium. May I ask why you do not wish to be espoused and what you consider wrong with connubial benediction?"

"I could not marry without love, Papa, and I do not think that it will ever reach me or venture into my unnoticed life."

"Then get yourself noticed, girl. Go out and shine and cut a dash as I have done. Why in God's name do you recede into the shade so much and keep forever in the background? Is it Henrietta's fault, is it she who is forcing you into retirement? Have you no dignity nor pride of person to fight her with?"

85

"I have plenty of pride, Papa, deep down inside of me."

"Then burrow it out, Susan, and bring it to the surface. You are very diminutive and demure, my dear, but you are not without a certain prettiness. Assert yourself, do not be so timid and mild-spoken as if you had no right upon the earth. God has given us all room to tread, Susan, and each of us has his or her road to travel. Well, then, walk with your head erect and your shoulders straightened, plant your feet firmly so that everyone will know in which direction you are going. Do not, for the Lord's sake, be as purposeless as I am. Open that pretty mouth of yours, open it wide, dear Susan, for out of the course of a little conversation great problems have been solved and great inspirations evolved. Have you not realized, my dear, what a power there is in speech?"

"It is easy for you, Papa, for you can talk."

"What you mean is, Susan, that I talk too much, but I am aware of it and I must confess I often do it purposely. It amuses me to see my guests wilt with boredom and droop in their chairs."

I looked at him and laughed; there was so much mischief in his face.

"Dearest Papa," I cried, "you are wicked, you are very very wicked indeed."

For a moment we were silent and then I told him how I had met Mrs. Abigail on my way to the village and that she had enquired after him.

"What is it like to be divorced, Papa?"

"As you do not seem to possess the slightest desire to be called to holy matrimony, Susan, it is hardly necessary for me to expatiate upon the sensations of judicial separation."

"Do you know what Henrietta says?"

"Henrietta might say anything, since she is unpredictable."

"She says I have but one vocation, one undertaking only, to become a nun."

"A what!"

"A nun, Papa. She says I will never like the world and that it is not for me."

"Have my ears deceived me?" shouted Papa, and his voice had so risen and he was so red in the face I thought he would well-nigh burst his collar.

"That was what Henrietta said, Papa."

For a moment he did not seem able to find words. He pushed me to one side and went over to the table where he always kept his favourite decanter. Pouring some port he drank it at a gulp and then came so rapidly towards me it seemed that he would strike me.

"Holy Orders in this house," he roared. "A nun of my flesh and blood. It is an outrage and how dare she speak of it. And you, Miss, what have you to say to this? Is it what you wish, is it what you want to be?"

"Suppose Henrietta is right, Papa? Suppose that is all I am really fitted for. Would I find happiness and peace?"

"And what about this transport of maternal love you regaled me with but a moment ago. This intense desire of yours to have a baby. Do you think that going into a nunnery will prevent that unborn child from standing at your elbow reproaching you for misusing life's opportunity? You love children, do you not, Susan?"

"Yes, Papa, I love them."

"And you would like to be a mother?"

"Y—yes . . . I think so."

"Merciful Heaven, then why this talk of Holy Orders?"

"I only thought . . ."

"No, Susan, you did not think. It was Henrietta who put this idea into your head. Come down to earth, child, and be yourself instead of a reflection of your sister. You only see yourself as Henrietta wants you to. You play with the image she presents to you. You weep over it, filled with self-pity, and you let it sway you this way and that whilst Henrietta pulls the strings."

"I have a weak character, I know, Papa, but . . ."

"To be sure, to be sure you have a weak character, Susan, but it is also that Henrietta is so infinitely stronger. Forget this foolishness, my dear, and drive these saintly yearnings from your mind. No Darlington has ever been enshrined in sanctity, nor ever will be."

"Very well, Papa."

"Very well what?"

"Very well I will not become a nun."

He dried my eyes and gave me a glass of port.

"Here's to life then," he said gaily.

"Here's to life, Papa."

And we clicked our glasses and solemnly we drank a toast to this momentous resolution.

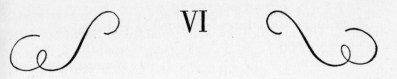

VI

This winter was an uncomfortably severe one and our withered garden, with its huddled shrubs and atmosphere of dead and blackened flowers, seemed to draw itself closer to the forest and shelter beneath the dishevelled branches that stretched in their weird nakedness across the angry sky.

When the snows came the flower beds were mottled with patches of white frost, and all over the horizon there was a dark and sombre greyness. The minikin country roads were swept clean by the village children and they looked like brown threads curling through a tapestry of tangled hedges and rambling over white clad hills.

Our attics became mildewed and clammy with the smell of wood hollowed by damp; but, by the aid of warming pans and small oil stoves, we were able to keep ourselves from shivering. For, strange as it may seem, Mamma still approved of our simple bedrooms and insisted that all young people should know the worst of life in order that they should appreciate the best when it came along.

I still stayed mostly in the library within the circle of my sad pursuits. More books, more melancholy reading weighing down my mind and bending my shoulders as I crouched to gain the melting light.

It was during this winter that both Papa and Mamma became busy with the preparations for our entry into society and how and when we should be presented at Court. At first there was ordinary talk to which we were permitted to listen, but later there were long discussions and conferences behind closed doors.

Mrs. Trouncer, with her eye to the keyhole and her ear to the cracks and crannies of the door, could both espy and listen to most that was going on; a pastime from which she contracted a cold from the draught and was obliged to take to her bed.

When I went to see how she was, I found she had tied up her head in an immense shawl from out of the folds of which peeked her nose, very red at the tip and shining from too much blowing. She informed me that Henrietta had been endeavouring to prevail upon Papa and Mamma that she should be the first to be presented.

"Just because she was given the wind of life a few hours earlier," said Mrs. Trouncer, sniffing and wheezing, "the young baggage considers she should be treated as a first born. I'll lay any wager you please, Miss Susan, that she kicked you back into your mother's womb to make sure she was delivered before you were."

"Mrs. Trouncer," I laughed at her, "even Henrietta could not do that, now could she?"

"I don't say how, being ignorant as it were in the manners of labour; all I do say is that Miss Henrietta is capable of anything when she wants her own way. She is all the devil ever painted a hussy, if I may say so, as sinful and selfish as ever you could meet. Did I not hear her say with my own ears that it was her due to go first into society and that she did not want you treading on her corns? There she sat as calm and unmoved as you please, and as lovely a creature as anyone could wish for, but with a twist on her like a hangman's knot, and she goes on about being

90

dressed alike and how, as you did not in any way resemble one another, she would be obliged to look a fright, or you like a clown in a frock which did not suit you."

"But what did Papa and Mamma say to this?"

Mrs. Trouncer chuckled and then sneezed and wiped her nose with a preposterously large handkerchief which seemed to envelop her entire head and shawl.

"You know how her Ladyship can look when she is on the fret about her darling. Cross as a crab she was with her brows knit and her face as tight as a nutcracker. 'My dear Edward,' she says, with her mouth so buttoned up the words could hardly fall from them, 'My dear Edward, I think Henrietta is right and it is also my opinion that our beloved child should come out before poor Susan.'"

"And Papa, what had he to say?"

"His Lordship likes nothing better than a quarrel with his wife, whatever the subject and whatever the time of day. There he was striding up and down with his face as red as a turkey cock, and he took to cursing and swearing by bell, book and candle he would have none of it. 'Confound, blast and the devil take it,' he shouts so that it comes through the crack of the door like a whip, 'either they are both presented together, Madam, or neither of them at all,' and then he clenches his fist in our dear Henrietta's face, blustering and scolding with his eyes flashing fire."

"And then what happened? How did it all end?"

"In the usual way, with a whirl of petticoats and a slam of the door."

"And Papa?"

"You know where his Lordship goes when the tantrums stir

up his bile, off to the dining room like a streak of lightning to his decanter and glasses of port."

"Poor Papa, poor, dear Papa. I will tell him I do not mind waiting if it will bring him any peace."

"And why should you be doing anything so silly as that, Miss Susan, when time is precious whatever age you are? Do you want to dry up like a leaf that has withered and look the same as those Miss Tinnerlies? There is no sadder sight in this word, child, than those futile spinsters, stale and sapless and not worth a straw to anyone or even to themselves. What do you think I wed Mr. Trouncer for, drunk as a goat and an idle good-for-nothing at that? Now I'm not afraid of a drunk, Miss Susan. On the contrary, I've always had an intense desire to spew right in their eyes and as soon as I see one coming along the street or lumbering out of the inn the saliva will rush to my mouth and well-nigh choke me. It's lucky for his Lordship that he's very seldom drunk, for I wouldn't want to so forget my manners as to unload on any gentleman. But with Mr. Trouncer it was different. Paralytic drunk he was when he walked under the wheels of a wagon as calm as you please. Diverting he was, too, in spite of his intemperance, and with a sense of humour as keen as a whistle. With all his faults, God rest his soul, he kept me from drying up."

Mrs. Trouncer began to weep. She always cried copiously whether from joy or from sorrow, and up to her eyes would go the corner of her apron and down her long nose would fall the drip.

"You want to get married, don't you?" she sobbed. "It's what God made us women for."

I still could not see any excellent reason why I should go out

92

of my way to be tied in holy matrimony, what with Mrs. Trouncer's grim experience and Papa and Mamma's unfortunate union for ever before my eyes. Papa and Mamma snip-snapping from morning till night, and Mrs. Trouncer's ne'er-do-well staggering beneath the wheels of a wagon; and then there was Mrs. Abigail, on top of it all, who had married so young and whose husband had eloped with a whore.

I went to Papa and informed him of what Mrs. Trouncer had told me.

"Listening again was she, Susan?" said Papa.

"Listening and spying as she always does, Papa, but you must admit there are times when it is useful, for neither you nor Mamma would have told me about Henrietta and I would never have known what she was planning."

"And now that you do know, what do you expect us to do?"

"I want you to let Henrietta have her own way in this; it matters so little."

Papa banged his fist on the table and replied that he was damned if he would.

"It may not matter to you, Susan," he cried, "but it is exceedingly important to me. It is unjust and insufferable and Henrietta had no right whatsoever to demand it."

"Dearest Papa, it is such a little matter. This waiting would not trouble me."

"But it would trouble me, Susan, it would trouble me sorely. Your sister is headstrong and selfish and we have sadly spoiled her. Cannot you see that if we let her have her own way in this there is no knowing what else she will attempt? Oh, I confess it is entirely our fault, your Mamma's and mine, but you see

93

our dear Henrietta has been like the sun shining in our eyes and dazzling our perception."

"But Papa . . ."

"Be silent, child, and leave this problem to me. You are twins, are you not, and I intend to honour this achievement. Two sprouts upon the same stalk, two fruit upon one branch ready for the plucking. I swear it is an unconformity which pleases me and no one can say the Darlingtons have not a rare originality."

Papa seemed to be far from well. It was not so much that he looked any older, for he still wore his gayest garments and was dressed with scrupulous care; but the flame in him was being painfully fanned, his breathing was heavy and there was something plaintive in his tiredness. The thing which struck me most was that his whole body appeared to have lost some of its vigour and his shoulders stooped as if the burden of this prolonged argument had been too heavy for him to bear.

A few days later Henrietta came to my room looking stern of face and cold as marble.

"I hear you have been to Papa again," she said.

"Yes, Henrietta, I have been to Papa."

"It seems you are always going to him, chattering like a magpie. Suppose I went and told him things about you?"

"What sort of things, Henrietta?"

"There is plenty I could tell him. The books you read, for instance. Mamma would not like to hear of them."

"I thought she already knew what books I read."

"Is it you who puts Mrs. Trouncer against the doors to listen and spy?"

"You know very well it is not, Henrietta. I only wanted to

94

help Papa by letting you do as you wished. It means so little to me when we go into society or how."

"Dear little Susan, sweet, obedient and loving," replied Henrietta, her voice like honey but with an edge to it like a broken nail against satin, "always the little peacemaker, the blessed saint. Take a load of my sins on your shoulders, Susan, and atone for them. There is a mission for you well worth while; but, in the meantime, you would oblige me very much if you minded your own business."

When Mrs. Trouncer heard I had been to Papa on Henrietta's behalf, she was most disapproving of what she called my doleful weakness of character. "Why, heart alive, child," she cried, "where is your pride? Are you such a chickenhearted weakling that you can't stand up against that sister of yours?"

It was not for the lack of trying, but I just did not seem to have it in me to oppose Henrietta's will. She continued to look upon me as her prey and was feline in her torture of me. Sometimes she was so pleasant I would begin to believe she was attempting to make it up with me, and then, out would come her claws to catch me again and again until she had me giving up the unequal struggle and following meekly at her heels.

After the winter, the spring seemed suddenly to waken and stretch long arms of sunshine across the countryside. Pinpricks of colour forced themselves through the brown earth, and there was a goodly smell in the air as if God had opened up His windows to freshen the whole world. The forest trees had little fringes of green covering their branches, and away in Springfield Town the painters were busy redecorating the small houses and shops. All was astir in the woods with the squirrels and birds shaking the winter from their minds and bodies. Throughout the fields there was the constant calling of the new-born lambs to their mothers who had strayed from them.

As spring took hold, Mamma went continually to London, hustling hither and thither on the search for appropriate gowns for us. Whenever she brought back a design or selection for us to choose from, Henrietta would say in her sweetest tones: "Not those, Mamma. They are all very well for me, but poor Susan will look a fright in them," and then both she and Mamma would look me up and down and sigh heavily as if they despaired of my appearance and would never find an adornment for me that would not be laughed to scorn and ridiculed.

As the time drew nearer to the presentation, Henrietta began to criticise these drawing rooms and abuse the fashionable world for no better reason than to fill my mind with fear of them. With venomous exactness she probed into their imperfections, painting so hateful a picture of society in general that I became imbued with a shuddering dread of entering into it.

"You will not like it, Susan," she said, her large dark eyes resting contemptuously upon my shrinking form. "I cannot see you up in the market when the great white sale is on, for that is all this presentation is, my dear, whatever other name they care to bestow upon it. It is a sale of white virgins, an exchange of young material for better or worse. A jumble sale most likely," she added with a rueful smile.

"But Papa says it is an elegant sight, Henrietta, with the ladies' wonderful dresses and gentlemen's fine clothes. He says the Queen is resplendent on her throne and that the music and lights are superb."

"It is elegant, it is magnificent, it is a blaze of glory and delicate refinement. It scintillates with quips and pleasantries.

96

Nevertheless, my dear misguided sister, the fact remains it is but a roomful of ninnies with but one idea in their heads. An assemblage of ogling sharp-set men on the search for a mate and with a thirst and an appetite for lust. You have read of the Romans with their slaves on pedestals for the crowd to bargain for; this is the same thing, Susan, only clothed in civilized garments. Will you like this, you, with your modesty and grace?"

"If others can do it, so can I, Henrietta."

"But you are not like other girls, Susan. You do not belong."

The sound of her voice as she told me these things, and the touch of her hand, made what little heart I had left in me pound in my ears and then stop, as if she had laid a finger on it, as one can take hold of the pendulum of a clock.

"You will not like it," she repeated firmly. "You are not fitted for it. Far, far better for you, Susan, if you had taken my advice and entered a convent. You would have been happy there praying for me and my sins."

Papa relied upon the social season to cut down his expenses, and Mamma was happy when other people's doors were open so that we could more frequently close our own.

"I like to watch society entertaining," said Papa, "because I can more readily see that if these avaricious parvenus are not given enough to drink they never come, and if they are given too much they never go. To strike the happy medium is an art I hope one day to attain; for perfect hosts, my dear Lucy, are few and far between, and it is a title I have always coveted."

And so in the fulness of time the great day arrived and beheld us on our way to London with a coach load of hatboxes and trunks.

We had been invited to stay with a certain Lady Bishop, a

close relative of Mamma's, who had gone wrong and run wild for a time and then married one of the most influential gentlemen of the Court. Mamma was obliged to accept the indiscretions of Lady Bishop because the Queen did so, but she always made it quite clear that it was against her better judgement.

Lady Bishop lived in an exclusive house in the most fashionable quarter of London, and from the windows we could see the trees of Kensington Palace. It was the first time we had ever slept out of our attic rooms, and the luxury of the furniture and the beauty of the draperies filled me with awe.

"This is the life," said Henrietta, stretching her full length upon the rich silk counterpane. "This is for me. Whatever I do or wherever I go, these are the things that I want."

On the evening of the presentation it seemed to take us hours and hours to attire. First one thing was wrong and then another, and all the while Mamma and Lady Bishop kept scurrying in and out of our rooms rearranging our hair and smoothing down our gowns.

At last we were completed. Mamma in a wine-coloured frock with so wide a skirt and so high a bustle she could hardly walk in it, and Lady Bishop with so low a corsage Papa could not take his eyes off her. Papa was most melodious in his gaily coloured coat and I did not think I had ever seen him look so handsome. Henrietta and I were softly voluminous in ivory white, with our bodices closed about our rounded bosoms like the folded wings of a dove. We wore long white veils and small feathers nestling in our hair. Everything about us was ivory white, even to our shoes, and we carried tight little bouquets of the purest white roses tied round with ivory ribbon.

Mamma was anxious and perturbed lest we should disarray

a single fold of our dresses or loosen a single tress. Papa was proud of us and said we were a handsome pair.

"It is remarkable what fine feathers will do even to the ugliest duckling," he said, looking laughingly at me.

The Queen had made up her mind to receive in person, and the drawing room in which we were to make our first curtsey was no longer at St. James's but at Buckingham Palace.

It was a rare occasion and the crowding almost beyond description. The air in the Palace was heavy and stale with flowers, and there was the continuous babble of excited talk and a fluttering of many coloured fans.

There was nothing momentous about our entry into society. We blended in to the procession of young maidens and curtseyed in unison with them. I saw no look of special interest in the Queen's calm eyes as they rested on us, and her hand, soft and slightly reddened, seemed extraordinarily small.

Mamma declared after it was over that, no matter how indifferent Her Majesty had seemed, she was after all the symbol of perfect womanhood and we could do no better than to model our lives upon hers.

That night Henrietta, yawning and stretching her white arms, said:

"So, the sale is now open and the rest is up to the bidder. What did my little sister think of this fancy fair?"

"It was very lovely, Henrietta, and I must confess I liked it very much."

"The dressing of a shop window when the display is new is always alluring," replied Henrietta. "It is later on, when the goods get old and faded and the prices have to be lowered—that is the saddest sight to see."

99

"There was no wrong in it this evening, Henrietta, whatever you may say. Mamma was in her best mood and so was Papa and there were no high words between them."

"It was tame, Susan, it was dull and I was bored. Everyone was so preoccupied with their appearance they had no time to notice anyone else. The gentlemen were pale faced and awkward. I saw no one there who would attract me. Remember the old saying, 'If your arms are empty the devil will fill them.' I would rather have Satan himself than a man of Mamma's choice. You see, I want to live . . . I want to live and love and be loved in return."

A great many social functions took place in Springfield Town. Round and about the countryside the large houses were free in entertainment. Mamma never missed a reception, a concert or a ball, and was most exacting as she drove hither and thither, or, as Henrietta put it, from market to market. Glittering jewels, old names, historic associations, the very cream of England's aristocracy was there, skimmed very carefully by Mamma before we were introduced. These evenings were a triumph of elegance and splendour, in spite of Henrietta's grim forebodings. We made new acquaintances, and there were so many dinings and dancings we began to find it burdensome and tiring. Those who indulged in this lambent merrymaking seemed apart from all Henrietta had told me, and I found the young men quite kindly and well disposed. But my shyness never left me and I was awkward and ill at ease. I had not Mamma's sedate tranquillity, nor Henrietta's perfect poise. When Henrietta danced the cotillion or waltz there were many who stopped and stood round that they might better watch her exquisite grace, the wild swish of her petticoats and the shimmer of her red-gold hair.

Was Henrietta right, and did I after a while notice the excess of ornament and tawdry falseness in this social vanity fair? Was there something expedient in this virginal parade, this violent desire of the old to get rid of their young, and did I indeed notice on the faces of the parents a tenseness of purpose, a determination that at least one of their daughters should be affianced their first Season, no matter who or whence the suitor came from?

Wherever the Queen was, the Abigails were not, but wherever the Abigails were, Mrs. Abigail would be sure to be surrounded by a swarm of gallants, including, of course, Papa. Mamma would sit with that tied-in expression of hers, as if she had snapped a window between herself and what was going on; but after we were home she would scold and upbraid Papa for his evident neglect of her.

"That woman," she cried, "always that woman, though what you see in her is past my comprehension."

"I see a sweet and noble creature, Lucy, whose lovely form entrances me. There is no harm in rhapsody and when I look at her I am in another world. Will you not allow me one brief moment of romance, my love, without a scene?"

"One! . . . What about the many conquests that you boast of and flourish in my face?"

"It is but bragging, my dear Lucy. Much cry and little wool. If, as you say, I exult and flourish my triumphs, it is but vanity and I do it to impress you. Fine talking can make heroes of us all, and a strutting jingoism keeps me young. I like to bray and bluster and show off. It feeds my ego. I wake up in the night and crow over my neighbours. It is a game I make a merit of, to forget my proper age."

"And Rosaline, was she a game?"

"Rosaline?"

"Do not begin to tell me you have forgotten the chambermaid I once found on your knees."

"An incident, my dear Lucy, agreeable but unimportant. An accident that anyone could fall into."

"And Mrs. Abigail, is she but a vaporous dream?"

"She is a very refreshing lady, my dear, who amuses me immensely, besides which she has a wondrous figure."

"To see you gaping and agog," replied Mamma most bitterly, "one would think it was the first time you had laid eyes upon a woman's shape."

When Mamma was jealous I thought it was unreasonable and I did not know then that the day was not far off when I myself would be consumed with it.

Henrietta would dance often with Kelvin Abigail, and they made so handsome a pair that everybody watched them and tongues began to wag as to whether something might not come of it. Mamma closed her ears to such suggestions because, she said, she would not hear of her darling mating with an Abigail. Sometimes the taciturn Henry would lead her to the floor, or Phillip with his strong full figure and birdlike eyes gleaming in his round red face; they all, so it seemed, admired Henrietta and could not keep away from her.

Geoffrey was my special friend and we would often sit against the ballroom wall and he would tell me in his strange shy way of his dreams about the future.

"Belonging to a large family such as ours," he said, "is like dwelling upon a small acre of land too widely built over so that one house gets squeezed in so tightly it is hardly noticeable.

I am like that with my brothers. I am the small quantity, the particle, the insignificant dribbling nobody cares for."

"Nonsense, Geoffrey, you know that is not true. I like you, I like you very much."

"I am indebted to you, Miss Susan," he replied, "for you have done me the honour of appearing interested in my simple pursuits. I have not, as you know, met with any particular success in anything I undertake. I enjoy tinkering with talents I do not in any way possess. I am in short a prodigious failure, which strangely enough does not disturb me. My health is excellent and I have a sufficient income to live respectably. Am I boring you, Miss Susan, with this specific narrative of my character?"

"Oh no, indeed no, but why do you so abuse your disposition? I find you charming, Geoffrey, and individual, and entertaining."

He looked at me with his eyebrows raised and in such openmouthed astonishment I could but laugh at his ingenuous simplicity.

"I am a solitary man, Miss Susan," he said, "a recluse, ascetic and austere, I have not my brothers' volubility. People bewilder me and I have no intimate acquaintances. It seems I have been cut in a rustic mould. Good fellowship and conviviality are not for me. I am like you and wish to be left alone."

And then one evening at a small unimportant party, Kelvin came over to me and asked me to do him the honour of a dance.

He was like a warm ray of sunshine that drew me from the shadows into the brilliant lighting of that room.

I endeavoured to be ladylike and calm in posture when all the time my heart was beating against his. I made pretence that I was well accustomed to the handsomest man in the room having his arm about my waist. I tried to attend to what he was saying to me and thereby destroy the disturbing thoughts which were racing through my mind; but all the time I was dancing with him I knew my world was in his arms, and all that I wished for was to go on dancing until I died, with him still holding me.

Henrietta was staring at us and I could feel her great dark eyes burning into me as we went by her on the floor. Kelvin was aware of it also and turned his head to smile at her.

"She is lovely, is she not?" I asked him, knowing so well what his answer would be.

"Yes, Miss Susan, she is lovely, but she is too aware of it. One day I mean to tell her."

"To tell her what?"

"To forget herself and remember me a little."

For a moment I could not hear the music and I could feel myself stumbling over him and breaking the smooth rhythm of our dance. With my voice trembling I asked him to forgive my clumsiness, but all he said was: "You are not awkward, Miss Susan. You are like a little feather blown this way and that, unable to settle. You have also the prettiest dimple, but you do not often show it. Your eyes could laugh if you would let them. Why do you cultivate so much sadness and live in a world of your own?"

Then, before I had time to answer, the dance was over, and with a bow and a smile he had returned me to Mamma.

That night before we went to bed and were dragging ourselves up the cedarwood stairway, I said to Henrietta how kind it had been of Mr. Abigail to spare a moment from her side to dance with me.

104

"The poor man could not very well do anything else," replied Henrietta, "since it was I who ordered him to."

"You asked him to dance with me, Henrietta?"

"I commanded it."

"Oh, Henrietta, how could you? . . . How could you shame me so? Am I so forbidding and inelegant that you have to plead partners for me?"

"I thought you would like to dance with Kelvin, Susan, since you never took your eyes from him. He dances quite well—do you not think so?—although you trod quite often on his feet."

I went to bed miserable, unable to bear the thought of the social season still ahead of us.

Gradually the invitations lessened and the great houses willingly closed their hospitable doors. Coaches went by with people for the country, and those who were more sporting went northward for the shoot.

The Queen left town, and blinds were pulled and shutters raised. The virgins put away their finery and compared notes, counting their conquests. A great peace settled over the social world.

The season's Season had finally come to an end.

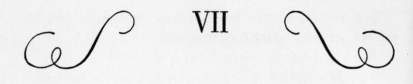

VII

Both Papa and Mamma were at first bewildered by their daughters' failure in the field of fashion, and then, when they had time to sit down and think about it, they were angry and offended.

"What did they think we were offering them," said Papa, with his customary plain spokenness, "stale meat instead of the very tenderest cut in the country?"

They had been so sure that Henrietta's beauty would sweep society off their feet and that she would take London and the towns by storm. As for myself, they had even gone so far as to imagine that some poor witless creature who wanted peace in his home would ask for me in marriage. It would not have mattered had they not been so genuinely concerned, so evidently eager to be rid of us, and I could not help thinking what a pity it was they laboured and aspired so assiduously for our welfare.

Whenever we met Papa he would pretend to be in a jocular mood and cry:

"Here come the prodigal daughters returning to the fold untouched by mortal man. Well, Henrietta, well, Susan, what have you to say for yourselves? A whole season spent and not a catch between you, not even a pick or a peck. Are you not ashamed of yourselves?"

"No, Papa."

"'No, Papa'—what kind of an answer is that, Henrietta?"

"Is it our fault that we have not been sought after? Would you not rather blame the men than us?"

"And why should you blame the men, my dear?"

"They bow and ask us to dance," said Henrietta, her lovely lips curling at the thought of it. "There is a flurry of virgins on the floor. I say something to my appropriate popinjay about the weather or the perfect lighting of the room. 'Dear Miss Darlington . . . Exquisite Miss Darlington,' he replies, and gives me the benefit of a coxcomical smile. He is certain to dance superbly and he will have all the stilted foppery of the nobleman so carefully selected. The dance being over, he returns me to Mamma. The other virgins are also being returned to their Mammas. Some are waiting for them, moving about the floor clucking like hens; others are propped against the wall in gilded chairs, scanning the faces of their daughters for hopeful news. The virgins cringe with the withering disappointment in their parents' eyes when there is nothing to report. Even Mamma's raised eyebrows indicate that it is time both Susan and I had something very special to announce. You, Papa, are always too busy with your own affairs to attend to either of your daughter's prowess. There was never anything to tell Mamma, except that one gentleman perhaps had danced better than another. Nor had the other virgins anything to recount. The Mammas become desperate and flutter their fans and frown upon their progeny, and so on and so forth, Papa, with interminable sameness, until at last the long sad evening comes to a close."

Papa was gasping, his eyes protruding from his head.

"God bless my soul," he cried. "God bless my long-suffering soul. I had no idea that you were so observant. Is that why you have been turning up your nose at everyone as if the whole world smelled sour as a sewer?"

"The social world does, Papa."

"In what way, may I ask, does it offend you?"

"In more ways that one, Papa. Its meaningless purpose and its utter waste of time."

"Society has a purpose, my dear, to those who have an eye to it and a mind to occupy the time of it."

"Society bores me, Papa."

"Society bores her. Did you hear that, Lucy? With one gesture our dear daughter wipes out the genius and beauty and hospitality that comprises it. What would you have us do, child, change all the laws, alter the fashion and create a new civilization just to amuse you?"

"Society only comprises one thing, Papa. A bow here and a curtsey there and a dance or two with such inanity I can hardly keep from yawning. You and Mamma standing like trussed turkeys, preening yourselves because you have twin daughters."

Mamma went over to her and tried to take her hand.

"My darling child," she said reproachfully, "whatever has come over you?"

But Henrietta flung herself away from her and went quickly from the room.

"If I did not know Henrietta," said Papa, "I would say there goes a girl exceedingly in love."

Then he looked at me. He seemed bewildered and confused and there was a hurt expression in his eyes I could not bear to see.

"We did our best," he muttered. "I am sure we did our best. You, Susan, do you find these drawing rooms dull?"

108

"I would rather be here at White Orchard Manor."

"For what purpose?"

"I am happy here."

"And you are not happy in London, is that it? But has it never occurred to either of you that you have a duty to your parents almost as essential as the Ten Commandments?"

"Thou shalt take unto thyself an obliging and appropriate husband. Is that it, Papa?"

"That is the context of it, Susan, but how do you propose to accomplish this with your eyes welded to the floor and Henrietta with her nose in the air?"

"Come, come, Edward," interrupted Mamma, "these paternal proddings will not help and are of no advantage."

"Strange," said Papa, shaking his head sadly, "strange indeed that we should have been endowed with daughters who find social entertainments irksome."

"But what can I do, Papa, since I have neither gifts nor capability?"

"You could smile occasionally, child, and be of happier countenance, as I have said many times before. Have you no play upon words, no retort, no nimble wit?"

Mamma laughed scornfully. "You cannot expect her to be a Mrs. Abigail," she said. "Susan is scarcely made in the same mould."

For a moment there was silence, with Mamma pursing up her lips with pleasure at her excellent retort.

"Sarcasm does not become you, Lucy," said Papa at last, "and a remark such as this I will ignore as being unworthy of my notice. Now what was I saying when I was so rudely interrupted?"

"You were finding fault with me, Papa."

"Yes, yes, to be sure I was, but what is the use? I do not mean to be exacting, Susan, but I must confess I am most confoundedly put about."

"Because I am not affianced?"

"And never will be, my dear, unless you put more effort into it. A man wants to lead a woman he is proud of to the altar, Susan, not a submissive drudge, a snail who dawdles at his heels."

Henrietta was indignant, and when I saw her later she was pacing up and down the corridor outside our rooms waiting for me.

"Men," she cried, "are they so wonderful? Divest them of their garments and you will see they are all alike."

"Henrietta!"

"Well, is it not so?"

"It is only our first season," I replied, "and I cannot see why Papa and Mamma are in such a dodder."

"It is my last season," said Henrietta firmly. "Never again will they drag me to the market. All those great ladies so tightly laced that when they ate a full meal you could see them praying that their corsets would hold, and the silk ribbons which hold their corpulence not burst asunder. And men like Papa with their eyes agog at so much flesh so artlessly displayed. No thank you, I have had enough. If I marry—if ever I marry, Susan, it will be someone of my own choice and no one else's."

"Papa thinks you are already in love."

"Papa is no fool, but on the other hand he is no wise man. He is only trying to find out."

"To find out what, Henrietta?"

"Oh, nothing," replied Henrietta and closed her door.

I was glad to return to the quiet of the country and to the shelter of my attic room. My little room was my confessional, and those four walls knew more of me than any living thing. It was there I would recite my grievances and pour forth my thoughts, wondering in Heaven's name what would become of me.

As the winter approached we began to busy ourselves in the search for gifts. Papa's birthday came just seven days before Christmas and the problem of finding two things to give him instead of one caused us great anxiety.

Papa always heralded the day he was born with an outburst of ill temper, and one had but to greet him with the best of wishes for him to grow red in the face and look as if he would well-nigh explode.

"Birthday be damned," he would say, shouting and stamping. "When you live to be my age you are only too glad to forget the day you were given birth to. It is a monstrous fallacy that when you wake up one morning with the knowledge that you are a whole year older than when you went to bed it is a matter for rejoicing. Everybody's birthday is supposed to be a chirruping anniversary however they may feel. Suppose they do not want to be any older, suppose they want to make believe they are still young. Along comes a fool of a friend with a parcel and gives the whole game away. Birthdays have to be honoured and they have to be humoured, though why the devil they should be, God in Heaven alone knows. I have not for the last twenty years come upon this day without the most profound melancholy, and the expressions of jubilation and revelry from my relations I regard as twiddle twaddle and I say to myself, 'What commemoration indeed is this when most everyone I know would have been far better off if I had never been born at all.' "

Springfield Town was the busiest place at Christmas time, with people hurrying to and fro with strange-shaped packages and an air of perplexed craft. There was much over shopping and exchange of money for goods that were of no particular value. But everyone felt obliged to give something to everybody else, whether suitable or totally unfit.

The townsfolk, I knew, worked very hard to earn a living. They gained their daily bread and saved and put by, eyeing one another suspiciously when anyone raised a new curtain or painted their doors. They had little time for leisure until the shops were closed, and it was then the gossip began. More mischief was made after dark when the lamps were lit and the taverns were open than at any other time, for the men gathered together and discussed their women, and the women sat by the fireside disparaging their men.

The bustle and urgency and the scurry and scramble as the townsfolk bestirred themselves to make short work of their shopping was a sight to see. It was dark then at about mid-afternoon, and sometimes there was a fog so that a few small boys earned an extra living by running about the town with flares, conducting the older people across the invisible streets. Close to the church there was a fire in a brazier placed there by the Reverend Barklett so that a few bedraggled ne'er-do-wells could gather together, warming their hands and complaining. The shop windows were garlanded with a great deal of holly and sprigs of fir, and there were turkeys and suckling pigs and a few scrawny chickens that looked so piercingly cold it seemed shameful to hang them outside. From great hooks in the ceilings large slabs of crimson meat dangled and the grocery shops were laden with currants and fruit and spices of every kind.

There was a gas lamp at either end of the main street which made faces look whiter, and noses redder, than they really were. It was not a becoming light and the fog splayed and splashed on it so that you could not see the lamp posts but only two globes of flame hanging, as it seemed, from nowhere.

Sometimes we met the Abigails, the entire family bent on the same purpose as ourselves. They would be laughing and talking and peering at one another's parcels, attempting to guess what was in them. If it was snowing, both Roger and Silvain would scoop some of it up in their hands and playfully throw it at us as we passed, and then a mock battle would ensue in which everyone joined.

Henrietta, in the midst of a wild and boisterous group, her cheeks flaming and her red hair loose about her face, was a sight indeed worth seeing. Shouting and throwing snow, the Abigails encircled her, even the solemn Henry all smiles and playing with the rest of them. The mad delight of Henrietta seemed to infect the brothers with its gaiety. Even Mrs. Trouncer was jovial and full of glee as she ran hither and thither, her skirt uplifted and her boots deep in the drifts.

But I had eyes for no one but Kelvin, with his handsome face aglow and his brown eyes sparkling, and I could not help noticing how Henrietta seemed always to be near him, forcing herself laughingly into his arms and concealing herself behind him for protection. In the end it was Henrietta and Kelvin against the rest of us, and there was I on the fringe of the group, well conscious that my nose was red and the tips of my fingers frozen blue.

When they had gone by, most of the happiness of shopping went with them, and Mrs. Trouncer, shaking her head, would look at Henrietta and say:

"That Master Kelvin is a bold one. I am told he has embraced and looked sweet upon every unmarried wench in Springfield. I am also told that his wild ways and fine talk will sweep them off their feet, and that he is so merry a rogue and so impenitent a rascal that few can resist him. Lord sakes, all I know is that if I was a younger woman and in need of a bit of nozzling, I would be after him myself as fast as a fox."

Silvain had grown considerably and had about him all the graces of youth. He was perhaps too comely for a boy, his hair too curled and his skin of too fine a texture. It was easy to see in him the dreams his mother must have had when she conceived him, of breaking at last the long male line by giving birth to a girl. His linen was of the very finest and whitest, and he was about as spoiled and indulged as anyone could be. Yet, there was not a soul in Springfield Town who could resist Master Silvain's broad ingenuous smile, and he was the heart and soul, and the warmth and gaiety, of any room that he entered.

Papa took to going more and more frequently to Wingmeadow Lodge, giving excuses that he had taken a liking to the Abigail lads and was giving them good advice. But the thing soon became a scandal and the tongues of the neighbours wagged incessantly like the interminable clanging of a rusty bell. Here at last was something they could talk about, and his Lordship's goings on with Mrs. Abigail was a cud they could chew with the fine rich juice of malice. To be sure they neither reproached nor criticised Papa, but they had not a good or a kind word for the beautiful wanton who had lured him to the lodge. She was the sorceress, the unworthy piece of whom they disapproved.

"Fie upon her," they said, "and for shame on her with her poor Ladyship moping and fretting whilst he is up there billing and cooing and philandering to his heart's content. She ought to be ashamed of herself, that Abigail hussy, for enticing a man well over his sixties."

When Mamma accused Papa of his perfidious unfairness and upbraided him for his infidelity, he refused to take either her or himself seriously.

"If I spoil the ladies and they ruin me, what then?" he said. "It is surely my own affair and no one else's."

"Your reputation is my affair as well as yours, Edward."

"Fiddlesticks, my dear," replied Papa. "If you would keep your delicate nose out of other people's business it would not get so twisted. I am afraid your regard for my welfare, my love, when tempered down from the meat to the bone, will be found to be derived from the feelings of others, and other opinion rather than your own."

Then Papa hummed and screwed up his face and looked at her sideways in the mischievous way that he had.

"You are too conscious of dishonour, my dear," he said, "not so much for me as for yourself. What, in Heaven's name, would you have me do? Pale my ineffectual fire which warms no other body but my own and recede into a grey old age in order to find favour in my neighbour's sight, or the Queen's or perhaps even your own? Would you have me sit by your side and twiddle my thumbs, twittering compliments in your shell-like ear and gallantly selecting the wools for your embroidery?"

"I would have you think more of me, Edward, and of the children."

"You are my wife. Therefore I am not likely to forget you; and the children, it seems, can well look after themselves. Why, then, may I not care for any other woman? I like Mrs. Abigail because she is gay. We have a lot in common. I tease her about Silvain, for instance. 'That beauty there,' I tell her, 'would look better as a girl,' and she replies, 'Your Henrietta could be wearing breeches and be none the worse for it,' and so we laugh and make a joke of it; it is good to laugh the way we do, Lucy, for God knows there is not much of it at home."

Papa was thoughtful for the rest of the evening and I saw him watching us from behind his book. When Mamma and Henrietta went upstairs to look over some old clothes which were to be distributed amongst the poor, he asked me to remain with him for a while.

"I have had a loadful of pleasant times," he said, "harmless times, most of them, but some with a wink here and there, but I am damned if I can see anything in my calendar to be ashamed of. Do you think I am a rogue, 'Go by the Ground'? Is that your opinion of me?"

I hesitated a moment, for he looked so repentant, so like a little boy who has been caught stealing apples from an orchard.

"Yes, Papa, I am afraid I do," I replied at last, smiling at him with the deepest affection.

"How much of a scapegrace am I, child? I live healthily, I am only rationally drunk, I do not eat to excess or dote upon rich pernicious foods. I am not perhaps the most important member of Springfield society, but I am looked up to and respected and made room for; whereas, on account of my somewhat precarious

116

moral code, I should be pushed aside and put under and pooh-poohed. That is the distressing outcome of this servile age, this fawning flattery, this gilded social pill, they are by force of circumstance induced to swallow me. If I had been born plain Edward Darlington, a butcher or a baker or an impecunious Jack-of-all-trades, I would have been reviled and abused and more than likely thrown out upon a dust bin."

"But, Papa, you are not really bad."

"I misconduct myself, Susan. Let us call it that and delight in it. It pleases me to be considered a game old bird, apart from the satisfaction of handling a buxom wench upon my knee. You cannot eliminate the fact, my dear, that I am an infamous old sinner long past praying for."

"Dearest Papa, I shall always pray for you, always and always."

"A beautiful effort, my sweet Susan, but a prodigious waste of words. Being so voluble a talker I might even have prayed for myself had it not been that the Reverend Barklett has put me off all spiritual humility. The sound of that suffering clergyman's voice jars upon my ears, and I say to myself, 'Does God indeed enjoy such moaning and lament as this? Is He of so doleful a disposition that He cannot countenance a hearty laugh, or a jolly reference to our sins?'"

"The Reverend Barklett disapproves of you, Papa."

"And what the devil has it got to do with him? Am I to be grudged a little amusement in my numbered days? You know it is hard to grow old, Susan, when your heart is still young. It is difficult to believe you have got to die when you still have so much life. To see yourself changing, a wrinkle here and a loose skin there. To watch time take hold of your face and mark it whether you like it or not. To feel time take hold of your body and cramp its muscles and lie heavy round your neck. The only compensation for old age, my dear, is memories, and I do most profoundly pity those people who have been too careful of their way of living. No past to rake up of an evening; no tablets filled with records of their sins. I am sorry for those people who die before they have properly or improperly lived and know nothing of tomfoolery and preposterous gallantry."

"Dearest Papa," I replied earnestly, "it does not seem possible that you will ever really get old. You seem to me to be always searching for something that you have never found."

"And what do you think that is, my wise daughter? An ideal perhaps intriguing and quixotic, or could it be a pearl at the bottom of Pandora's box?"

"Whatever it is, Papa, it keeps you young."

He looked at me strangely, I thought, and then he smiled.

"Tell me, Susan, how much have you learned about sexual things since I last spoke to you?"

"Only what Henrietta has told me, and from the books that I have read."

"Henrietta. . . . What does she know, I wonder? By the Lord, I would give anything to listen to her immature version of the greatest problem upon earth."

"I think you would be surprised, Papa. Unfortunately I do not care about the subject. It . . . it embarrasses me."

"It embarrasses you. What nonsense do you talk! Have you not realized, Susan, that sex is the greatest material for thought that God ever presented to a living world?"

"Yes, I know, Papa."

"And still you do not like it?"

"No, Papa, I do not like it."

Papa shrugged his shoulders and turned away from me and I could see by his attitude he was no longer interested in me. I wanted to tell him that it was not all my fault, it was Henrietta's; but what would have been the use when he would not and could not understand me.

Papa spent most of his birthday at Wingmeadow Lodge and returned in the evening with a host of small presents the Abigails had given him.

"All the mumbo-jumbo and hocus-pocus of good will," he grumbled, "just because a rogue like I am falls from a mother's womb. Can people change over night and think no more of my sins because I have a birthday? We are what we are by the grace of God and the workings of the devil, whatever day of the year, and handing a package from one to the other of us will not convert nor purify our lives. Dear Mrs. Abigail gives me a book when my library is already choked with literature; my charming spouse presents me with a pipe I am unable to smoke. Henrietta's woollen muffler might well become the oldest inhabitant of Springfield Town; and you, Susan, with your little box of scented cachou which was intended, I feel sure, for the sole purpose of concealing the port-fogged odour of my breath."

And so from Papa's birthday we passed on to Christmas which did not concern him so much because the whole world was wrapped up in it. We all gathered round an immense and festive tree upon which hung our gifts for the entire household. Papa as a matter of course conducted the ceremony of distribution as solemnly as if he were at a sacred ritual, making an appropriate speech to each and every one of the domestics. Mamma even went so far as to help us decorate, and, unbending as far as her corsets and her character would allow, became almost human as she festooned the tree with parcels and garlands of crimson berries and tiny sprays of mistletoe.

Always on Christmas day both she and Papa refused to quarrel, and when the tree was ready we sat in a goodly circle round it singing carols. Papa always made a good resolution every New Year's Eve. He would do *this,* he declared emphatically, and he would not do *that,* so help him God. But in a week he forgot what month it was and the reformation never seemed to materialize. He was like a small boy breaking a rule and chuckling and chortling as he cheated. "Resolutions are fiddlesticks," he said. "Put them up and somebody comes along and knocks them down again. It is a fool's game, that is all, to try and hoodwink our own conscience."

"Every New Year," said Mrs. Trouncer, "I would give up listening at doors and peering through keyholes were it not for the fact that I might miss something. For, you must admit, you can't go on peeking and peering all your life without finding something of the utmost importance you shouldn't really know. It's what people do behind closed doors which counts. People change behind closed doors and you see them with their minds exposed as well as their bodies. It's a wonderful sight, that's what it is, to catch a creature unawares; and it's a different world you can see through the slit of a keyhole."

On this particular Christmas there was a look in Henrietta's dark eyes I could not fathom, and she seemed kinder and closer to all of us than she had ever been. What was in that cold heart of hers, I wondered, and what was in that calculating mind? What was she up to, and why was she so magnanimous to me?

When at last we retired to bed I found the answer.

Henrietta asked me humbly if she could speak to me for a moment and if I objected to her coming to my room.

She watched me for a while as I was undressing and then she said:

"Are you a pious hypocrite, Susan, or have you indeed the quality of being divine?"

"What an extraordinary thing to ask me, Henrietta. Have you not always told me that I am what you yourself have made me?"

"Why cannot we be friends, Susan, and let bygones be bygones. I am sure I am willing enough."

"Is this a New Year's resolution?"

"Perhaps. All I know is I am sorry with all my heart if ever I have hurt you. Why not let us kiss and make up this Christmas night, what do you say?"

"I would say that you were ill, Henrietta, and send for Doctor Wiffin."

This was a dangerous Henrietta, a girl I did not know, and as I brushed my long hair I watched her closely in the mirror.

"What do you want with me, Henrietta," I asked her, "that you take this unusual tone?"

"You have the power to make me happy, that is all, or plunge me into despair."

"I have as much power as that? In what way? In what way have I become so suddenly useful?"

"There is something you can do for me, you only, Susan. You will help me, sweet Susan, say that you will."

"'Sweet Susan,' is it now, Henrietta? I cannot recognize myself in those kind words. Are you sure you are well, that you have no fever?"

121

She took a small parcel from the bosom of her gown and held it out to me.

"It is a gift," she said gently. "Just a trifling thing I have purchased in the town for Kelvin. I dare not go with it to Wingmeadow Lodge with Mrs. Trouncer spying and listening and telling Mamma. If Mamma was to know she would send me away from here, and this I could not endure. If you are caught, Susan, they will think nothing of it, for Mamma would not believe you up to mischief. If you do this I will give you my new gold bracelet, and return you the pearl necklace which is rightfully yours. You can have anything of mine, Susan, if you will deliver this parcel into Kelvin's hands."

I looked at her coldly.

"I do not want anything of yours, Henrietta," I said firmly. "Surely you must be aware of that."

"I promise I will never say things to you again, Susan. From now on you are free of me."

"I shall never be free of you, Henrietta."

"Susan, I beg . . . I will even go on my knees."

And I, poor weak fool that I was, consented. What else could I do when I knew she would give me no peace, that she would plead and then threaten and then plead again and doubtless weep. But I knew all the time it was not so much my will that made me do this thing as Henrietta's.

And so, on the morning after Christmas, I sallied forth, a thick cloak about my shoulders and a hood covering my whole head.

It was one of those mornings clean and crisp, with the trees sharply outlined. The snow, slowly melting from the branches, was dripping on to the white carpet below, leaving little dark holes where each drop had fallen so that the ground looked as if a fine lace veil had been placed over it.

Across the fields thin threads of smoke rose from the cottage chimneys, and everywhere round and about was the smell of freshly lit wood.

I had never been abroad at this hour before, when yesterday's footsteps had not properly thawed or been disturbed and the ghosts of those who had walked seemed still to be going hither and thither in their different pursuits. I interested myself in endeavouring to imagine who had been along the lane before me. The postman, the small boy who drove his goats to pasture. A horse and cart, and the portly woman from the farm with her basket of eggs. How many times I fluttered to and fro fitting my footsteps into theirs, following them in the snow and slush as I went on my way by the edge of the forest.

I seemed to be the only person in the world who was awake; even the birds sat huddled on their branches with their heads under their wings, refusing to be disturbed. Henrietta had told me the gate where I should stand and where Kelvin, always the first to rise, went out for a walk with his dogs.

I could see Wingmeadow Lodge gradually bestirring and shutters being drawn back like eyes slowly wakening from sleep. I could see windows being lighted and the maids shaking out the mats and moving round the rooms, dusting them.

A great sense of joy and freedom came instantly upon me. I felt that I was resting upon the brooding clouds and being taken for a sweep across the sky. Then, in what seemed only a moment, the sun appeared, a pale ineffectual sun with no warmth to it, and no strength to do more than just hang there, spoiling what had seemed so crisp and clean by revealing the plainness of a wintry morn.

The winding lane ended in a mixture of tangled branches and weird shapes, like long lean arms stretching towards the mounds of driven snow. Very soon Kelvin came through the quiet garden and out into the roadway, and I could catch a glimpse of his tall figure and the thick clustering hair about his brow. I loved the way he strode with his stick tucked under his arm, his hands behind him and his head raised as if the whole world belonged to him. I loved the way he whistled to his dogs and called them each by name as they bounded to him, following at his heels.

He did not at first notice me standing by the side of the lane, concealed by brushwood, and he would most certainly have passed me by had I not said loudly:

"Master Abigail."

Most truly there was nothing in his name, nothing to make my heart pound and beat wildly in my breast.

"I must keep very quiet and calm," I said to myself, "and conceal my secret from him; he is after all but an ordinary man who will in a moment wish me good morning."

"Miss Susan," he cried, "by all that is wonderful, what in the name of Heaven are you doing out so early and in this windy, icy place?"

I looked at him with a lustreless smile in which he could not possibly have guessed the measure of my affection and my fear. I remembered what Mrs. Trouncer had said about him, how he had embraced and looked sweet upon the wenches and what a rogue and impenitent rascal he really was. I felt that when I hated him most I loved him best; such was my troubled passion.

"I . . . I have something for you," I stammered, "something from Henrietta."

"Henrietta sent you out here? She dared to?"

"Oh, but I wanted to come, indeed I agreed to it. Henrietta did not have to force me. I came of my own free will."

He looked me up and down with a broad stare.

"You liked it! In all this slush and in those little boots," he said. "You must be crazed. It is a coldish morning to give a man like me a gift I am unworthy of."

"It is a very important gift, so Henrietta says."

"Then, if it is of such importance, why did she not bring it to me herself?"

"You mean you wish that she had come instead of . . ."

"I said no such thing, Miss Susan. I only wondered why she sent you as her messenger."

"Henrietta was afraid that Mamma might get to hear of it and there would be trouble."

"And what about you? Will there be no question raised, no hue and cry?"

"I am not noticed as Henrietta is. No one suspects me of . . ."

"Of what, Miss Susan?"

"Of anything," I whispered lamely, and I could feel the colour rushing to my face.

I handed him the package and for a moment he looked embarrassed. He did not open it but stood twisting and turning it about in his hands.

"I am curious about you," he said at last. "About what you think and how you feel. Sometimes I believe I am beginning to know you, and then of a sudden I realize I do not know you at all."

"I am very simple really."

"Are you, Miss Susan? Are you indeed?"

He looked down at me and saw that I was trembling.

"Why, you are half frozen!" he said, and taking his cloak from him, he placed it on my shoulders, and with his arm still round me he led me down the lane.

The warmth of his body and the closeness of his hold upon me was almost more than I could bear. I found myself praying fervently, "God loosen his hands from me, oh dear God, make him let go." But still we walked, and still his arm was laid upon my shoulder.

"You know I have dreams," he said, "whilst I walk here with my dogs. I have dreams and many minds but never the heart to accomplish anything. I have the ambition to make progressive laws, to tear aching cities apart and give the massed people a chance to breathe such air as this. You see, Miss Susan, in spite of what they say of me, I have heroic moments, though I do admit they may not often last the length of a day."

When we reached the end of the lane, he paused for a moment and there was a puzzled look upon his face. He seemed about to ask me a question and then with a shrug thought better of it.

Quickly I slipped from his grasp and, without so much as another glance in his direction, left him standing with the cloak dragging limply in his hands.

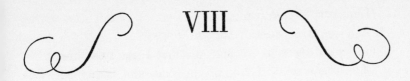

VIII

AFTER THAT it was easy for Henrietta to make use of me. I became her frequent messenger and began to look forward to these mornings with a frantic fervour which consumed me through each preceding night. I began to count upon the touch of Kelvin's hand as he took the letters from me, and the tenderness of his voice as he thanked me for them. I rambled over the countryside and through the fields and into the forest, anywhere and everywhere and at any time of the day in the hopes that I might meet him. And he, did he care? Did he put himself out to look for me? Not Kelvin Abigail. He merely went his way whistling carelessly to his dogs or throwing sticks for them to chase, completely unaware that a certain Miss Susan Darlington of White Orchard Manor was hopelessly and helplessly in love with him.

On some of my ramblings I would often meet the little goat boy driving his animals to pasture. I noticed once that the goat boy had a serious old-world look about him, as if his task lay heavy on his shoulders and the responsibility was more than he could carry. Upon questioning him he told me that Master Abigail had warned him that if he drove his goats too fiercely the milk would run out their udders and be lost, so he must keep his eyes fixed upon their bellies. That was his constant worry.

When next I saw Kelvin I chided him for bullying this boy,

but he merely laughed at me and said, "He reminds me of my brother Shelly, one who seems born to be teased."

"But he believes you. He believes everything you say and thinks you are wonderful."

"And so I am. Do you not think so too, Miss Susan?"

"I think you are horrid," I replied indignantly, and I could hear him laughing as I hurried from him.

One evening I met Papa returning from Wingmeadow Lodge with a book which he said he had lent to Mrs. Abigail.

"A book, Papa! Are you quite sure it was a book?"

"Why do you ask, child? Do you doubt my word?"

"Of course not, Papa, and yet I do not see the volume in your hand."

"To be sure . . . to be sure, since it is in my pocket. Do you wish to search me, Susan?"

"Dearest Papa, of course I would not dream of such a thing."

He grunted and then looked at me doubtfully with his head on one side and after a while he laughed.

"You are a little devil, 'Go by the Ground,'" he said, "and I cannot get past those solemn eyes of yours. There is no book, there never has been a book, and there never will be a book, but do not tell Mamma so. It is too excellent an alibi."

Kelvin did not often reply to Henrietta, but now and again he would thrust a letter into the pocket of my muff. When Henrietta received one of these epistles she would rip open the envelope with eager fingers and devour the contents.

"Oh Susan, Susan," she would cry, "never has there been such happiness. He is so tender and affectionate, so deeply attached, it seems that he must die for love of me. Listen to how he addresses me, 'My dearest love . . .'"

"He calls you that?"

" 'My dearest love . . . My dearly beloved,' and more and more, Susan, so that he whirls me off my feet. There is no end to his love for me; there are no words, so he says, to express his absolute devotion. Soon we will be married and you will be my bridesmaid, will you not? You are my only sister and it is right and befitting that you should."

"But, Henrietta, he has not yet proposed. He has not yet been to Papa and asked for your hand in marriage."

"Not yet, Susan, but he will. . . . He will. You wait and see."

"But . . ."

"Is anything the matter, Susan?" she asked, showing false concern as she thrust the letter into the bosom of her gown. "You look so white and strange."

"The room is cold," I replied, my teeth chattering. "Can we not go where it is warmer?"

"I do not feel cold," said Henrietta and gazed at me in wonder. "I could not feel cold with Kelvin's letter resting on my heart."

One morning, when I was making my way into the house from an early excursion on Henrietta's behalf, I heard a strange noise coming from the stairs.

"Hist," . . . it went, and then again, "hist," and looking up I saw it was Mrs. Trouncer with a shawl about her head.

"What is it?" I whispered. "Is anything the matter?"

"I woke up wondering," she said, "and I have been awake ever since. Are you not yearning and burning to know what is in the letter you have in your muff, Miss Susan? Are your fingers not twitching to open it?"

"Certainly not, Mrs. Trouncer. I assure you I have never thought of such a thing."

"It isn't natural, little Missie, it isn't natural at all to be holding a thing like that and not want to know what's in it."

"You mean to say you would . . ."

"Steam it open, Miss Susan . . . steam it open. It's as easy as blowing your nose when you have the manner of it."

"But it would be wrong. It would be wicked. It is none of my business or yours. You mean to say you would read someone else's letters? You . . . you would actually open and read them, Mrs. Trouncer?"

"To be sure I would. How else can I know what's going on when everyone in this house is as closed as an oyster shell?"

"But that is cheating; it is unfair. Suppose there was something in the letter you were not meant to know?"

"All the better, Miss Susan, all the better, for it's secrets like those that make trouble. Suppose it's a love letter, for instance. Wouldn't that be more than a body could bear, the temptation, I mean, of seeing what's in it? Not that I haven't seen plenty of love letters in my time, Miss Susan, for Mr. Trouncer had as pretty a way with his pen as anyone could wish for until, poor soul, he took to the bottle and it cramped his style something cruel. But, when you get to my age and love is over with and as dead as a dried-up salt fish, then it's time to take an interest in other people's affairs if you see what I mean, and that's exactly what I am doing. You think too much of what is right and what is wrong, child, to make much of a juicy morsel out of life."

"But I could never—I could never open a closed letter."

"Or look in at a fastened door, I suppose? Why then do you think there are keyholes in doors as well as bolts, if they aren't there to peep through. Temptation, that's what they are, and the invention of Satan himself. If doors had only bolts to them there wouldn't be any desire to see on the other side, now would there? It's the same with a kettle. You can sit and wait for a kettle to boil with no more mischief in your mind than wishing for a cup of tea; and then, just as the steam starts bursting out of the spout all pretty and warm, you remember a letter there is on the table beside the front door. An interesting letter maybe, with an enticing smell to it and an air of being unusual. Temptation again, Miss Susan, and again it's Satan himself who invented a kettle with a string of steam in the spout of it just asking for trouble. Then it starts to whistle and whisper, the kettle, I mean; it's telling you all the things it can do besides boiling, and the uses it can be put to, and before you know where you are, the letter is under the spout, and snick . . . snack . . . with the blade of a knife, the envelope is open. Well, that's that. It's not your fault nor the kettle's; it's just human nature. It's the same when you pass a door, Miss Susan, which has a light through the keyhole like the wink of an eye. So what do you do? Down on your knees you go with your face glued on to it, and the wind rushing through it as sharp as a needle."

"Mrs. Trouncer!" I cried, horrified at this revelation of her character. "You mean to say you have read Papa's letters, or Mamma's, or mine? Oh, how could you, how could you?"

"I don't rightly know, Miss Susan, and that's the truth," replied Mrs. Trouncer solemnly. "But there's a weakness in my belly somewhere that makes me do things against my mind. Nevertheless, what I reckon is, the Lord brought us into this world to have a good time, and nosing and ferreting, and peering and prying is, in a manner of speaking, the very best time a body could have, so help me God."

I went up to my room with Henrietta's letter burning a hole in my muff, and I thrust it into a drawer and locked the drawer, and put the key in a secret corner for fear of myself. As soon as it was evening I would tell Henrietta it was there; in the meantime I would try and forget it, and the kettle, and the steam from the spout. Snick . . . snack . . . with the blade of a knife and the letter was mine for the reading.

It was a strange winter.

A long time of waiting and watching and temptation, for me, with many a tear. No matter what was my mood, or how tortured my mind was, Henrietta's demands upon me came first. Sometimes I was afraid of betraying my feelings for Kelvin. Sometimes I wished she could see what was in my heart and have it over with. But no one ever thought of me, never considered that perhaps I could be in love. They were only solicitous for Henrietta and her strange looks and the manner in which she was behaving. Their darling was ill; her cheeks were pale and she had moods of passionate disorder. They fretted and fussed over her and even went so far as to send for Doctor Wiffin, who told them that he thought I was the little lady who wanted his attention more than Henrietta.

Every night after I was in bed and the great house round me was silent, I imagined I could hear Henrietta's voice saying, 'my dearest darling . . . my dearly beloved,' until the words loomed out of the darkness and there seemed to be nothing else in my attic room but Kelvin's love for my sister, driving me mad.

It is an established fact that the postman can belabour a door day upon day, week upon week, year upon year, and have noth-

132

ing more gladsome to offer than a gazette, or an appeal from the parson, or a few vague pages from an almost forgotten friend; and then, of a sudden, he hands in a packet as cool as you please which will turn the whole household topsy-turvy and create enough hubbub to raise the dead from their graves.

This is precisely what happened at White Orchard Manor.

In at the door there fluttered so redolent an envelope, so perfumed an epistle, that Mamma went sniffing and nosing about the house in an endeavour to determine what manner of thing it could be that was so outraging her distinguished nostrils.

She picked up the offending missive and holding it arm's length between the extreme tips of her fingers, as if it were of too noisome a character to endure, hastened with it to the music room where Papa was playing over to us some of the old melodies we loved.

"I believe this suffocating communication is addressed to you, Edward," she said coldly and handed it to him.

"If it is addressed to me it is doubtless intended for me, my dove," replied Papa and laid it on the table beside him.

"Are you not going to open it, Edward, and see who it is from?"

"I am already aware, Lucy, who it is from as well as you are!"

"A woman, of course."

"A lady most assuredly. Would you have me acquainted with a gentleman who smelled as sweet?"

Henrietta and I started to laugh, but Mamma frowned so heavily upon us we were obliged to conceal our exultation.

"Is it that woman again, Edward?" she asked Papa, her eyes glinting and her voice as sharp as a sour fruit.

"If by that stark inference you are alluding to Mrs. Abigail, your assumption is correct, Lucy. The letter is from her. I presume, my dear, that you have no objection?"

"Is there any reason why I should have, Edward?"

"None on my soul, my dear. I swear to that."

Mamma drew herself up from her corsets as stiffly as a cobra will stretch from its coils, and so she waited, tapping her fingers together and her foot upon the floor as Papa continued his playing, the letter lying on the table between them.

I do not know what were Henrietta's feelings, but as far as I was concerned I had already made up my mind that Mrs. Abigail's epistle had something to do with us. Perhaps she had discovered the intrigue with her son? Perhaps Mrs. Trouncer had informed her of my weekly excursions to Wingmeadow Lane. I could feel my cheeks burning and the tears smart in my eyes. What should I say? What could I say if they questioned or accused me? Suppose I told them it was Henrietta who was responsible, would they believe me? Would they for one moment listen to a word against their darling, and what hope had I of freeing myself from Henrietta's guilt?

"Well," broke in Mamma, "are you going to read the letter, Edward, or are you going to leave it stifling up this room?"

"Forgive me, my dear," replied Papa with a twinkle, "I did not know you were so impatient. Can it be, my love, that you wish to see what is in it, or would you prefer me to recite it?"

He took the envelope and smiled as he caught its flowered perfume.

"Delightful. . . . Delicious Mrs. Abigail, so distinctive. Do you not think so, my love?"

Mamma snorted and tossed her head as, unfolding the document, Papa began slowly to read it aloud.

" 'My dear and esteemed Lord Darlington . . .' "

"What a ridiculously extravagant manner of address."

"I will be obliged, Lucy, if you do not interrupt. 'My dear and esteemed Lord Darlington:

'I have for a long time been considering the reason of our apathy and dullness and I have come to the conclusion it is because of the sad lack of harmony and unity between us; in other words, dear Lord Darlington, we do not mix.

'Our hospitality in Wingmeadow and Springfield Town is tempered with prejudice and petty likes and dislikes which are likely to divide us and close our doors to one another. This, on the face of it, does not conform with our Lord's maxim to "Love thy neighbour"; moreover, I decline to be bored to extinction and am indifferent if I shock. Prudery, as you know, I despise, and it would surprise even myself were I to blush. I therefore present this somewhat unusual suggestion to you in the hopes that it will meet with your pleasure and Lady Darlington's approval.

In order to relieve and enliven these tedious wintry evenings I have in mind to establish a ladies' choral society which will, I sincerely hope, perform at various charitable concerts and within the safety of our homes. The society will assemble for the purpose of practice once or even twice a week at Wingmeadow Lodge, and it will be I can assure you a most decorous and drawing room affair of which we need not be ashamed. I have consulted the Reverend Barklett upon this subject and attained his approval of it, although I have not the slightest doubt that there will be many whose hands will be upraised in condemnation of it.

'I would deem it a great honour if you would permit your Henrietta and of course the little Susan to attend, and I can assure you they will be made most welcome in my humble home.

'Your most attached and devoted friend,
Ann Abigail.'

There was a long silence, each of us attending to our varied thoughts. There was Henrietta, with such rapture in her face, and her hands clasped and her eyes shining like stars; and there was I, treading upon air because I would at least see Kelvin; and there was Mamma, with a look as sour as a green apple, plying her needle with vexatious vigilance, and last of all there was Papa, chuckling and chortling with the devil of mischief in his eyes.

"Gad, what a woman!" he exclaimed, "*What* a woman! By all the stars in Heaven, I love her!"

Then Mamma bestirred herself and her voice was as sharp as steel upon stone.

"She must be insane," she said, "completely and utterly insane. Whoever heard of a choral society of young ladies; it is a monstrous breach of etiquette."

"It is magnificent," replied Papa. "Just think of them. Blond, brunette, all sizes and all shapes and most of them virgins, I will swear. Nice healthy simple wenches unspoilt and unscathed, rich bargains in young flesh voluptuously garmented. . . . It is an inspiration."

"There is no occasion to be coarse, Edward, and I can see nothing inspired in such a project. The folly of a frivolous woman about to violate the fashion and break convention is

136

hardly a salubrious sight; and a gathering of females raising bedlam once or twice a week is a proceeding in which I see no sapience or discernment."

"There is another complexion to it, Lucy, you have doubtless overlooked."

"Such as?"

"Such as Mrs. Abigail's seven sons . . . seven unmarried sons, Lucy, just think of that. Is it not possible she is becoming anxious? Can you not imagine her fuming and fretting over what is to become of them? The entry of so many local ladies for them to look over twice a week is as skilful and neat-handed an idea as you could wish for."

"If you are suggesting that even Mrs. Abigail would sink to such a level I am amazed at you, Edward."

"If you had seven unmarried sons, my dove, instead of two unaffianced daughters you would not be so critical. There is no harm as far as I can see in combing out the countryside for suitable and agreeable wives. On the contrary, it seems to me to have the fire of genius."

"I am sorry you should think so, Edward, and I wish to inform you here and now I will take no part in this irregular affair."

"Consider for Heaven's sake our daughters' happiness, Lucy, and reflect upon their future. Are they to live for ever in this stagnant pigeon hole, confined to our hearth and family alliance, are they? Is that what you want for them? For the love of God I ask you to be reasonable for their sakes as well as for our own."

"I do not think even you, Edward, can accuse me of being thoughtless where the children are concerned."

"But they are no longer children, Lucy; by Christ they are young women with the flesh and blood of our own making.

"Without the aid of blasphemy, Edward, I am fully aware of the facts of their creation; but I cannot for the life of me see how they or their future can benefit by a caterwauling community such as Mrs. Abigail suggests."

Mopping his brow and between the most vehement oaths, Papa proceeded to deliver an edifying discourse upon the merits of the milk of human kindness and the benefit of a charitable viewpoint; but as Mamma's benevolence and bounty had dried with the milk within her long ago, the more he spoke of it the more inexorable and determined she became, asserting that Mrs. Abigail was but a modern upstart, that she was attempting to ape the manners and customs of a certain undesirable group who called themselves the gloss of novelty, people who set themselves to outrage and scandalize all those who came in contact with them. Mrs. Abigail was aspiring no doubt to exhibit Wingmeadow Lodge as a parade ground for the display of her seven progeny; it was not only repellent but disgraceful, and it was up to them to put her in her place.

"These so-called concerts will be an innovation, Edward, they will be a laughing stock to some and a stench in the nostrils to those of a higher standard who live near Springfield and in the lane. As for myself I refuse to become a party to such nonsense. I have my friends to think of and the position that we hold here, besides which there is the Queen to be considered who, as you know, disapproves of progress, especially in women, and . . ."

"Confound the Queen."

"Edward!"

138

"Well, you force me to say it, you drive me to it, Lucy, you madden me into saying things I do not mean, pig-prodding at Mrs. Abigail as if she were some common slut. From what can we derive amusement, may I ask? I swear I see no pleasure in this retired and gloomy circle round the Queen. If you were a close friend of Her Majesty's, my dear Lucy, I might better understand your point of view, but I think I am correct in saying that the only connection you have with this gracious lady is the slender circumstance that you both frequent the same costumier and milliner."

And so the controversy raged with their voices rising and falling in monotonous dispute. First Mamma would score a point and then Papa, and all the while Henrietta and I remained and listened to them, praying fervently that our dear Papa would win.

I do not know what it was that suddenly came over me as I sat there waiting for the verdict; but of a sudden a great wave of resolution surged up within me and I no longer felt afraid. All I knew was that if I did not attend these practices I would die . . . die because the very reason for living would have been taken from me. I was inspired by my secret love for Kelvin and my heart was strong.

Without another moment's thought of what the consequence might be, I began to speak.

"Papa . . . Mamma."

"Yes, Susan, what is it?"

"You will let us go . . . to . . . to Wingmeadow Lodge I mean. You must let us go, you must . . . you must, do you hear?"

They all turned and looked at me, their mouths agape and the most profound amazement in their eyes.

"What is that, Susan?" murmured Mamma. "What is that you say?"

"I want you to let us go, I want you to let us join this choir."

Then I poured forth a torrent of words, my voice at times rising to a scream. I told them how starved we were for occupation and at a loss to know what to do with our days. I told them about the books I was reading, the sordid, perverted literature with which I filled my mind. I insisted it was their fault, it was their parental suppression which was driving me to the lowest depths of thought.

"Neither you nor Papa have treated us fairly," I screamed at Mamma. "Even with the rooms we have, along where the maids work. We are like prisoners within high walls. We are like cattle penned in for the market. All you have ever thought of is that we should wed, and yet, when the one chance comes our way you want to take it from us. What are we to do? Where are we to go if you are for ever possessive of our bodies and our souls?"

Papa remained very quiet during this outbreak, looking first at Henrietta and then somewhat sheepishly at Mamma. His face was flushed and he seemed to be distressed and far from well. The light from the window by him caught his handsome genial countenance, and with a pang I noticed lines in it I had never seen there before.

Mamma had dropped her embroidery and was patting the lace upon the bosom of her gown with affected concentration; her expression had not altered except that her cheekbones seemed a little higher and her eyes a little smaller.

"Have you quite finished, Susan?" she said.

"Yes, Mamma, that is all I have to say."

"If you are endeavouring to suggest that you might one day wed an Abigail," she continued icily, "you had better free from your mind any such idea, for I would not under any circumstances tolerate it. I am surprised that you have not more to tell me of how dull and bored you have been, and how cruel and unnatural we have been to you. Good gracious, child, in listening to you one might imagine you had been starved and beaten and confined to your rooms; and yet, I do not seem to remember ever questioning either you or Henrietta as to where you go or how you spend your days, and never once have we commanded that you should not walk alone without a chaperon."

"I know, Mamma. It is not that, it is something deeper, not the little things."

"I am afraid I do not understand you, Susan."

"What Susan means," interrupted Papa, "is that we have neglected their occupations in our eagerness to find them husbands. In London, for instance, we aired our social life in Rotten Row and the fashionable quarter of Hyde Park. We went to invitation parties, picnics, tea-tattles and musicals. Because we had two comely and well-dowried daughters we wished to see them wed in their first season for our edification, my dear, rather than their own, and now, when the great houses have closed their doors and the shooting and hunting is occupying men's minds, we have provided nothing to take the place of entertainment."

"But did they not say they disliked society and all that it composed?"

"A whim, my love; young girls will have their fancies."

"And what are we supposed to do, humour their vapours, and because of their contrary moods throw them into the laps of the seven Abigails?"

"You must admit, my dear Lucy, it has the flavour of an excellent idea."

Mamma turned and looked at me coldly.

"I am surprised at you, Susan," she said, "and your conduct quite amazes me. I must confess I did not think you had it in you to protest with such vehement unreserve. I cannot say that I admire your taste in words and I think at this moment you would oblige me if you would kindly leave the room."

"Stay where you are, Susan," commanded Papa, "for I wish to settle this matter once and for all."

The passion was slowly passing from me and I now felt that if the floor had opened and engulfed me I would indeed have been most thankful. Henrietta was nudging me to continue and grimacing at Mamma behind her bustle; but my heart ached for Papa and the tired look he had and how sorrowful he seemed to be at what I had said to them.

"You must forgive me, Lucy," he said, "but in this I am determined to go against you. Whatever doubts I may have had about this project, the eloquence of Susan has convinced me. We have been wrong to treat them as we have, half girls, half children, for it is a life of their own they are after, not ours. I have therefore made up my mind, I have definitely made up my mind we will without any more ado or argument, accept Mrs. Abigail's kind invitation and write her a courteous letter to that effect."

Mamma swept out of the room with a swish of her skirts and a toss of her head and a snort you would have thought might well-nigh choke her; her slam of the door was enough to raise the dead.

Papa lay back in his chair with his eyes closed as if the scene had been too much for him, whilst Henrietta was acting a pantomine of exultation over the gaining of this end. But I was too alarmed at the lassitude of Papa to triumph over him, his shortness of breath and the slight sweat upon his brow. I went over to him and sat on the arm of his chair.

"Dearest Papa, you are tired, you do not feel well and it is all my fault."

"Confusion seize all women," he replied smiling at me, "and their perpetual jangle. Such a storm about so small an issue as a women's choir. Let them all caterwaul to their hearts' content, say I, and leave the men alone."

"Mamma will not reason."

"Mamma has no will to, that is why. She has no wisdom either with a man. When words are at a loss she should swoon upon her failure. It is unarguable and most becoming if well done. Many a fainting female, my dear, has reached a decision far quicker and more easily than by the clatter of her tongue."

"But you are sick, Papa?"

"Not really, Susan, not really. Have you ever thought of the world as a human clock with thousands of hearts to keep wound in it. Have you ever considered the labour of keeping each clock regulated, with some of them with their main spring on the wane."

"You mean?"

"I mean my heart is tired and needs remodelling."

"What sort of a clock am I, Papa?"

"A very little one, Susan, a gilded toy set high upon a mantel.

A very little one with puny chimes that no one heeded until today. May I ask, child, what in Heaven's name possessed you?"

"I do not know, Papa, I suddenly felt that I must speak."

"Can it be that you have grown up more than I imagined?"

"In what way, dearest Papa?"

"The only way, Susan. Are you in love?"

"With whom, Papa? With whom?"

"With perhaps an Abigail. God knows, there are seven of them to choose from."

I could feel my cheeks burning when Henrietta interrupted with a strange fierce recklessness I could not understand.

"I am the one, Papa. . . . It is I who am in love."

Papa looked at her and then threw back his head and laughed. The blue came back into his eyes so that he was once more the dear vain lightsome man we knew so well.

"By all that is wonderful! Henrietta has a suitor," he cried. "The Lord have mercy on his soul, poor Abigail, whichever one it is."

"And why should you suppose it is an Abigail, Papa? Are there no other men in the world but them? And why do you laugh at me?—am I so undesirable?"

"Were I a young man I must confess you would take the edge a little off my appetite."

"You flatter me, Papa."

"Which of them is it, girl? Tell me his name so that I can send the poor fellow a harness and whip, for I swear to God he will be sorely in need of both to tame you. It is an Abigail I presume?"

"Yes, Papa, it is an Abigail."

"And am I to know no more than that?"

144

"With you in the mellow moments of a glass of port gabbling my secret to Mamma? Oh, no, thank you, Papa, I dare not trust you."

"Do you know which one it is, Susan?"

"Yes . . . Susan knows."

Papa sighed. "When I think of Mamma hearing about this," he said, "I can feel the draught of a storm whistling about my ears. God help us all, that is what I say, God help us all when she gets hold of it."

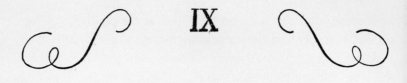

IX

THUS IT WAS that a letter to the effect that we would join
Mrs. Abigail's choral society was despatched to Wingmeadow
Lodge. Afterwards, there was a sullen silence from Mamma for
many days. No more conversation was held upon the point and
the talks at meals became trivial and dull. Papa, full of mischief,
would wink his eye first at Henrietta and then at me, or else
sigh and place his hand upon his heart so that Henrietta, flushed,
her eyes flashing fire, would tap her foot incessantly beneath
the table.

It did not take Mrs. Abigail many weeks to assort and set up
the society for the great day when the first practice was to be
held.

Henrietta attired herself in her most becoming gown and
I could hear her singing as she dressed; as for myself, there was
but one thought in my mind, one feeling in my heart, one
apprehension. Would Kelvin Abigail be there?

Papa insisted we should take the chaise on account of the
wet ground and icy wind; Mamma, enclosed within her room,
refused to make note of our departure; Mrs. Trouncer alone
patted us down, declaring us both as pretty as a picture.

All the way to Wingmeadow Lodge, Henrietta sat with her
large eyes glowing as she gazed at the dismal weather we could
see outside us. She talked so much of Kelvin and his love for
her that it was all I could do not to cover my ears and scream
out to her, "Let him alone, for God's sake, let him alone for

he is mine." But she saw nothing of this as she prattled, driving the knife deeper and deeper into my heart.

As we entered Mrs. Abigail's drawing room it seemed full to the brim of eager chattering voices.

Ladies both old and young, pretty and homely, pressed round her, all talking at once and anxious to impress her.

Mrs. Abigail most evidently believed in the abolishment of class distinction and had therefore selected from her circle of acquaintances a variety and assortment of persons from almost every sphere of life. Some were in calicos and simple garments, whilst others were lavishly arrayed in silks and laces. Tall and short, dark and fair, sombre and gay, they stood round, waiting for Mrs. Abigail to tell them what to do.

There were two of Lady Garmington's three granddaughters, whose noble features were scarcely embellished by their spectacles, and whose thin lips seemed set as if their teeth were perpetually on edge. There was also Lady Agatha Swann's sole offspring, very gay and sprightly, whose voice sounded incessantly about nothing like the persistent tinkling of a bell.

Those who came from Springfield Town stood out from the Wingmeadow neighbours and at first it appeared as if Mrs. Abigail had made a mistake in attempting to be too convivial; for in that goodly company she had poured plebeians and rank, skipjacks and gentlefolk, the exalted with the underlings and earthborn.

For instance, on the further side of the room, sat the two Miss Tinnerlies, timid and ill at ease, and perched on their chairs like birds on a rail watching for worms. They were untidy, insignificant creatures who looked, all in all, as if they had selected their wardrobe from an out-of-town jumble sale. Their dresses, shabbily held together by voluminous dusty flounces and a great deal of ribbon and tattered lace all fastened with pins, plainly showed that they had little of the luxuries of life or the comforts of a family home. Their parents were dead and they lived in a tolerable but sparsely furnished house, the large rooms of which they let out to lodgers.

"We only let our rooms because we are lonely," they were careful to explain. "It is not so much the money we need as the companionship. As ladies at large there were few who came to visit us, but as landladies we get a rare variety of guests."

They did not consider it lowering to keep lodgers, although some of their neighbours looked down their noses at them. They were only embarrassed and uncomfortable when rent day came round and there would be sure to be some argument.

They always asked for three months' payment in advance, thus assuring themselves some days and nights of comparative peace; then there would be a few hours of tears and protestations as the tenants renewed their obligations, some haggling and bartering, whilst others whined and complained of a holdup at the bank which they could not account for. They kept a little diary about their tenants, jotting down notes as to their habits and appearance. The good conduct guests were at the beginning of the book and had complimentary bracketings and flattering marginal notes. But the bad tenants were in the back pages, written heavily in ink. "Mrs. Wiggles does not wash . . . Miss Isobel Blimbark keeps biscuits under her bed," etc., etc., and they would read this little diary of theirs to anyone they met.

Standing erectly beside them was Miss Amelia Pinchbeck, a most respectable and respected woman of about thirty-five. Her features were strikingly handsome, and she wore her hair most elaborately turned up behind. Miss Pinchbeck bestowed a great deal of time upon the dressing of her hair, and it was so moulded and flattened and patted and pressed that it looked like a doll's wig which had somehow been fastened to her head with glue. She was surprisingly amiable and beamed upon all and one, except of course the Miss Tinnerlies, whom she secretly despised. She was taking advantage of the choral society to improve upon her own. Her mother was bedridden and her father a retired sea captain on half pay who had travelled all over the world. This gave to Miss Pinchbeck an enlightened expression, although she herself had never been farther than Springfield Town.

Gathered round Mrs. Abigail I observed Miss Kettlewell who was spick and span and owned a small vanity establishment at the end of the lane. Her face was so fat and her mouth so small, she looked like an ivory powder puff with a little red button in the middle of it. Then there were the Gimp girls, with their round black eyes and snub noses, who were sufficiently wealthy to do nothing at all; and, with them, Miss Bertha and Miss Georgina Baffit, who went in for croquet and archery and refused to wear bustles or colour their faces or seek the seventeen-inch waist. We were presented to Miss Withering, a painter in oils, whose father was the head of a linen draper's store; and, last of all, we met the Honorable Diana Quirk, a writer of essays of a most advanced order and a young woman who prided herself on calling a spade a spade with such rusticity that she shocked all the neighbours nearby. It was the Honorable Diana Quirk who defiled all arguments, and who even made a flower show seem like a farmyard for fertilizing pollen. She would stand before one of the loveliest of roses and expatiate upon the quantity of stamens and pistils so that those attending to her dissertation turned away their heads with a blush. It was all rather fearful and indecorous, but the Honorable Diana Quirk declared there was no more interesting pursuit than being stud groom to a rose.

Mrs. Abigail was flushed and eloquent as she welcomed us to Wingmeadow Lodge, but I could not help noticing the hoity-toity raising of eyebrows and the brushing to one side and the haughty staring of the social lights for those less well born than themselves.

"Now, ladies," said Mrs. Abigail, as she unfolded her plans for the choir, "I think for this afternoon we will just sing a short chorus together so that we can become acquainted with the tone of one another's voices. Henrietta, my dear, will you be so obliging as to accompany us upon the piano? And if all the sopranos will kindly group themselves together, and you, Susan, come here and stand beside me."

The little Miss Tinnerlies rose meekly to their feet and scuttled across the room. They were so used to trotting up and down stairs with trays that their movements were always fluttering and hurried. It may have been my imagination, but I thought I perceived a slight shifting away from them as they stood at the edge of the group with their eyes lowered and their hands folded nervously before them.

"What will it be?" asked Miss Amelia, beginning to hum an ending with a stentorian trill.

"Something gay," replied the two Gimp girls, with their small snub noses turned up to the chandelier.

"Something old-fashioned," said Henrietta. "All about lilac and love, to fit in to my sentimental mood."

"What about 'John Peel'," suggested Miss Georgina Baffit.

"Too rollicking . . . far, far too rollicking," replied Miss Kettlewell with a shudder.

"As Christmas has not long been over," said Mrs. Abigail,

"I propose that we try 'Silent Night.' We have been singing it so often in church of late I feel sure you must all know it by heart."

There was a great deal of rustling of petticoats and unfolding of music and then Mrs. Abigail raised her hand.

"I will count up to three, ladies," she said, "and then please all of you begin. Now here we are, one . . . two . . . three."

With a resplendent chord from Henrietta we strained our throats and opened our lungs and started.

It was a combination of incredible sounds which soared up to the ceiling and sank with a strange despairing wail upon the ground; yet, considering how many of us there were, we made uncommonly little noise; only Miss Amelia Pinchbeck's impressive voice tore through the choir, and the two Miss Tinnerlies punctuated their notes with such incisiveness that when they sang the words, "holy night," it was as if they were indeed stabbing the syllables with a gimlet. Miss Kettlewell's voice was like the piping of a new-born bird, and when she opened her button of a mouth her manifold chins closed it up again with a snap.

The choir left off in a flourish of high notes, each voice dead set against the other. In vain Mrs. Abigail implored us to be more in unison, to get in concert and not in opposition.

"It is a choir of contradictions," she said with a laugh. "A musical controversy. Why so much rivalry, ladies? I have not brought you here to wage a war."

Then she patted us down and assured us that with practice we would take the town by storm. "And you especially, my dear," she said, folding me in her arms. "You have the loveliest fresh young voice I have ever heard, and when you come next week I implore you to bring some special song with you so that we can hear you sing alone."

Smiling and encouraging us, she said she was sure we would care for some tea after our exertions, and the strange assembly followed her in a long thin trail to the dining room where her seven sons had been waiting.

The moment they all caught sight of the brothers the choir appeared to brighten as if a cloud had been removed from the sun, and there was a great deal of tossing of heads and drooping of eyelids as they undertook to entice and allure.

Henrietta began immediately to assert herself and spread out her beauty. As the young men handed round hot muffins and tea she displayed herself artfully, and I could not fail to notice the admiration she called forth. I hated her then, I hated her so much I could feel my nails cutting the flesh as I pressed them into my hands.

The dining room was well warmed and snug and there were bright plates and shining dishes all over the table. Mrs. Abigail had laid out most bountiful provisions which the choir set upon with voracious gluttony. They stodged and stuffed, gobbled and devoured, as if faced with their first decent meal for many a day. Through it all, Silvain, with the air of a perfect publican, moved amongst them saying, "Give your orders, ladies. What shall it be now, hot rum, a smattering of port, or a cup of freshly brewed tea?"

Such a giggling and wriggling then ensued. Such a shaking of curls and rolling of eyes as they tittered their requests. And what a roguish gentleman that master Silvain was to be sure, what mischief. But they managed him well enough, I noticed, to get several glasses of rum, which was, after all, just what they wanted.

Sated and flushed, the choristers eventually leaned back in their chairs to contemplate this magnanimous family who had given them so much pleasure. They felt mellow now that they had fed, and even the Miss Tinnerlies were allowed to make an occasional remark.

The utmost hilarity and vivacity now prevailed, with everyone in the best imaginable humour. Phillip's round red face seemed rounder and redder than ever as he bent over the ladies, and even Henry's sharp-angled features had broken into a smile. Henry had a way of standing as if he was awaiting a jury, and he seldom seemed to throw off the grave expectancy of the law. It was easy to imagine him in wig and gown, condemning some poor prisoner, and he hummed and hawed his way through the choir as if each one of them was his client.

I caught a brief glimpse of Kelvin and Henrietta with their heads very close together, and it was not until we were leaving that he at last came over to me.

"Forgive me, Miss Susan," he said, "for not having claimed your attention somewhat earlier."

"You were otherwise occupied," I replied politely, "and no man can be in two places at once."

"Henrietta was particularly exacting, Miss Susan, and she has, as you know, a will of her own. I tried several times to reach you but . . ."

"But what, Mr. Abigail?"

Before he had time to answer me I was swept from his side by the exuberance of Mrs. Abigail and her fulsome praise of my voice.

"This child sings like an angel," she cried, "and I can assure you will be one of my most cherished pupils."

We were both silent in the chaise going back and I thought

153

Henrietta looked flushed as with fever. She stared at me from beneath her stormy brows and said:

"I would not be too elated at Mrs. Abigail's honeyed words if I were you, Susan. Blandishments and rosewater pour easily from her, you must always remember that."

"But it was an enjoyable afternoon," I replied. "Did you not think so, Henrietta?"

"It was passable," she said, "and will fill in our time, which is after all what we both wanted; but you need not have sung so loudly, need you? It was hardly in good taste. Kelvin told me that he could hear your voice as far as the dining room."

My heart leapt.

"Did he say that, Henrietta, did he indeed tell you that?"

"Yes, he told me that," replied Henrietta, and there was a look on her face I could not understand.

Mamma never once enquired about our evenings at Wingmeadow Lodge, and, indeed, she made it quite evident that the subject was distasteful to her. She remained decisively affronted by the unwonted flightiness of Mrs. Abigail who, she vehemently asserted, had so outraged the Victorian era.

But with Papa it was different. He desired to know in every detail how we had fared, and of course Henrietta made much of what she assured him was my uncalled-for display and how Mrs. Abigail had showered compliments upon me like summer rain.

"And you, Henrietta, had you no praise for your playing? No admiration? Was there not at least one Abigail who gave you his applause?"

"There was too much noise for anyone to notice me, Papa. Never have I heard such discord, such screechings as there were like wounded peacocks."

"So no one heard you, eh? And you were twinged with jealousy and spite? Poor Henrietta, it is not like you, my love, to be ignored."

"Do you not think, Papa, it was in grievous taste to acclaim Susan as the matchless singer? The others were much put out by it and disappointed. I noticed how they shrugged, and I heard a few of them say that as a matter of course Lord Darlington's daughter would be sure to be in favour."

"Henrietta," I cried indignantly, "you know that is not true. Do not listen to her, Papa. It is not true."

"How could you hear them, Susan," replied Henrietta, "since you were so concerned with Mrs. Abigail's good opinion of your voice, so elated and twittering with conceit."

"I was nothing of the sort, Henrietta. Indeed, Papa, I was not. Mrs. Abigail asked me to bring some music with me next time I came in order that she could hear me sing alone. There was no harm in that, now was there?"

"Of course there was no harm in it, Susan. And you, Henrietta, my dear, will kindly hold your tongue. I will not have these bitter words whenever there is praise for Susan. Upon my soul, one would believe when listening to you that you wanted the whole world for yourself."

"Myself and one other, Papa."

"You mean that ambiguous lover of yours? Well, that may or may not be."

"You mean you do not believe it?"

"I am inclined to think he may be but a dream suitor whom you have conjured up to be important."

Henrietta reddened.

"If you do not believe me, Papa," she replied, "ask Susan. She does not lie."

Papa turned to me, his face full of mischief.

"Has she indeed a lover, Susan? And do you really know who he is?"

"Yes, Papa, I know."

"But do not tell him," interrupted Henrietta hastily. "Please do not tell him. He cannot keep anything to himself and is sure to spread it abroad."

"You need not concern yourself, my dear," replied Papa, "for in the course of time it is natural that the young man will conform to the dictates of society and ask me formally for your hand. Alas for him, poor blinded devil, I shall be obliged to give it. You have a lovely hand, Henrietta, but with nails that are too sharp. I presume you think yourself in love?"

A strange smile curved Henrietta's lips as she fingered the ribbons of her gown.

"I presume so too, Papa," she said.

"*Are* you in love, Henrietta?"

"I do not know, Papa. Pride of conquest and possession make up part of it, and I doubt if it is in me to love to distraction. It is the weakness of a man which pleases me, the fact that I can play upon his heart. The wondering when I have driven him beyond endurance, whether he will rape me or wring my neck."

"Henrietta!"

"There, I have shocked dear Susan. I did not remember she was there."

As soon as she closed the door I could control myself no longer.

"She is a cruel and heartless girl," I cried passionately, "and she has no right to speak of Kelvin so."

The words slipped out before I had time to stop them, and in a flash I knew I had now given away Henrietta's secret.

156

"Kelvin!" said Papa. "So, it is Kelvin Abigail. The devil confound and seize my soul; it surely is not possible."

And then I told him.

I told Papa of my love for Kelvin Abigail.

There were moments when he tried to stop me as if he could no longer bear it. Moments when he put his hand over my mouth and pressed my face against him. For this was not the Susan he had known. This young girl kneeling at his feet with the tears streaming from her eyes was not the Susan he was used to. This was an abandoned creature—a shameless creature, a small child crying in the wilderness with dishevelled hair and crumpled clothes.

I had to tell him everything, now that I had broken down, not that there was any special reason that I then knew for me to hold my tongue. Still I wanted to convey to some sympathetic ear those torturing hours at Wingmeadow Lodge during which I had sat and watched Henrietta wooing and being wooed by the only man I would, or ever could, love; I even went on to speak of the times I had hated her and even wished her dead.

"Why should she have everything?" I sobbed. "Why should I be starved of love because of her amusement? Am I so homely and dull still, Papa? What is wrong with me that I can give so much and gain so little?"

And so it went on and on, and as I unfolded my confession with such eloquence and such a flow of words and tears, Papa lay back in his chair with his mouth agape.

"I wonder if you can understand what Kelvin means to me?" I continued, still kneeling humbly by his chair. "I am really and truly deeply in love, Papa. Kelvin means existence, he means happiness, laughter and tears. He is indeed the very heart of me. What am I to do? Am I to allow Henrietta to destroy what is left of my life? Am I to permit her to break my heart and watch me grow old before her eyes? Always she has come between me and everything I wish for. If I was to tell her what I have told you now, Papa, she would not be sorry but gloat on my misfortune. You love her I know, both you and Mamma have always believed that she is sweet and good. But you have been wrong, God knows how wrong you have both been, for Henrietta is evil and corrupt and venomous and made of stone. Although I say this of my own sister it is the truth, Papa."

Papa took me in his arms, stroked my hair and let me weep awhile.

"Poor little Susan," he said at last. "Poor little come-by-nothing Susan with her stillborn love. If only I had known of this I might have helped you, but even now it may not be too late. I know how much we are to blame for spoiling Henrietta, and it is more our fault than hers that she is as she is. We should have been less tender with her and more considerate of you; but there was always Henrietta bewitching us and twisting us round her little finger, playing with us as if we were but puppets on a string. Love is like that, Susan. You see no wrong in anything they do. Can you forgive us and can we make amends? I wonder if it is humanly possible for a man by one good deed to atone for his whole life."

He was so deeply in earnest, so filled with understanding, and when he had soothed me and dried my tears he sat for a moment lost in thought.

"A woman is made for man's comfort," he said at last, "and to bear him children; that is the way of our inscrutable God, but it is not the measure of the women of this house. It is not Henrietta's way nor her conception of a wife. She is a spirited madcap and would lead a man a dance just for the fun and cruelty of it, and think nothing of it if she drove him to his death. What a world of pity it is she had to light upon the only man, my dear, that I have ever known you to care for. Tell me, my child, what kind of a fellow is this Kelvin Abigail?"

"If there were more like him in this world, Papa, there would be more sunshine and gladness and contented hearts. He is handsome and headstrong and at first I was repelled by him and almost afraid. Then something seemed to draw me to him; and do you know what it was, Papa? It was because I found he was extraordinarily like you. He has your gaiety, your heart and mind, even his eyes often look at me the way you do."

"Is he as good as all that, Susan? Is he really?"

"He is even better, Papa."

"And yet he loved Henrietta. You amaze me."

"Do you not love Henrietta, so how can you blame him for that? You also are aware, Papa, of how Henrietta can assume a gentleness and kindness as easily as she can change her gown, and yet you dote upon her. She seems to have everything a man can want, and I have nothing."

"You are too good, little Susan."

"Can any woman be entirely and absolutely good without being also most profoundly dull?—answer me that, Papa."

"I do not think so, Susan."

"Shall I become wicked then? Shall I become hopelessly and heartlessly depraved?"

Papa's eyes twinkled into mine and he could not keep from smiling.

"Is this indeed the young lady who could not say boo to a goose?" he said teasingly. "The very same young lady who could not lift her eyes without a blush. A chaste and decorous miss without appetite for love, wishing at one time to take Holy

159

Orders? Has God so tricked me that I cannot even recognize my own spawn? I used to reverence your goodness, Susan, although I could not understand it and it wearied me out of all patience. I said to myself that perhaps you were from another world where you seemed beyond the passions of mankind."

"Oh, Papa . . . dearest Papa, I do love you so."

"We know one another better, that is all, and perhaps seeing me in Kelvin and Kelvin in me helps a little."

"What shall I do, Papa, whatever shall I do?"

"Go out and give your heart a fling. Fight for this man with everything that is in you. Fight for him, child, so that in the years to come whether you win or lose him you will know that with God's help you did your best."

The confession done, I felt the better for it. It was as if a great weight had been lifted from my mind and a deep shadow from my heart.

That night when I went to my room I prayed for courage. I prayed for the strength to do as Papa had told me.

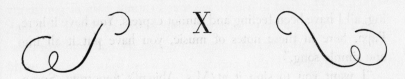

X

It was only two days later that Papa called me to the Music Room.

"I have something here, my love," he said, "which you will like and which I think will please you."

He held a script of music in his hand and, taking it over to the piano, he started to play and speak the words softly as he went along:

> Can't you see it in my eyes
> You're the one I adore.
> It may seem a big surprise
> Wish I'd told you before.
> Since you first raised your hat and smiled
> You're all I've been thinking of.
> Can't you see it in my eyes
> I've never been so much in love.

"Oh, Papa," I breathed, "dearest Papa, it is the loveliest thing . . . it is the loveliest thing I have ever heard you play."

"I wrote it for you, Susan. It is your song."

"It is Springfield, Papa. It is the narrow street and the great coach swinging round the corner of it. I can hear the jingle of harness and the clatter of the horses' hooves, and I can see Kelvin himself riding into my heart. It is all I have been thinking, all I have been feeling and cannot express. You have it here, Papa, here in these notes of music, you have put it all into one simple song."

"I want you to sing it at Mrs. Abigail's tomorrow, Susan. Will you do so?"

"Of course I will sing it, Papa, I will sing it wherever I go. Play it again for me. Please will you play it again?"

He smiled at my eagerness and started to do so when all of a sudden, and without any warning, he fell heavily forward and lay across the notes.

He appeared to be in a paroxysm of agony. His countenance was of the deadliest pallor and I could see that he was shivering. His left arm was crooked with pain and he seemed to be breathing with the utmost difficulty. I tried to raise him, wild and incoherent with fear, but he was too massive for my frail arms. Again and again I tried to hold him to me, but he slipped from my puny strength with a crash onto the piano.

And then in a second it was over and he was smiling at my anxious and tortured face.

"Do not look so alarmed, child," he said. "This is not the first time, I can assure you. You remember what I told you about the world being like a clock shop. Too much good living, my dear, and fast loving, has run me down; and with all God's winding I am finding it increasingly difficult to keep time."

I helped him to his comfortable chair and wiped the sweat from his brow. His pulse was still feeble and the surface of his hands ice cold.

"Let me send for Doctor Wiffin, dearest Papa, for you are ill. You should not be here. The good doctor will put you to bed and order you rest. I beg of you."

But he shook his head.

"God forbid that I should ever be put to bed," he replied.
"I do not like being stroked and pawed and commiserated—you
know how women are. There is nothing they enjoy so much
as a man laid so low they can say and do what they like with
him. I beg that you will not inform either Mamma or Henrietta
or Mrs. Trouncer of this unless you wish me to be killed out-
right. Do not look so perturbed, little Susan. You see I am quite
well again. My mode of life needs a little fresh air, that is all,
and my body must be put in order."

Nevertheless, whilst we were at supper I noticed how much
he had aged of late. He was trying so hard to keep up a flow
of his usual light conversation, avoiding all subjects which would
disturb Mamma. She had been shopping in Springfield Town
and was tired and cross. Moreover, she had encountered old
Lady Garmington who had ill-naturedly informed her that the
whole community considered Mrs. Abigail's choir a monstrous
blunder, and that the Queen herself had been heard to say she
sincerely disapproved of such a bourgeois innovation so close to
Windsor Castle.

"Who cares what Lady Garmington has to say," replied Papa,
"and as for the Queen I am sure she has better things to do
than criticise a village choir. I am surprised at you, Lucy, for
listening to such unpolished ramblings."

"There is a story going that Mrs. Abigail . . ."

"I do not wish to hear it."

"But you should hear it, Edward, since it concerns us all.
We have ourselves to consider and what people say and think."

"Curiosity and enquiring and keeping your eyes open and
your ears pricked is the salt of living to you, Lucy, is it not?"

"I like to know what is going on, Edward, if that is what you mean. If we knew more about our friends before we took them to our bosom, we might be less encumbered with undesirable acquaintances."

"I do not agree with you, my dear. I think people should be permitted to reveal themselves, either by their good or their bad conduct, rather than be torn apart by their next-door neighbour's tongue."

"Even your precious Mrs. Abigail?"

"Precious she is, my dear Lucy, and rare in this community. As for the gossip round her, I daresay she pays no more attention to it than to a fly upon her shoulder. To live happily above scandal, as she does, is verily a great achievement."

"I am glad you think so, Edward," replied Mamma, and snapped her lips upon all further conversation.

It was not until the following morning whilst Mamma went about her household duties that Papa and Henrietta and I assembled in the Music Room. Henrietta appeared sullen and resentful when asked to rehearse Papa's song. She pouted and sulked and was in so ill a humour that Papa was obliged to remark upon it and ask her if anything was seriously the matter.

"Do you not like my music?" he said. "Is it indeed as bad as all that?"

"As bad as all what, Papa?"

"As your contemptuous countenance, my dear. To look at you one would think I had written so inane a verse and so discordant a melody that it disagreed with your digestion."

"I am hurt that you did not write it for me, Papa, that is all."

"And might I enquire why your feelings have been so wounded?"

164

"Because of what I told you. Because I am in love."

"But you were not sure of this when I last spoke to you, Henrietta."

"And Susan! Do you think the song is suitable for her?"

"It comes to us all at one time or another."

"But not to Susan, Papa. Never to Susan."

Papa shook his head and sighed.

"Alas, my poor Henrietta," he said, "such jealousy does not become you. Have you not enough of the good things of this world that you begrudge even this song to Susan?"

Shrugging her shoulders Henrietta continued practising the offending melody, but now and again she would turn her eyes accusingly towards me as if it was my fault Papa had chided her. When we had finished we retired to our rooms, and on the way up the long cedar stairway Henrietta said bitterly to me:

"It seems you are in favour, Susan, and I am in disgrace. I wonder what little bird has been singing into Papa's ear."

"If you think that I . . ."

"My dear Susan, I do not think, I know; however, it is of little consequence. What matters is that you are getting out of hand."

"Out of your hands you mean, do you not, Henrietta?"

Henrietta stared at me in astonishment.

"What makes my little sister so declaratory all of a sudden? What mood is this which has in it a suggestion of impertinence? Always remember this, Susan. Nothing will harm you if you do as you are told."

"If I do as you tell me, Henrietta?"

"Yes, Susan, as I tell you, and I think it will be wiser for you if you do not forget this. It will make life easier for us all."

Nevertheless, that afternoon on our way to Wingmeadow Lodge, Henrietta was vivacious and talkative with all traces of her temper gone. She expatiated upon the choir and what she most disliked about it with its jumbled intermixture.

"Those Miss Tinnerlies, for instance," she said scornfully. "With the pittance of money earned from their infrequent lodgers. What in Heaven's name made those misguided creatures think that they could sing, and did you ever in your life behold such scarecrows? And Miss Kettlewell with her corpulent frippery aping the airs and graces of the Court. I cannot say that I am enamoured of Miss Withering, excellent though her art may be. She smells prodigiously of paint and pigment and does not clean her nails. Of course it is most commendable of Mrs. Abigail to invite such people to her house, but I think she would have been wiser to reserve the choir for those of her own class."

I did not agree with Henrietta but hardly thought it worth my while to inform her of this. Mrs. Abigail had not undertaken the choral society casually, but with the utmost zest and for the purpose of making the country lives of people more congenial, and it seemed to me worthy of admiration the way she handled these frustrated spinsters and put a ray of lightness into their everyday monotony.

The practice was more proficient this time and even Miss Amelia Pinchbeck's resounding clamour was restrained. At the end of it all Mrs. Abigail expressed her delight in our improvement and assured us that if we went on as well as we were doing she would have us upon a platform in no time.

"And now," she said, "I have a little surprise for you. Lord

Darlington, as some of you may know, is, besides his many other qualities, a most distinguished and excellent composer. He has, I am happy to say, written a song for our especial benefit, and I am going to call upon little Susan here to kindly sing it for us. Henrietta, are you ready, and Susan, my dear, will you please stand close to me so that all of us can see you?"

I sang nervously at first, partly because of the dark frown upon Henrietta's face, and partly because I was standing in the midst of that critical assembly, exposed to the cold eyes of the choir. But after a while I seemed to forget the room full of people, and I was once more back in Springfield Town on that burning day in June when the Abigails first came there. I could see the sunlight tingeing the cottages, and I could feel the cool trees and follow the small clouds as they made their way to the horizon. And then, as the great coach swung into my life, I could see Kelvin with his strong clean beauty at the window of it.

The door at the far end of the room opened and Kelvin himself stood there, leaning against the wall with folded arms. The moment I caught sight of him the hot colour rose to my cheeks, for I could feel him looking at me with a strange intentness as if indeed he was seeing me for the first time.

I sang the song then only for him. There did not seem to be anyone else in the room; and he came closer and closer to me, drawn by my love for him, first frowning a little as if amazed at his own willingness. All that I wanted but could never have expressed was in those words as I stood there, singing out my heart to him, and then, quite suddenly, with a single chord, it ended, and Henrietta's clear cool voice cut through the scene as a sharp knife.

"Hark to my little sister warbling of love," she said. "Could anything in this world be more incongruous? Susan does not care for love. She is too chaste, too pure. She lives in a world of her own amongst dreams and books, do you not, dearest Susan?"

For a moment there was silence and a little consternation, and then Mrs. Abigail interrupted with her sweet discrimination.

"Nobody cares for love until they have a lover," she said, laughing, and the rest of the choir smiled and the tension was over.

I saw Kelvin stop with Henrietta's hand upon his arm. She whispered something to him, looking across at me, and he half shrugged his shoulders, turning away from me.

Whispering can hurt like a heavy blow between the eyes, and, however soft the sound may be, each unheard word can rap upon the mind like a hammer. For whispering means things are being said that are disparaging and cannot be revealed; it means mischief and cruelty and trouble. It leaves a trail of discomfort in its wake, each person thinking it is him or her who is being spoken of. So it was that in that well-filled room many a baleful look was cast upon Henrietta and upon the man I loved.

On the way home in the chaise Henrietta spoke of what she said was a to-do about next to nothing.

"Such a storm in a teacup about a song," she deplored, "the raves and delight of that frouzy company, as if indeed Papa had composed a masterpiece. And as for you, Susan, I wonder you were not ashamed of yourself, flaunting and parading an emotion you could never endure. But perhaps you were unaware

168

of Miss Pinchbeck's evident displeasure, and the smirking derision of the Gimps."

"What were you saying to Kelvin, Henrietta? He wanted to come to me, but you prevented him. What were you saying to him about me?"

"Really, Susan, I have no idea. It was of no importance."

"It was important enough to lower your voice and to stop him coming to me. What was it, Henrietta?"

Henrietta looked into her reticule. She smoothed her hair and drew on her gloves and looked everywhere except at me.

"Is this a court of law?" she replied lightly. "If so, we had better send for Henry to put us both on trial. Am I to remember everything I say?"

"And how dared you make fun of me before them all," I cried quivering with rage and my unhappiness. "How dared you, Henrietta?"

"I dare anything," replied Henrietta, "at any time and in any place. Surely you know that."

"Why did Kelvin smile and shrug his shoulders? Why did you both turn away with your heads close together, whispering?"

"I cannot remember, Susan. We are too much in love to know what words we use. Perhaps he was asking me to marry him, perhaps Papa's song had made him feel emotional. I really cannot say."

Henrietta swept out of the chaise and into the house and up the stairs, whilst I followed her slowly endeavouring to calm myself. When Papa asked me how it had passed, I burst into tears. There, in his arms, I told him of how Henrietta had ridiculed my singing, how she had made fun of me and whispered and nudged with Kelvin. "Your lovely song, Papa," I wept, "she has spoiled it all. It will never be the same again."

"Nonsense, Susan. What difference can it make?"

"She destroyed it, Papa, and she made me feel small and cheap. It was our song, yours and mine and Kelvin's, and now she has come between it as she comes between everything I do, and think, and say."

But Papa laughed and started to play it once more, and very soon we sang it together and I was happy and forgot my torment.

And so twice a week now the choral society assembled, and every second week there was a change of programme, except for Papa's song which, much to Henrietta's vexation, I was asked each time to sing.

Sometimes a few of us remained after the practice for an intimate sit-down supper, with the servants all retired and the seven Abigails fetching and carrying and making themselves generally useful. Under the influence of glasses of warm rum, the choir would expand and the elderly ones spoke of the good old times, whilst the young girls prattled of the present. They did not like the age they were in and blamed the Queen for it. It was too prim and formal, so they said, and there were great arguments as to what they would like to be if they only had one wish.

Miss Pinchbeck so far abandoned herself as to admit that all she wanted was to get married. "I need protection," she explained archly, patting her well-coiffed hair, "and a man to attend to me."

"Instead of taking in lodgers," said the Miss Tinnerlies, "we would like to be ladies at large."

"If I could have been Joan of Arc," cried Miss Kettlewell, "I would have been perfectly content."

Geoffery said that all he wanted to do was to paint a truly great picture, and Shelly, in a torrent of words, announced that he could never be really happy until he had discovered a country where no human being had ever been before.

"I would like to be a highwayman," said Silvain, "for I cannot imagine a more palatable thrill than kissing a lovely lady's neck and at the same time biting through the string of her pearl pendant."

It took Mrs. Abigail a considerable time after that to quieten and compose the disconcerted choir.

They were gay, those evenings at Wingmeadow Lodge, and full of cheer, and as the conversation turned this way and that, and the laughter rose and fell, I could not help noticing that Henrietta and Kelvin were not present. Where had they gone? What were they doing? Was he at that moment asking her to marry him, and would she return elated and affianced?

Phillip, it seemed, had already fallen into the delicate trap Mrs. Abigail had laid out for him, and it was one of the Miss Gimps whose turned-up nose had beckoned him to her side. Poor simple-hearted Phillip who looked, so I thought, a little bewildered as he paid court to his love whilst his brothers winked and nudged and teased him. Roger was away most of the time studying in London to become a medical practitioner. Doctors and solicitors were considered of the middle classes and consequently looked down upon by those who were in other services. It was as a rule the youngest son of a considerable family such as the Abigails who was forced to enter the church, but it was very evident that Silvain had no such leanings. He wanted an easy life, and Mrs. Abigail, doting creature that she was, would allow him to indulge in idleness. She wanted him near her, he

171

pleased her with his beauty, and after all she had plenty of sons who could scatter in professions.

Everyone seemed to take it for granted that Henrietta and Kelvin would become affianced, and even if they had not thought so, Henrietta herself would have very plainly told them. It was Kelvin's attitude I could not understand, for he did not seem to be like a man inflamed with ardour. It was she who kept him dangling at her heels, and he would treat her possessiveness with careless inattention.

Every time we returned from the gaiety of Wingmeadow Lodge, I could see that Papa was far from well; his eyes were less blue and his upright body slightly frailer. His whitening hair was scanty now, and the laughter and devil-may-care way of him seemed as if it came from a long way off. I watched him so tenderly, so carefully, afraid that he might once more fall in an attack. I even ventured to mention to Mamma my anxiety as she sat by the window with her embroidery.

"Have you not noticed something about Papa?" I asked her.

She looked at me coldly. "To what manner of thing are you referring?" she said. "Cannot you make yourself a little more explicit, Susan?"

"I am alluding to his health, Mamma. I do not think he is well."

"He would be better if he stayed at home more," replied Mamma. "Wearing the road down between here and Wingmeadow Lodge at his age is hardly conducive to good health. Ask Mrs. Abigail if he is sick, for she sees more of him than I do."

"I wish you did not dislike Mrs. Abigail so much, Mamma."

172

"Can you give me any good reason why I should not do so, Susan?"

"Mrs. Abigail is the kindest, the . . ."

"The kindest and cleverest and wittiest of women. God knows I hear her praises sung in every key. How gracious she is and a proficient hostess. Her lovely manners and her charming ways. Do you think I am not sick and tired, child, of this drawing-room divinity?"

I then asked Henrietta if she did not think that Papa seemed unwell and wasting away, and her only answer was that as far as she could see he was but enfeebled by his dissipation.

"If you burn a candle at both ends," she said, "what else can you expect? If anything happens to Papa, it will be of his own making, for he will not give way to his old age."

Mrs. Trouncer was even more emphatic.

"Wine, woman and song," she grumbled, "will murder many a man. Assassins all three of them. Wine is a monster that chokes a man's blood, and women run through a man's body as keen as a knife; as for singing, not even a fool could chant a cantata unless he was a tosspot and as drunk as a wheelbarrow. You can't have it all ways, Miss Susan. If you live as his Lordship wishes to, you must die as God wills it."

We had not long to wait.

It was one of those winter afternoons when all we could hear was the moaning and screeching of the wind. Papa had said that he was on his way to Wingmeadow Lodge, and he had seemed strangely perturbed and put out. He hovered round the library for a while, fingering the books and first taking out one and then another, whilst the little lamps grinned and the fire

173

chuckled. Then he came and leaned over my chair. He was unquiet and restless and unlike himself.

"Where is Mamma?" he said.

"She is upstairs in her room, Papa, as usual at this hour."

"To be sure, to be sure, she has not changed the pattern of her life has she, Susan? For the last thirty years that I have known her she has always rested at this time. Again and again she has done the same thing at the same hour. I doubt if any occasion in this world, not even death, would turn her from her measured day. Strange, is it not, when I am so unlike her and ring the changes as often as I wake? She is a good woman, Susan, according to her own lights she is an honest woman with a strong, cold purity of heart. I often think, had she not been so strictly virtuous, I might not have become so outrageously unfaithful. It is the disapproval of a man that will send him into another woman's arms, and the effort to reform him which drives him to those beyond redemption. Never try and correct and mend those whom you love, my little 'Go-by-the-Ground', for they will only fare worse for it. I have sown my wild oats and reaped them and gathered them in, and there is little else for me to do than to watch them lie there, sheaves of memories."

"Dearest Papa, I wish you had been happier."

"Had I been God Himself, Susan, I could not have lived more pleasurable a life."

He then told me that after considerable thought he had made up his mind to something.

"I have a part to play, Susan, and I may not be back to tea. Please tell Mamma not to wait one moment for me. I will return as quickly as I can."

Embracing me hastily as if eager to avoid emotion, he was gone.

The vision of him flushed and faltering remained in my mind, and I could not rid myself of the feeling of impending trouble. Why had he set out on such a night, and why had he spoken so strangely of Mamma? What could there possibly be of such importance that he could not wait for better weather?

Then it was tea-time and still no Papa, and still the wind shrieked and howled about the house. Mamma and Henrietta and I sat down to eat our sweet cakes and sip our cups of tea in silence, until at last I could bear it no longer and sped up to my room.

There, by the window, where so many years before I had tried to end my life, in the little attic amongst the tiles, I waited for Papa. The gloom which had settled on my soul matched well with the black storm raging down below. The profound darkness of the night and the lashing rain prevented my seeing very far along the road, and I could hear little but the torment of the storm.

The roaring in the chimneys and the tremble of the house alarmed me. It was as if the wind and the house were battling for supremacy. Would the house stand, or would the storm tear it to pieces with its lusty force?

Then I heard the sound of a horse galloping and, even between the screeching of the gale and the wild tossing of the branches, there was something prophetic in the clatter of those flying hoofs. Who could it be who was under so much press of speed? What visitor was it who had so little time to spare?

I ran shivering down from my attic and hurried through the unwarmed corridors with a feeling of some fearful evil that awaited me. Pale and trembling, I went straight in to Mamma and stood, scarce breathing, by her chair.

Presently there was a thunderous blow upon the outer door, and then another and another. As soon as the door was opened a man's spurred footstep came running from stair to stair. Into our peaceful drawing room where the cups were yet warm, and the crumbs of our sweet cakes scattered on the plates, strode Kelvin Abigail with pools of water seeping from his cloak onto the floor and the moisture hanging in heavy drops upon his hair.

"You must all of you come at once," he said breathlessly. "Something has happened up at the lodge."

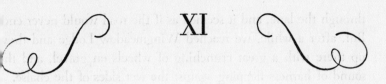

XI

We did not lose a moment. Urgently the chaise was ordered, and without a word to one another we wrapped ourselves round in our cloaks and were gone. But, on the way, Mamma kept repeating over and over again:

"I will not go to this house. I protest against this intrusion into my own. This is some trick that is being played upon me by Papa."

I curled myself miserably in a corner of the chaise endeavouring to keep my teeth from chattering. For, in spite of the warmth of my cloak and the fustiness of the carriage, I could not keep from shivering.

The wind blew the sharp-edged rain against the windows and splattered it from the horses' backs. Pools of water upon the road ahead looked like sheets of ghostly glass. Our ride, as we rocked and swayed and slashed on our way, was a comfortless one, the horses throwing up steam and hot breath so that we could not clearly see where we were.

Henrietta, in order to look upon Kelvin, attempted to lower the window nearest her, but, with one imperious gesture, Mamma ordered her to close it again so that all Henrietta could do was to press her nose against the streaming pane.

The chaise rocked and rumbled through the storm and we could hardly keep our seats, whilst Kelvin was urging his tired horse to keep pace with us. It was farther by carriage than through the lane, and it seemed as if the road would never end. But, after a while, we reached Wingmeadow Lodge and drew up there with a great crunching of wheels on gravel, and the sound of harness flapping against the wet sides of the chaise.

As we entered the house Mrs. Abigail was there to meet us. She was very pale and appeared to have been crying. Both Roger and Silvain stood awkwardly upon the stairs and the servants seemed to be staring from the shadows of the large dim-lit hall, weird now and shrouded in gloom.

Mrs. Abigail took us silently upstairs, Mamma with her nose in the air, refusing to speak. As we brushed by the brothers on the staircase I could not help thinking how Silvain's golden curls seemed almost disrespectful in that sombre and darkened house.

There, in a large-sized room and upon an immense four-poster bed, lay Papa, and a scream rose to my lips as I looked at him, for I knew he was dead.

On the table close by there was some water and a flagon of brandy with which Mrs. Abigail no doubt had been attempting to revive him, and beside the bed, with a stethoscope in his hand, stood Doctor Wiffin. The good doctor was as I remembered him, with his ridiculous puffed up belly, and his little white whiskers that looked so like a brush drooped on his fallen chin. There was not the slightest expression whatsoever in his face, and without any visible sign of emotion he took Mamma's hand in his own and started to pat it professionally.

"My dear Lady Darlington," he said in a hollow voice, for Doctor Wiffin always spoke in this low tone whether his patients were dead or alive, "my dear Lady Darlington, this is a sorry sight indeed and enough to rend the heart."

He spoke automatically, as one only prescribing for physic

or pills, whilst he held onto Mamma's hand as if he had nothing better to do than caress it. "You have my deepest pity," he continued, "as well as Miss Henrietta and Miss Susan. To be struck down in the prime of life, and he was still in his prime, was he not, is a calamity no words of mine can atone for."

"How did it happen?" said Mamma.

Doctor Wiffin cleared his throat and was preparing for a long dissertation when Mrs. Abigail interrupted him. It appeared that Papa had arrived in the house in the highest of spirits, and yet all the time she had had the feeling that his liveliness was unnatural. He had talked incessantly in an easy airy way upon various subjects, all tending strangely enough to bear upon religion.

"I could make nothing from his incoherent wanderings," she said. "First Susan's name was spoken and then some carelessness of action he felt bound in duty to atone for. Over and over again he muttered something about Susan. It was as if two thoughts were struggling for release. One thought about himself and one of Susan. 'I have a part to play,' he kept repeating over and over again, 'but I have forgotten what it is.' I begged him not to worry, but he became more and more frenzied, walking up and down the room with violent gestures. At last I persuaded him to come upstairs and rest, but once he lay down upon the bed he seemed in the greatest pain and I could see that the effort to tell me something or even speak to me was costing him his life. I called to Kelvin to ride in to Springfield and fetch the doctor at once, and then go on to you, Lady Darlington. When I returned into the room I heard Lord Darlington cry out, 'Poor Susan . . . poor little come-by-nothing Susan,' and then with a violent shiver he relaxed. . . . My dearest friend was dead."

Mamma stood as one turned into stone gazing upon the still figure of her husband. Henrietta recoiled from the bed and would not look at Papa, and when I stooped to kiss his forehead I saw her shudder and cover her face with her hands.

"There is nothing more irregular than death," said Doctor Wiffin. "One day you think you are alive and kicking for many a year to come, and then, hey presto, all of a sudden you are no longer a mortal man."

"How was it that you could not save him?" replied Mamma. "Had you no stimulant, no remedy to revive him?"

Doctor Wiffin coughed uncomfortably. "My dear lady," he said, "no one is infallible, no indeed, not even we are the Almighty."

I shall never forget Mamma and the way she held herself, assuming command and showing no sign of trouble as she issued her orders and thanked Mrs. Abigail for all she had done.

"I found him a very cherished friend," replied Mrs. Abigail, "attractive and kindly. No words will tell you how much I am bound to miss him. He was so highly developed and such a debonair brilliant man."

On the way home in the chaise Henrietta and I dared not speak to Mamma, for there was a look on her face which alarmed us. She sat upright in the carriage, tearing her handkerchief with so much rage and temper in the destruction of it that we gazed at her open-mouthed. Then she ended by beating her hands together and silently weeping. It was only after she had entered the house that she said stiffly:

"I am better now. It was the shock of seeing him in somebody else's house . . . her house, of all people. I am going to my room and I do not wish to be disturbed. Please inform Mrs. Trouncer that I will see her in the morning."

Henrietta followed me and sat in her usual way uninvited upon the bed.

"It is difficult to imagine Papa not being here," she said. "His natural term of life could have been so much longer had he not so abused it. And yet, suppose there was no wickedness, no harlots, no libertines, life would not be worth living, at least not for Papa. He had the very essence of existence at his finger tips. He made an art out of iniquity, and a god out of wrongdoing."

"But he was kind, Henrietta. There never was a better-natured man."

"He was not kind to Mamma."

"Nor she to him."

"No, Susan, nor she to him."

"He had a way of making people love him."

"Everyone except Mamma."

"But then she . . ."

"Do you know why she was angry, Susan, and why she wept? It was not with sorrow but with rage. Rage because even at the end Papa had managed to offend her. She was right when she said it was the shock of seeing him dead in somebody else's house . . . her house. All her life she will remember with the bitterest resentment that he did not draw his last breath in the bosom of his own family, but upon the bed of a woman she abhors. That, my dear Susan, you can be sure, is the thorn in her flesh and will disturb and torment her for ever. The fact that Papa died at Wingmeadow Lodge instead of at White Orchard Manor. The servants will talk of it, and you know how much Mamma dislikes the chatter of domestics. High society will chew the cud of it. Some will pity Mamma whilst others will deride her. The Queen will consider it unorthodox and shocking for a husband to die in any other arms than those of his wife, but most of them will blame Mamma rather than offer her condolence; for a woman who cannot keep her man, Susan, is a poor creature indeed."

There was silence for a moment, each of us thinking in our different way of Papa. Henrietta seemed to be staring at me in a strange disquieting manner, and I wanted to tell her to go away and leave me with my tears and with my grief. Her very presence at that moment disturbed and provoked me, and I was in no mood for her philosophy.

Then Henrietta's cool, incisive voice began again.

"Why did he go to Wingmeadow Lodge, I wonder, on such a night as this, and why was he sorrowful for you? I was his favourite child and it is of me he should have spoken. Do you not think it strange that he only uttered your name? What was he trying to say about you, Susan? What was he trying to say?"

I could feel my face reddening and I dared not meet her eyes.

"Papa was not responsible, Henrietta," I replied. "He was confused and ill."

"He was not too ill to go to Wingmeadow Lodge," said Henrietta, "and not too confused to know there was a part for him to play. What kind of a part, what did he mean, was there anything going on between you and Papa, any secrets, I mean, of things that I was not to know? Sometimes of late I have thought that Papa was concealing something, something against me."

"Leave me alone, Henrietta," I cried, "and leave Papa alone. Do we have to quarrel and tear him apart whilst his body is yet warm?"

When she had gone I could not help remembering that even now Henrietta had not shown one spark of human feeling. There was no one in our house who would wholeheartedly mourn Papa, not even Mrs. Trouncer who would be sure to say in that manner of hers born out of intimacy, "What else could you expect from that old reprobate? If he could have mastered the forces of nature as well as he conquered his mistresses, he would be alive and kicking to this day."

No . . . there was to be no kindness over the passing of Papa.

The news of his death spread rapidly from house to house, and the manner of his dying caused many a comment. This was the greatest event that had happened for many a year in Springfield Town. The street corners and public houses were filled with the talkative neighbours and, as Henrietta had predicted, the busybodies prattled and expatiated, their tongues running fast, as to why his Lordship had breathed his last out of his own bed. The townsfolk turned their inquisitive countenances this way and that in search of more scandal than was on the surface of it, chewed up the titbits and licked their uncharitable lips.

"So sudden," said one. "He carried his years so well I would not have deemed it possible."

"Those who live easily die easily," said another.

"It is very fair," said Mrs. Smooth, who owned the post-office store and was embittered because she handled so many letters and never received one of her own, "it is very fair and fitting that what you sow you will reap. He was of too loose a character, too fast a man. A high-spirited animal, that's what he was."

"And why should he not be? Weeping won't get anyone anywhere. I say it's a pity that those who moan and groan don't die and let the world be a happier place. Not that his Lordship did not overdo it, because he did; he was a bad example and there's no denying it."

"Heaven keep him happy," said a little unknown woman on the outskirts of the crowd, "and if he can get up there what he had down here, there's no real cause for grieving."

A funeral in Wingmeadow was a serious undertaking, particularly as death there seemed most uncommon, for Wingmeadow's people clung to their lives. The countryside was filled with ageless ancients who seemed for ever to be defying the grave!

Papa was buried in the little churchyard close to the high surrounding wall, and the Reverend Harper Barklett twittered a few consoling prayers over his grave.

There were so many who attended the ceremony that some were obliged to remain outside the church.

Most of the people walked to the funeral along the mud-splashed roads, whilst others crowded into hired carriages. There was a low-lying mist after the rain and it was clammy and intensely cold. The townfolk plodded up the hill from Springfield wrapped to the ears and with drooping heads. This was an outing they would not be likely to forget, a woebegone dolorous affair which would end in hot cups of tea, so they hoped, and wagging tongues.

The lower pews of the church seemed to be craning their necks to see what the upper pews were doing, and a few straggling seats in the minute gallery gazed dimly upon those beneath them.

There could not have been more snobbery than in this church at Wingmeadow. People who went there, presumably to pray, would kneel with the consciousness of who they were and from whence they came. Their pews were allotted in accordance with how much they had in their banks; it was a rigid dividing line of sheep from goats. Strange, I thought, how that deeply rooted sense of superiority was more evident on Sundays than at any other time of the week.

It seemed that all the parish was there, the well-to-do and those of small earnings. The choral society could be seen scattered throughout the church, and the domestics from White Orchard Manor and Wingmeadow Lodge were clustered in a small subdued group round Mrs. Trouncer.

The entrance of Mrs. Abigail and her sons caused a ripple of interest and, as they settled themselves in their pew, the congregation stared first at Mrs. Abigail and then at Mamma. They watched Mamma for the rise and fall of her bosom if she should weep, and they waited for the flicker of an eyelid or a sigh from the lady of whom they so much disapproved.

Mamma's face was shrouded by a thick black veil and she looked unnaturally tall in her deep mourning. We were like a gathering of crows come to a certain spot because there was something to feed upon. But whatver it was we awaited the Reverend Harper Barklett, with his ponderous supplications, could not give it to us. His funeral recitation seemed bland and without significance. When he came to the words "desolate and oppressed," the choir and the whole congregation looked sideways at Mamma; and when the usual words of comfort and help for the weak-hearted, and for the raising of them that were fallen could be heard, they turned their baleful glances upon Mrs. Abigail and her prolific brood.

It was getting dark when we left the church and stood snivelling and blowing our noses round the grave, and the churchyard looked mournful enough with the newly turned earth shiny and soggy with the rain that had fallen in the night. There was an air of solitary desolation, and the stone monuments and wooden crosses dripped with the damp. I noticed some children peering with natural curiosity over the high wall and whispering together at the strange goings on as the coffin was carefully lowered to its resting place.

The flowers we placed upon the grave were the only bits of colour in that dismal yard, and I could not help thinking what a sad farewell it was for such a jovial man.

The Abigails did not approach us but stood in a separate group with their eyes averted, but the villagers lingered by the roadside as we came out, unable to resist the temptation of seeing her Ladyship and the femal voodoo who had brought such ill luck to Wingmeadow Lane.

"He died in her arms, so they say," was the whisper. "He could not even go to rest under his own roof. Infamous, that's what it is, for a woman to be away from her husband at such a time, and downright wicked that he should have been lured away from his rightful home."

"I knew this would happen," said a very old man who was not unlike the twisted branch of a tree; "last time I saw his Lordship I said to myself, 'he's for it.' You see I am a death diviner, I can tell who the next one will be."

The crowd edged away, eyeing him fearfully.

"You needn't be alarmed," he cackled. "I looked in the mirror," and he went off laughing to himself as if it was the greatest jest in the world.

"What kind of a funeral was it?" asked those who had been unable to see over the church wall.

"Uneventful," replied one who had evidently wished for some violence of emotion.

"But pleasant," said another, "as funerals go."

"I don't like black," grumbled a third. "It gives me the creeps. Depressing, that's what it is."

"Funerals are not meant to be hilarious," replied the first speaker. "There's nothing inspiring about the dead."

The Queen wrote simply and sincerely to Mamma as from one widow to another. She knew how Mamma must be feeling, so she said, and she commiserated with her for her untimely loss. This letter was of the utmost consolation to Mamma and she went about the house with a rapt expression on her face, almost of awe, as if she had been blessed by some holy touch.

The half of our house that had once been Papa's was closed, and the blinds pulled down so that the whole face of the house looked like a man perpetually winking. I could not even then believe that our happy, good-for-nothing Papa was really and truly dead, that that warm and tender heart had ceased to beat. All I could think of was his noble but final gesture in trying to make amends for his neglect of me. I was glad I had not been obliged to witness the approach of death, and yet I deeply regretted I had not been with him at the last. And now the grave had closed his laughter and the shadow of Papa lay for ever across the churchyard of our home.

Mrs. Trouncer did not often comment upon the death of Papa but, whenever she did, she would say:

"I won't express anything good nor bad against either of them now that he's gone and she is in trouble. I daresay it was a lot her fault that he went flitting and flirting all over the town. But then she had a lot to put up with, poor dear, and no mistake, and so, poor devil, had he."

When we wound up Papa's affairs we found that we were, as he had predicted we should be, most prodigiously wealthy. There were many bills and charges to be paid, for our dear Papa had been as careless and vague in these matters as he had indeed in all others.

Mamma was now a solitary woman, still handsome, but of a hard sadness which could not be approached. She wore the deepest black and went into retirement, plying her needle when indoors, and walking only in the garden, withdrawn from all who knew her. Her voice when she spoke to us was purposely suppressed, her actions quietly controlled. To look at her one might have believed that she both honoured and revered Papa's memory and that her heart was genuinely broken. It was a magnificent pretence, a vain and glorious conceit to stare the gossips out of countenance.

Of course for a while we could no longer attend the choir practice and Henrietta became restless and tormented. She began to write letters to Kelvin once more, and once again I went upon her errands.

"We are so different, you and I, Susan," she said in that half-pitying, superior way of hers. "You think and dream too much, so that your blood runs cold. You cannot keep warm with books and shadows. It is a man you need, my dear. You have lived too long in other people's minds, including mine, to have one of your own. But there will come a day when you will suddenly realize with bitter discontent your life is over."

I was glad she could not read my heart with its aching passionate desire. How could she with her beauty know the agony of love unreturned, the yearning for just one look, one gesture of affection.

Once in a while we went secretly to Wingmeadow Lodge, creeping from the house to the lane whilst Mrs. Trouncer occupied Mamma, but these varied visits brought with them more unhappiness for me, more fevered heartaches and pained imagination. For sometimes only Kelvin would be there, his brothers having gone to town and Mrs. Abigail set out upon some errand, and Henrietta and he would retire to the little boudoir that led out of the drawing room and close the door between them and me.

There I was left with nothing more to do but listen to the murmur of their voices in the room beyond. Sometimes they laughed, and I would press my ear against the wall for all the world like Mrs. Trouncer, listening and prying. I was fiercely and insanely jealous of every moment they were there together. What were they doing? What were they saying? I walked up and down, up and down the drawing room wringing my hands and muttering foolish incoherent words that held no meaning. I felt I would indeed go mad, and my whole body ached with incredible suspicion. I pictured them clinging together, she with her dark treacherous eyes raised lovingly to his and her red hair pressed against his face. "Dearest . . . darling . . . dearly beloved." Was that what he was saying? Sometimes I was obliged to stifle the scream that would rise to my lips. "Let them come out," I moaned, "dear God, let them come out."

But, by the time Kelvin and Henrietta appeared, I was quiet again and there was not a single trace of the storm that had raged over me.

"I am sorry," Kelvin would say with his most charming smile. "We should not have kept you waiting, Susan."

But Henrietta would laugh and interrupt him and say:

"Oh, Susan does not mind. She will do anything, this simple willing sister of mine. She does not live in our world, Kelvin, but in regions of her own. It is time you should know that Susan is a saint."

The winter was gradually passing and the countryside drawing from its mud-soaked garments and its cloth of snow into a pale covering of green. Buds were lighting up the trees, and now and again there was a fine enough day when the weather was warm for the people to stand by their doors and gossip.

The rich and noble rolled back to London in their carriages because it was early March and the social season which had been slowly opening since January was pulling back its shutters and polishing its doors.

There was a steady flow of grandeur and flunkies and band-boxes of furbelows and hats. Henrietta and I watched from our house of mourning, thinking how much Papa would have liked to have been there. Mamma condescended that we should go on a visit to London to see Lady Belinda Bishop, but with the strictest instructions to observe and conform to our period of lament. So we sat in the park on little chairs waiting for friends and acquaintances who might happen to be passing, and we behaved with such customary correctness that Henrietta declared she would rather be down at White Orchard Manor where at least we could be free.

"There is only one thing to do," she said firmly. "I must marry at once before this retirement of Mamma's has driven me insane."

My heart stopped beating.

"Marry!" I repeated dully. "Oh, Henrietta, you cannot . . . you dare not."

"And why, may I ask, should I be so poor spirited? Do you think I am afraid of Mamma?"

"She . . . she will not permit you to marry an Abigail. She will forbid it, Henrietta."

My lovely sister laughed me to scorn; she tossed her red curls and said she would like to see anyone tell her what to do.

"But suppose Kelvin does not wish to marry, what then?"

"Are you so blind, Susan, that you cannot see how much he desires me?"

"Nevertheless, Henrietta, he does not seem to me to be a man overanxious to settle down."

Henrietta looked at me closely.

"And what exactly do you mean by that?" she asked. "Do you think he is not sufficiently in love?"

"I know nothing of his innermost feelings," I replied desperately, "except what you tell me, Henrietta."

"And have I ever told you that he does not love me."

"No . . . no."

"But you do not believe me, is that it?"

"Oh yes, I believe you, Henrietta. I have no reason to doubt. I only thought that Kelvin did not seem to be a man half crazed with longing to get wed."

Henrietta was angry. I had not seen her so enraged for many a moon. She stamped her foot and cried feverishly that Kelvin would do as she wished and that he would obey her in every thought and action. I could not help wondering if she really and truly believed that a man like Kelvin Abigail, with his broad forehead and forceful chin, would be tied to a woman's apron strings, and had she indeed so convinced herself that she had him bound to her hand and foot?

As I went from the door I fell straight into Mrs. Trouncer who was bent half in two with her ear pressed close to the keyhole.

"So you are at it again, Mrs. Trouncer," I cried, laughing inwardly at the dismay in her face. "And what is it this time?"

"Nothing," replied Mrs. Trouncer, "nothing that is in particular."

"But what did you hope to hear? What did you expect to see?"

"Something, Miss Susan."

"But what?"

"Just something. You can go on peeping and prying and listening year after year, and then, all of a sudden you hear something, and you see something of stupendous importance."

How well I was to remember those words, and how little I knew then there would come a time when I would thank God on my knees for Mrs. Trouncer's overcurious thirst for information.

XII

To SEE HOW strangely things come about and the wheels of fortune turn in devious ways.

It was not long after this conversation upon Henrietta's marriage, on an evening when we were sitting quietly after dinner, my sister writing no doubt to her lover, and I with my nose in a book, that Mamma raised her head from her embroidery and said:

"You remember Mr. Bemrose, do you not?"

The mention of this man's name sent the colour flooding to my face, and all at once it seemed I was a minnow of a girl again, following this sleek young whelp with adoring eyes. I could hear his soft voice saying, "I would like to go into society. My ambition is to be a gentleman very much at large. I could be, you know. I have got it in me. I could be almost anything I wanted if I had the money his Lordship has. Oh yes, I have got it in me all right, more than most I should say. It is this having no money that is the devil's curse."

I could hear myself asking ingenuous artless questions such as, "Why do cows have milk?" "Can you lay an egg, Mr. Bemrose, and where do babies come from?" The old fear of the woods swept over me. I could smell the damp grass and feel the tall ferns holding me back. I could feel my heart panting and pounding as Mr. Bemrose's kisses scorched my face.

Then Henrietta's voice brought me back into the drawing room.

"I do not think we have forgotten Mr. Bemrose, have we, Susan?" she said.

I mumbled an answer and appeared to continue my reading, but I was listening with my whole being trembling with fear for what Mamma was about to tell us.

"I have been making enquiries," she said, "and it seems he has been out of work for some time and eked out a miserable pittance wherever he could. I am told he is badly in need. There is room for a man like him to be bailiff again, now that we are alone, and I am sure you will both be delighted to hear that I am taking him back into my service."

We neither of us answered, only Henrietta looked across at me and I could see in her large dark eyes that she was laughing at me.

Thus it was that Mr. Bemrose came back to White Orchard Manor.

In addition to his box and innumerable small parcels he brought with him a runt whose name was Incubus.

Incubus was a foundling who had been picked up in a rabbit hole at the foot of a tree close by the Squirrel Inn. The word, "Incubus," had been written on the broken paper in which he was wrapped.

Mr. Cattlewig, the proprietor of that particular tavern, came upon him one morning when he was on his way to the village, and bending over this amazing discovery he said to himself:

"Dear me . . . tut tut, what a horrible apparition! I had better go and show it to Mrs. Cattlewig."

Yet, several times he walked away from it with the intention of leaving it where it was, until his conscience smote him with so fierce an intensity he was obliged to return to the tree, pick up the parcel and go with it to his wife.

Mrs. Cattlewig was a cheerful homely woman who took such extraordinary events as just part of the day's work. "The rough with the smooth," she would always say. "It balances in the end."

Nothing ever surprised her, although she had round goggle eyes under raised eyebrows and a mouth that seemed always to be saying "O," even when it was in repose.

She was by no means put out by this extra strain upon her life, and had crooned and gurgled over this unprofitable offering as if a lump of gold had been deposited at her door; and in spite of the fact that "Incubus" was hardly the name to bestow upon any child, she insisted that he should be so named without even so much as a christening.

"It was a queer enough thing to pick up a parcel in the root of a tree," said Mrs. Cattlewig, "but to find a babe in it is even more than I could expect. But let me tell you one thing, not for one moment have we regretted it."

God had laid the merriest trap for Mr. Cattlewig, a trap with a smile that went straight to the landlady's heart and which even Mr. Cattlewig himself could not resist. If Mr. Cattlewig had not gone by that tree on that particular morning, Incubus would never have been discovered. "And if we had not found Incubus," said Mrs. Cattlewig, emphatically, "we would have lost half of what now makes our lives worth living. Indeed, when I come to think of it, I say to myself that if ever God had His hands on a miracle it was this one."

Incubus was a misshapen gnome of a runt with a face as flat as a bulldog's and arms so long that they reached well below his knees. Yet he was by no means repulsive, having as broad a grin as anyone could wish for, and something extremely kindly at the back of his eyes. He knew how to play upon a little guitar which he carried swung about his neck, and the most human thing about him was this musical instrument, upon which he strummed at any odd moment of the day.

Mr. Bemrose explained that he had brought the runt with him on the chance that he might find some work. "He is as handy a bastard as ever I've seen," he told Mamma, "and could be an asset to White Orchard Manor."

Mamma agreed that perhaps there was some use he could be put to, and Incubus settled down on the farm and helped with the milking and the hay-making and pig-feeding and a hundred small jobs that his weight and size could manage.

Incubus liked hard work. He said that it made him feel wanted.

"Being left at the root of a tree is a solitary business when you come to think of it," he solemnly assured me, and he did think of it quite a lot. I could not help feeling sorry for the runt whom his parents had abandoned in such a callous manner.

"I am nobody," he said, "and yet who can tell, my parents might have been somebody."

Incubus had no prospects beyond his work, and he knew that as long as his short legs supported him and his small active body obeyed what was demanded of him, he had nothing to fear for the future. And so, with Incubus whistling and playing his guitar we found there was a cheerfulness about the estate, and even Mrs. Trouncer was forced to admit that the new farm hand was indeed an asset.

Mr. Bemrose was greatly changed by the years and by the way

he had been living. This penurious existence, this hand-to-mouth, down-in-the-world way of passing the time had aged him, and he bore the unwholesome traces of malnutrition and debauchery most visibly upon his countenance. Circumstance had set a mark upon him and sinning shaded his face. He had grown into a tall untidy shape of a man, with hair that was thinning on the top, and pallid cheeks. But the uncertain moustache had settled itself quite firmly upon his upper lip and his whiskers curled about his ears; he was also in a strange way extremely mindful of his personal appearance.

Mr. Bemrose lived, as it were, by a side wind with no sincerity of purpose, seeming to prefer a crooked path and to ·derive amusement by astute and intriguing conduct. He had never been obliged to beg his bread, even when things had been at their worst, for there were always odd jobs to be had about the countryside. He had never borrowed or got into debt, but had just paid as he went with never an extra coin in his pocket. He had no possessions, so Mrs. Trouncer informed us, and no definite place of abode; he had slept where he worked and had then moved on so that no one could trace his whereabouts.

"I am a man who cannot do without civilized comforts," he pleaded to Mamma, "and having to shake down in odd rooms and outhouses has soured my disposition. When his Lordship died I thought so much of you and how you might need someone like me to help you with the estate."

What power of persuasion he used upon Mamma we never rightly knew, for she had never been overfond of him in the first place. Nevertheless, the next thing we heard was that he was back in his rooms and at his old job again and that Mamma seemed more than delighted to have him there.

197

"He is an unsavoury morsel to swallow," said Mrs. Trouncer, "and leaves as nasty a taste in the mouth as you could find. He is a harmful, offensive and evil-natured being, not very highly rated either here or in Springfield Town."

"He has better manners than he used to have," replied Henrietta, "and he is a finer figure of a man."

"He is an ill-disciplined and ill-conditioned fellow," grumbled Mrs. Trouncer, "for he doesn't believe in cribbed control, not he, or that thoughts should be curbed. 'A man's tongue is for making words with,' he declares. 'It is the means of expression, the voice of the mind.' That's all very fine and well, I say, when a man's mind is wholesome and clean, and not backsliding and defective as his is. As for that runt with his ungodly guitar and his way of getting round women, my advice to you young ladies is to keep out of their way, for no good can come from being with the likes of them."

It was well over a week after Mr. Bemrose and his strange companion arrived that I was able to encounter him.

He worked in a room close to the library and he always kept the door ajar so that he could not fail to see me pass. When he noticed me giving him a wide berth he laughed ironically, and more ironically still he kissed his hand to me. He would sit at his table, feigning to write in a large important book, but every time I went by the door he would throw a sidelong glance at me or twist round in his chair so that he could more fully face me.

On this particular morning he called out to me to come into his room.

"I have time on my hands, Miss Susan," he said pleasantly, "and I would deem it an honour if you would spare me a little of yours. There would be no harm in your attempting to amuse

198

me now and again, would there? It would help me considerably to be able to get away from myself."

"I am not a very sociable person, Mr. Bemrose."

"Of that I am fully aware," he said smiling, "but I thought in my case you might perhaps make an exception."

"For any particular reason, Mr. Bemrose?"

"For old time's sake, Miss Susan, for surely I deserve more notice than you usually bestow upon my sex."

I could feel his eyes sweeping over me; the eyes I remembered so well that seemed to take the clothes from me and leave me naked, and tear away my flesh and expose my frightened heart. Mr. Bemrose was never in a hurry; everything he did was slowly and perfectly timed as if he were licking his lips and gloating over it. He had developed a technique of pausing between words so that their full meaning could be more thoroughly digested. It was no use concealing things from Mr. Bemrose, for he had eyes at the back of his head. It was useless to disguise one's thoughts from him, for he could read them as quickly as they came into one's mind.

I steadied my voice and asked him politely how he liked being back as our bailiff, and with equally cool courtesy he replied that he was indeed happy to be once more entrusted with the family affairs and to make a few shillings to get himself going again.

"If you will be seated, Miss Susan," he said, "I will endeavour to entertain you with a narration of my past, and how excellent and gracious her Ladyship has been to have given me this chance. To execute her wishes," he continued with fawning obsequiousness, "will ever be my constant wish, for it is her that I have to thank, not you nor Miss Henrietta, for having given me back my self-esteem."

I was perched upon the extreme edge of a chair whilst he was leaning on his hand and biting the tip end of his pen with his eyes intent upon me.

"Time has flown, Miss Susan, since I saw you last, and a deal of sand has been shifted. The Lord has kept my memory green. I trust it is the same with you?"

"I have not forgotten, Mr. Bemrose, if that is what you mean."

"I am delighted to hear it, Miss Susan, for I would not like to think I had left such a poor impression. Time has taken its toll of me, has it not?"

"No more than it has of most of us."

"Human nature is weak. Even you should acknowledge that."

"For you to talk of humanity, Mr. Bemrose, seems hardly necessary since you have not, and never will, have the slightest idea or conception of it."

"And why should I have?" he replied. "May I ask you that, Miss Susan? Why should I have, when nothing has ever happened to me to make me human. All I have had in life is the pie crust. The real meat of it I have not chewed, and there has been no gravy in it to wet my palate. A man cannot live on crumbs, Miss Susan. He needs blood and bone to sharpen his wits. You cannot treat a savage as a suckling."

"There are many others besides you who have been less fortunate."

"That may or may not be, yet you have no idea into what extremity I sank. I had no recommendation from her Ladyship, no written word from either of them, telling of past services. Thrown out like a dog I did not know where to go or which way I should turn. Have you any idea which way I went, Miss Susan, or where I have been since last I saw you?"

200

"Indeed, Mr. Bemrose, I have not even given it a thought."

He scowled at me and there was a sneer on his mouth beneath the small moustache.

"I have been to the devil," he continued calmly. "It was an easy enough journey once I had set my mind to it. There were, no doubt, innumerable places where I could have gone, but, of my own free will I chose to go to the devil."

"And how did it profit you, Mr. Bemrose? Were you happy?"

"I was and am the most miserable man upon earth," he replied mournfully, seeking the pity I could not feel for him. "I know it has been mostly my own fault that my energies were misdirected, but I was forced into this mode of living by circumstances beyond my control. Do you not think it unfortunate that a man of my character should be brought so low by a family of quality such as yours?"

"Do you blame us for your misfortune?"

"Who else, who else, Miss Susan? I have now, in spite of my position, allowed myself to become the possessor of an opinion, and my opinion is that you yourself are mostly responsible for my downfall."

"In what way, Mr. Bemrose?"

"I would like to have rioted in riches as you know. I thought I was sitting safely in an excellent position. You took that seat right from under me, Miss Susan, and left me lying on my backsides. A little more play upon her Ladyship and I might have inherited this estate, who knows? She liked me enough, even his Lordship admired me, and I had almost deceived him into believing I was the son that they had never borne. Her Ladyship had no wit to combat my duplicity, and Lord Darlington was too intent upon himself to see much farther than his own aroma."

"How dare you speak of Papa and Mamma like that, how dare you?"

"My dear Miss Susan, I am a man of mettle and you have brought this on yourself. Little girls who cannot hold their tongues have to be punished. Little girls who kiss and tell and blab out of school must pay the penalty. Each of us must pay what we owe, and you have a debt to me of quite long standing, a debt, dear Miss Susan, I expect you to pay with interest."

I rose quickly to my feet and went towards the door, but he shouted after me:

"Loneliness brings trouble, Miss Susan, and when a man is without company his mind begins to work and his thoughts run riot. It is then, when he realizes no one is going to help him, that he determines to help himself. Remember that. If he is not given, then he will take."

I could hear him laughing as I slammed the door in his face.

There was nothing decent about Mr. Bemrose, I could see that now. There was not one drop of blood in him that was not poison. He had reached the excess of sin and dreamed only of the fulfilment of revenge.

"There is a stench of sewer gas about him," said Mrs. Trouncer.

"I am not afraid of him," replied Henrietta, "which is more than can be said of my dear sister. You are still afraid of him, are you not, Susan?"

"That was long enough ago to be forgotten," cried Mrs. Trouncer before I had time to speak, "so there's no need reminding Miss Susan of things that are over and done with. She is not afraid of anything now—not even of you, my dear—so that is that."

"But is it, Mrs. Trouncer, is it? It would be good news indeed if it were true."

"And what reason have you to doubt my word, Miss Henrietta? I am sure your sister can take care of herself the same as you can."

"Is it so, Mrs. Trouncer? Is it, Susan?" said Henrietta, a strange smile playing upon her face. "You must forgive me for my lack of observation. If I had been asked, I would have said that she was still the pigeon-hearted sister I remember so well."

"Nobody has asked you, Miss Henrietta," snapped Mrs. Trouncer, and there the conversation ended.

There were days when Mr. Bemrose had a frank and easy way with him, when he would talk to Mamma about the garden and the flowers without so much as a glance in our direction, and Mamma seemed to have taken a liking to him and was constantly with him on his walks round the estate. Mr. Bemrose was a contriving diplomat who played an ingenious game; anything reprehensible he could twist into a lamblike penitence, and yet I could scarcely believe that this cold and haughty Mamma of ours with her greying hair was actually humble and submissive before this smooth-tongued rascal for ever at her heels.

"Her Ladyship's sharp-sightedness is dimmed," said Mrs. Trouncer. "She has only half the sagacity she used to have."

But it was not entirely that. It was the care with which Mr. Bemrose treated her, such deference, such respect. He bowed and kissed her hand and paid her compliments. A well-planned scheme enhanced, no doubt, by the fine reward he hoped for and expected.

Sometimes I would come upon him skulking in the lane or leaning across a gate, scowling heavily at all he saw before him.

"My life has rolled on and on, Miss Susan," he would say. "Just as the rivers never change their course, I have not been able to make head against the flow of it. Nevertheless, I have, I think, made an impression, and time will remember me as a traveller of some consequence."

He was a man with a grievance against the world, a sore-headed, sick-minded creature with his back to the wall.

It was his confidence which held Mamma, for even she realized that her assurance had considerably waned and he inspired and emboldened her every purpose.

"Mamma's senses must have forsaken her more than we imagined," grumbled Henrietta after she had been watching them together, "or she would not be so bent upon this clod. She nibbles at every bait he sets for her, and it would seem as if the house, the garden and the whole estate was his by the way he struts about and gives orders."

"Mamma is enchanted by his flummery," I replied bitterly, "and her eyes are blinded by his seeming softness to her. Mr. Bemrose is a habitual liar and has the oily tongue of a flatterer who knows just the way to Mamma's heart. Moreover, she is ageing, Henrietta, and relies upon his hardihood; if only Papa had lived this never would have happened."

"You fear him," replied Henrietta, "and that, my dear sister, is all there is to it as far as you are concerned."

Sometimes in the night I would start from my sleep with the feeling that Mr. Bemrose was somewhere in the room. It seemed that it must be so because of the rancid smell of perfume which followed him wherever he went.

As the days passed, everyone could see my face grow paler, and both Mamma and Mrs. Trouncer remarked upon it, although they could not determine the cause. But Henrietta knew. She knew and was amused at my misgivings, and my restless disquietude filled her with secret mirth.

XIII

I<small>T WAS</small> <small>NOW</small> full summer and the Abigails were away a great deal concerning themselves with social activities and their professions. Whilst they were gone there was no reason for me to frequent Wingmeadow Lane in the hopes of a chance meeting with Kelvin, and Henrietta sulked and moped about the garden, finding this bereavement for Papa a vastly tedious business now that the sadness of his death had softened.

It was Mrs. Trouncer who brought us bits of tittle-tattle now and again of how Mrs. Abigail had announced that the choir was by no means the same without us, and how Master Kelvin was making quite a name for himself as a public speaker.

"He has a wild, wide notion of how the world should be controlled," said Mrs. Trouncer. "He thinks that each of the peoples should rule their own nations and not let a party of individuals make laws for them. He is what you might call a free thinker, with a mind of his own and views beyond the age we live in. 'The survival of the fittest,' says he. 'That would be my world, with the weak ones thrown out as waste, and the witless ones destroyed.' A purge of uselessness—that's what he's after, that's what he wants; with room enough left for those who are worth while."

"But, Mrs. Trouncer, we cannot all be strong, we cannot all be useful. There must be futility somewhere."

"Not in his world, Miss Susan, and what is more, do you

know what his impudence says? He says that even God Himself would sit back on His heels and gaze with wonder at his inspired way of living. He says that what is wrong is that God did not reckon with progress and men thinking of things. Blasphemy, that's what I call it, and nothing more nor less."

"Mr. Abigail does not tolerate blockheads, that is all," said Henrietta. "Can you blame him when he is made the way he is?"

"He is only a man pitting himself against the Almighty," replied Mrs. Trouncer, "and if that isn't blasphemy I don't know what is."

"He is a man," said Henrietta, "and that is enough for me."

"Being a man, Miss Henrietta, doesn't amount to much, not to me, it doesn't."

"You have been soured," replied Henrietta, and there the matter ended.

We heard that Kelvin was sometimes gay and disorderly in the town and that his love of gambling might one day lead him into trouble. He was the most colourful figure in Springfield, so they said, and his doings and misdoings were the talk of the town.

Mr. Bemrose seemed to know about Henrietta and Kelvin and what he did not know he suspected. He would watch her walk proudly through the garden or from the iron gates with ill-concealed admiration in his eyes. He scarcely ever addressed more than one word to her, and would always stand with his hat respectfully held whenever she went by. Henrietta was perfectly aware of this and of the wild, warm looks he gave her; but, with a flourish of her skirts and a twist of a smile she would pass him by as if he was no better and no bigger than the runt.

It was my timid approach, my evident fear of him, that made him insolent. I could see that he both pitied and despised me, and I could sense as I went near him that I struck some chord of cruelty in his wicked heart which made him want to hurt me.

"You have a fascination for me, Miss Susan," he would say, with what was meant to be an enticing leer, "that I cannot put into words. Your timidity urges me to frighten you more, your aloofness draws me to you. Is it because you are so unapproachable that I long to crush you in my arms?"

On a certain afternoon I made up my mind to speak to Mamma about Mr. Bemrose and beg her to dismiss him; and so I ventured into her strictest hour of seclusion and in a storm of nervousness I implored her to reconsider her employment of this man.

"You do not know how evil and corrupt he is, Mamma," I told her, "and what is said of him in Springfield Town. Everyone knows how bad he is and the reputation that pursues him. Everyone knows but you. He flatters and cajoles you, Mamma, and if he stays on here I have a premonition of something dreadful happening to us. This is not mere fancy. I can feel it, I can feel it round us everywhere."

Mamma gazed at me coldly as if she was endeavouring to pierce my trepidation and find the true reason of it.

"Nonsense, child," she replied. "This supposition is unworthy of you, Susan, and I am very much surprised. The way Mr. Bemrose has striven and suffered to overcome his misfortune is most creditable; he is, moreover, most assiduous in his work, and to me his manners are without doubt faultless. What have you against him, Susan? Never before have I been treated with such deference and respect. Gracious powers, am I to dismiss a man on account of your whims and premonitions, or whatever you may call them? Would that not be a little hard on Mr. Bemrose and exceedingly unfair to me? Do not heed evil rumours, my dear child, but wait for the proof of wrongdoing. Then, and then only, will it be time enough to act."

It was not long after this that a small travelling fair settled upon Wingmeadow Common, with gypsy vans and booths and entertainment of all kinds. It had a noisy, wheezy gaiety to it which we could hear as far as White Orchard Manor, and in the evenings we could see it by the light of its flares.

Mrs. Trouncer heard rumours of the young gentlemen from Wingmeadow Lodge having the devil of a time frequenting the fair as soon as they returned from their work, and Mr. Bemrose and the runt came with tales of how wild the Abigails were, especially Kelvin and Silvain. But Henrietta laughed when she heard these things and tossed her red hair and declared that she liked them to be this way and that there would be time enough to tame Kelvin when he was hers to command.

"Let him sow his wild oats," she cried, "for he will have none of them with me. Let him rid himself of his spleen, by all means, so that I do not find myself wedded to a mad brain."

"Why not go to Wingmeadow Fair," suggested Mrs. Trouncer, "and find out for yourself? Why not see with your own eyes what we have heard?"

"You mean go to Wingmeadow Fair ourselves?"

"Why not? Is there any law against it? It is an open fair for everyone and all. How would you like to come with me one early evening, you and Miss Susan of course? A thing like this will not hurt his Lordship's memory, nor damage his dead soul."

And so we went to Wingmeadow Fair, leaving Mamma embroidering in her window, completely ignorant of the whereabouts of her daughters. I do not say that Mrs. Trouncer was altogether right in permitting us to do this thing, but on the other hand there was no genuine harm in it. We had mourned Papa and the loss of him seemed now to be very far away. It was only when we passed his rooms or found some small possession he had treasured that the sorrow of his not being with us forced its way into our hearts.

What a wondrous sight the fair was, what an uproar of delight.

It seemed at first as if all the noisiest people in the world were there, each determined to make himself heard. Those who had been working together all day now greeted one another as heartily as if they had not met for years; and all along the way we had observed the quietest dwellings lit up with the excited faces of those too young or too old to be out so late.

We saw many people we knew there. The Misses Tinnerlies, for instance, standing in rapture before a man in tights and preposterous muscles who was lifting incredible weights. "Who would like to take me on for a crown?" he kept shouting, stretching out his arms so that the muscles stood out like writhing cobras from his shoulders downwards. I could see by the look in the Misses Tinnerlies' eyes that they would have been more than willing to take him on for nothing.

Phillip was there with his snub-nosed sweetheart on his arm, and Silvain of course was playing at every booth and diving his way into every tent he could find. Now and again there was a boisterous laugh from the crowd as a clown turned a somersault or tied himself up in a knot.

There was no air, and the atmosphere was hot and heavy with the giddy crowd for ever pushing and jostling to see what was going on. Nobody wanted to miss anything. They were like little waves on a restless sea, lapping first this way and then that. Along the lane there were carts of all sizes either leaving the fair or else bringing more company to it; such hilarity had seldom been seen in Wingmeadow, and the village folk were taking advantage of it.

"Welcome to the fair," bellowed a portly individual who had nothing whatever to do with the place but was somewhat the worse for drink.

"And who might you be, may I ask?" replied Mrs. Trouncer, adjusting her bonnet and eyeing him severely.

"I am the Lord of Hosts," said the red-faced gentleman, solemnly drawing himself up to his full height and thereby nearly falling prone upon his back, "sent by Divine Providence to be extremely at your service." He swept off his hat with a bow that almost threw him at Mrs. Trouncer's feet, and continued:

"What do you wish of me, ladies? Pray allow me to be your escort for I am completely yours to command."

"What you can do for us," replied Mrs. Trouncer, prodding him with the end of her umbrella, "is to get out of our way. Moreover, my good fellow, if in your present state of reprehensible intoxication you can understand what I am saying, my advice to you, Sir, is now to go home and put your head under the pump."

His air of profound astonishment, his wide open mouth and protruding eyes made him look as if he was about to weep, and long after we had left him we looked back and could see his round red face like a crimson moon on the edge of the common.

"I won't stand no nonsense," said Mrs. Trouncer firmly. "I never have, not even with Mr. Trouncer, and I don't intend starting it now. I am no more afraid of a looby like that than I am of a newly born babe."

A thick cloud of tobacco smoke hung over the trees, and the wavering flares made of it a golden network of leaves. In a corner of the green there was a small stage with a crowd round it as thick as a hive of bees. In the midst of the crowd stood Kelvin Abigail and, as we approached, we saw him lift the runt onto the platform and heard him shout, "Here is a player of great renown. Get out your guitar, my friend Incubus, and give us a song."

Kelvin was mellow. He was merrily, unconcernedly mellow, with his face flushed and his dark eyes shining like stars; and as I looked at him I kept saying over and over again to myself, "Why do I love this man?" And the answer was always the same, "Because he reminds me of Papa."

It was evident that the runt was not quite himself and his grotesque body swayed this way and that as he grabbed at his guitar. With a grin all over his face he started to play, and one or two people went out in the open to dance. Before we had time to look round, Mrs. Trouncer was swept from our side and by no other person than the weight carrier with the rippling muscles.

Kelvin was calling to all the roisterers he knew to go back to the inn where he would stand them a tankard, when, quite suddenly, he saw us and his jaw fell like that of a little bo

212

caught unawares out of school. I shall never forget the look on his face as he came towards us, and it was to me that he turned, not Henrietta.

"Miss Susan!" he cried. "I did not expect to see you out here. What in Heaven's name are you doing and why are you alone?"

"It is my fault," gasped Mrs. Trouncer who had by some miracle escaped from the strong man. "I brought the young ladies for a breather, seeing as they's been choked in retirement for so long. I thought it would do them a power of good to be mixed up in a little relaxation away from her Ladyship's rigid control. How did I know that the fair was to be like a tavern on a drinking bout with all these befuddled tosspots not heeding which way they are going."

"But Miss Susan, of all people?"

"And what is wrong with my sister being here?" cried Henrietta furiously. "If it is good enough for me it is good enough for her, is it not? Or perhaps you had not even noticed, Mr. Abigail, that I am here as well?"

Kelvin turned and they looked at one another. Henrietta's cheeks were flaming and her eyes flashed with such fire that I trembled for what might take place. Then she laughed. It was not a very pleasant laugh, being sardonic and contemptuous, but it lifted the tension, and she said, "There, there, I will forgive you this time," and she flicked his face lightly with the tip of her gloves.

For a moment Kelvin looked the same as when she had stepped in front of the coach, and he put out his hands as if he would take hold of her and shake her, but before he had time to do anything she turned on her heel, and with Mrs.

Trouncer and me following meekly behind her she stormed through the lane.

"Well," said Mrs. Trouncer, after we had entered the house and Henrietta had flounced into her room, "was there ever such a to-do about nothing. Miss Henrietta is as jaundiced and horn mad as a Barbary pigeon, and if you take my advice, Miss Susan, you'll keep out of her way until the bile's gone out of her liver."

Henrietta did not speak to me for two days after that, and of course Mr. Bemrose had something to say about it as I passed his room.

"It is a pity about Mr. Abigail being the worse for liquor," he sneered.

"Indeed," I replied coldly, "and what makes you think that he was?"

"I have eyes, Miss Susan, and I saw what I saw, for I was also there you know, and had you been more observant you would have noticed me under the platform."

"I had better things to do, Mr. Bemrose."

"How true," replied Mr. Bemrose, stroking his moustache, "but the affair has given Miss Henrietta some food for thought. He had better be careful, that young man, for she is by no means a lady to be trifled with."

"Mr. Abigail can take care of himself," I said sharply, and Mr. Bemrose looked up at me and laughed and replied:

"I wonder."

It was the following evening that Henrietta came into my room with a letter in her hand. The cloud had gone from her face and she was all blandishment and smiles.

"You know the little hut," she said, "the one we used to call *our hut?* I have sent a message to Kelvin to meet you there, as it will be safer than in the lane. You will go, dear Susan, will you not? It is of the utmost importance to me."

"But I . . ."

"I swear here and now this will be the very last time I shall ask this favour of you, for I may as well tell you I have asked Kelvin to marry me before the summer is out."

"You have asked him to marry you?"

"I must, I have to. I do not like his attitude, Susan, and he is becoming out of hand. You saw how he was the other evening, pretending he did not see me, so ill-mannered and so wild. I will not tolerate such conduct, not from him or any other man. When we are married it will be different. He will be mine, and once he is mine, my dear sister, I will teach him a lesson he is not likely to forget."

My whole being seemed to stand still so that I could not think, and when Henrietta thrust the letter into my hands I could not feel it.

"I am sick and tired of this sorrowful house," continued Henrietta. "It has never been the same without Papa. Whatever his faults may have been he knew how to warm a house and fill it, as if with friends. Unless Kelvin marries me soon I now I will go mad. There is nothing I would not do to get away."

She looked at my stricken face and laughed and asked me what, in Heaven's name, was the matter. "Please wake up, dear Susan," she said. "You look crack-brained and shattered and there is much for you to do. The night is not young and Kelvin, as you know, does not like waiting."

"You want me to go to the hut tonight. Is that it?"

"Yes, Susan, that is it."

"It is very dark," I stammered, "and I do not care for the darkness, Henrietta. Why cannot you wait until tomorrow?"

Henrietta patted my arm with pretended kindness.

"Dearest Susan," she said, "you need not be perturbed. You will not be alone, I promise you. I have arranged it all and Incubus is to keep you company."

"Incubus!"

"You like him, you know you do, and he will take great care of you. All he will do is to accompany you as far as the hut and the rest will be in Kelvin's hands, who will more than likely see you home as far as he is able. Please Susan . . . *please*, my dear, I beg of you."

"Why cannot Incubus take it? Why does the letter have to be delivered by me?"

"I dare not entrust even Incubus with anything so precious. It is my whole future, Susan, that rests with you and this letter. I swear by all that is holy you will never have to do this thing again."

It ended in the usual way. What other choice had I? We were a strangely assorted pair, the runt and I, as we crept out of the house and along the red brick pathway. Incubus was walking in front of me with a minute lantern that made him look weird and uncanny, like a small twisted branch. He still had his guitar slung over his shoulder and he hummed and whistled as soon as we had gone outside the gates.

"What's in the wind?" he asked, looking back at me with every line in his bulldog face twinkling and merry as if life was a perpetual jest. "Mischief, I'll be bound, and mischief means a man or my name isn't Incubus."

216

"Your name is not really Incubus," I replied, and then we both laughed, for I was happy then at the thought of seeing my love, and was no longer afraid of the dark, or of Henrietta, or the letter that lay in my cloak.

"What colour is virtue, Miss Susan?" said Incubus.

"Has it a colour?"

"Yes, it is green," he replied, and chuckled and chortled as if he had made the cleverest remark in the world.

It was the same shabby hut, only a little shabbier and more woebegone than I remembered it. The same tattered remains of a home hung about it. As we entered the door a shower of crumbled woodwork and dust fell down upon us, and the door creaked sadly on its hinges.

It was so dark that even by the aid of our lantern there was little we could see. The very denseness of its nooks and crannies filled my nostrils. I could not touch anything without my fingers encountering a quivering ghostly web wherein some spider had gathered its gruesome meal.

"Here we are at last," said Incubus cheerfully, "and a nice place it is, to be sure. A pretty place, so merry and gay for a dainty lady like you. Such an earth-smelling hole of a hut to make free with and maybe plight a troth."

He swung the lantern onto a nail, the little lantern that was hardly alive and could not give me comfort. Then he made towards the door.

"God give you joy and a good time and keep you safe, Miss Susan," he said, and I could hear him whistling as he went on his way.

The wood of the hut was worm eaten and broken beams crossed the low ceiling. Now that Incubus had gone I was conscious of a great fear round and about me, an almost imperceptible trembling of the very earth itself. There seemed to be a heavy heart pounding wildly inside these four walls, a panic-stricken pulse which after a while I realized was mine. I could not separate the present from the past and my old recollections with this hut. They seemed to be looking at me, cowering over me, thousands of thoughts peering at me from the dark.

It was not so much the hut I was afraid of as what had taken place there. From the first wakening of reason this place was connected with cruelty and the dark realities of life. It did not seem so many years ago that two little girls were here, one timid, the other infinitely bold. The bold one drew the timid one onto the wooden bench beside her and sat there telling her the facts of life with a grip on her arm to prevent her from running away. Words ugly and distorted echoed in my memory, wicked tales of rape and lust hung in the shadows. I looked fearfully about me. What a coward I was! What a poor weak-willed midget, dreaming up things that were long over and done with!

"Ho, ho," screamed the past, "I have scared you, have I not? Ha, ha, it is a fine thing to frighten human beings to death."

The remains of a low cinder fire were scattered upon the floor. So many years had they been there that they had been winded and drafted into the very openings of the brick. In the centre of the hut there was a rough and rickety table and a broken chair and the bench I remembered so well. A pile of faggots remained as if some ghostly company had heaped them for a future fire. A few pieces of matting were crumpled across the hearth, and I was sure there were bats hanging dismally to the low beams. The whole place smelled of rotting woodwork

218

and fungus and dust, and it was so stifling hot I could hardly breathe.

There were hideous crawling beetles playing in and out of the torn matting; moths and spiders clung to the rafters. I could hear the rats pattering upon the roof, and now and again there was a squeaking fight between them and such hurrying and scurrying that the dust fell through the ceiling.

Where was Kelvin and why had he not come? Why had he left me waiting alone when he knew how I hated the dark? Perhaps he had been waylaid and would never turn up? How would I ever know, what would I do? I dared not go back to Henrietta with the undelivered letter in my hand.

As I stood and waited the years rolled back once more and the terror of the woods swept over me. I could feel the trees closing in on me, and the branches holding me down. I could not stay here. . . . I could not stay one moment longer or I would go mad.

Then I heard his footstep and all was well with me again. His steady even tread brought me to my senses.

With a happy laugh I turned to the door to meet him. I turned with my arms outstretched, abandoned and glorified with the love I had for him.

And there, filling the open space, was not Kelvin Abigail at all, but Mr. Bemrose with a smile on his evil face.

XIV

Mr. Bemrose stopped short at the door in order that he might survey me at his ease, and for a moment we stared at one another and not even the sound of our breathing could be heard within the hut.

I could see it all now; how simply Henrietta had deceived and tricked me, how she had baited the hook with her honeyed words.

"You will go, dear Susan," she had said. "Dearest Susan, you need not be perturbed. Please, Susan, please, my dear, it is the last time I will ask it of you."

Why had I trusted her so implicitly and believed that Kelvin would be here to meet me? Why had I not been more suspicious when she told me it was the hut? And then Incubus—what about him?—was he also part of this frightful nightmare?

"What colour is virtue?" he had asked me, and I had questioned as to whether it had a colour or no. "Yes, Miss Susan, it is green," he had replied and laughed. What had Incubus meant by his, "God give you joy and a good time and keep you safe?" Had he known then the danger I was in?

A good time, Mr. Bemrose, that was a smart saying. How they must have mocked and made fun of me in the forming of this plan.

My heart was beating wildly as I stood there gazing at the man I hated, and waves of memories swept over me of things

that had been done and had been said. "Why do you not become a nun, Susan? It is not for you, this savage routine of sex."
And then I could feel that the spirit of the dead was with me,
Papa's love reaching me from the grave. "Go out and give your
heart a fling, Susan. Fight for this man with everything that
is in you; fight for him, child, so that in the years to come,
whether you win him or lose him, you will have something to
remember."

I shrank from Mr. Bemrose closer and closer to the dusty
woodwork. We still had not said a word. I could not bear the
feel of him there in the hut. The smell of him, the look on his
white face and the sweat shining on his hands.

"Do you have to hunt and persecute me so?" I whispered at
last. "Why cannot you leave me alone?"

He came a little closer to me.

"Because I love you, Susan."

"Love . . ."

"You do not think me capable of such an emotion, do you?
You think that a word like that belongs only to fine gentlemen
and easy living."

"I do not think it belongs to you and me. Have mercy, Mr.
Bemrose, and for pity's sake leave me alone."

"Did you or your family have mercy upon me when I was
thrown out on a dung heap for one harmless kiss? Had you any
pity then?"

"I was a child. You frightened me."

"And now you are grown up you are no longer afraid, is that
it? Why then do you colour so deeply? Why does your lip
tremble if it is not with fear? Why do you sicken at the sight

221

of me, recoil from me as if I was some monstrous beast? Why am I so insufferably repugnant to you, for God's sake why?"

His voice had risen and he was shaking violently so that for a moment it flashed across my mind that this man might well be insane. He moved towards me until he reached the table, and there he paused and with an effort calmed himself.

"Most people shun me," he said in that sorrowful voice that Mamma found so entrancing, "but this dislike of me gives me powerful satisfaction. It makes me feel that I am not as other men are, and gloat in my apartness. But it is lonely and a man does not wish always to be alone. I do not like to see you pale and trembling, and to hear you stammer and falter in your speech at my approach. I want you to like me, Miss Susan. The measure of my loneliness you cannot fathom. No one to care or cook for me, or mend my clothes. When I open a door it is of someone else's home. No welcome waits for me. No arms encircle me and there are no kisses on my lips. All these things I need, Miss Susan. I need them from you. Your coldness and indifference maddens me and sinks into my mind so that I can think of nothing else . . . *nothing else but you.*"

I was pressed so far against the wooden wall my frock was creasing and crushing, and my cloak slid from my shoulders. I tried to scream, but there was no sound. I tried to pray, but there were no words of any prayer I could remember. He was close to me now. I could feel his breath stirring my hair. He kept licking his lips with the point of his tongue, his damp hands were brushing my cheek, and the strange bitter smell of him filled my nostrils.

"By the Lord, you have grown a beauty," he said. "You are

enough to make the earth heaven, and religion a glory. What are you thinking of, Miss Susan?"

"Let me go," I moaned. "Please, Mr. Bemrose, for God's sake let me go."

Then he took me in his arms. I struggled and fought and beat my hands uselessly against him, but he only laughed.

"You are like a little mouse that I have caught alone in the fields. A little field mouse, Miss Susan, fluttering against my heart."

My whole being was rocking with fear. It was a constant aching movement, eyes rolling, head turning this way and that to avoid the pressure of his lips. I kept mumbling over and over again to myself, "I must not swoon. . . . I must not fall down," when suddenly there was a shout, and Mr. Bemrose's arms were torn away from me, and there, tall, strong and complete, stood Kelvin Abigail.

For a moment they measured one another and then Kelvin struck the jeering man before him a heavy blow across the face so that a crimson stain drained slowly down his chin and spurted from his nose. I had never seen two men fight before, nor realized the savage cruelty which lies so closely to the dictates of society, and how, when their passions are let loose, men are but animals . . . Kelvin and Mr. Bemrose were now only two fighting dogs with their teeth bared and their eyes ablaze. Mr. Bemrose was ghastly pale, and the blood still ran from his chin and dripped upon his clothes. Each time he struck at Kelvin the blow did not seem to harm, for he was well knit, this Abigail, and light of foot, and so able to evade each desperate assault.

Again and again Mr. Bemrose rushed towards the door and

hurled himself against the strength of Kelvin, and each time with a fierce swift movement Kelvin Abigail struck him down. Mr. Bemrose became maddened by his failure to overthrow his enemy and hit wildly, swinging his long arms this way and that in his blind endeavour. Then there was a sudden scuffle and a noise like thunder in my ears. The next thing I knew was that Kelvin was holding me closely, and Mr. Bemrose lay on the grass outside the hut with the blood pouring from his mouth.

And so we stood waiting and watching until the tall lank figure rose first to his knees and then onto his feet. His eyes were smouldering with rage and his hands clenching and un-clenching with a strange monotony of movement. He shouted and mouthed at Kelvin, and then he said clearly:

"You will live to regret this day. . . . You will both of you live to regret it. Remember what I have told you, and God have mercy on your souls, for I will have none."

Long after Mr. Bemrose had gone I still clung to Kelvin, trembling and crying and uttering incoherent words; and he soothed me as if I was a child, stroking my hair and whispering, "Hush, my pretty, it is all over. You are safe, little Susan. No one can hurt you now."

"Oh, but I love you," I sobbed, "I love you so. You are the only living thing I have really and truly loved."

He held me from him and there was a look on his face I could not fathom.

"Do you know what you are saying?" he asked, "or are you still distraught with what has happened?"

I threw all caution to the winds. My pride was at his feet. I did not care any more about Henrietta and his passion for her.

224

This was my moment, the time that I had waited for and dreamed about so often.

"I love you," I repeated over and over again. "I know what I am saying, Kelvin. There is nothing in me but love of you. There never has been since the day you drove into Springfield Town."

He took my face between his hands, unassured and doubtful, as if he still could not believe what he was hearing.

"I wonder," he said softly. "I wonder."

"You wonder what, Kelvin?"

"Can anyone change so easily as this. Can a whole way of thinking and feeling be altered in an hour. Henrietta told me, she has always told me, she has always said . . ."

"What has she always said?"

"She told me you hated men, that all men were repugnant to you and that you held them in abomination. She told me you wished to be a nun and that rather than wed you would take Holy Orders."

"Did she tell you why, Kelvin? Did she say what part she herself had played in this?"

"She said that if any man was to speak to you of love, you would of your own free will leave Wingmeadow. I believed her, I believed every word she said. Why, in God's name, why, Susan, I do not know."

We sat upon the wooden bench, Kelvin and I, he with his arms about me and my head against his shoulder, and we talked and unfolded all that had passed these many moons.

"I dared not speak to you those early mornings," he said, "for the fear that I would never set eyes on you again. Many

225

and many a time my arms ached to hold you like this, my dearest, and yet, by doing so I should have lost you perhaps for ever."

"How did you know I was here, Kelvin? What brought you to this hut just when I needed you most?"

"The runt told me. He said you were waiting for me."

"I am glad it was Incubus. I did not like to think that he had duped me."

For a moment we were silent and then I said:

"But you love Henrietta."

"Do I? Is that what she has told you?"

"She said you were so tender and affectionate, so deeply attached, it seemed that you might die for love of her. You called her your dearest dear and . . ."

"Listen to me, Susan. A man will come to a crossroad, and one way to him looks the right way and full of promise, whilst the other is concealed by shadows and lacks enticement. So, what does a man do? A man who, as you know, surpasses an animal in his capacity for love: he takes the easy way. He takes the sun and the moon and the stars, thinking that there is no more he can ask of life than this. Yet, all the while he is not truly content; he has an uneasy feeling he should have taken that more secluded road. But still, weak fool that he is, he cannot get away. Then at last he becomes sated and sick of it, for there is no man in this world who can live for ever with the sun and the moon and the stars. I admit I was bewitched by Henrietta. It was so easy for me to turn to her when she half turned to meet me. But you stood on one side, you were the road without enticement, wrapped round by prejudice and fear. Was it my fault that you were so afraid, Susan, and so against the course of men? If you had only looked at me, held out your hand to me, it might have been so different. Henrietta is very, very lovely and a man has little strength to fight against a beauty such as hers. But she is spoilt. All her life she has been given what she wished for. She is like a strong fierce animal lying in wait for whatever prey she can devour."

Then I told him about Henrietta and the immeasurable harm she had done me. I told him of the hold she had over me and what a waste my life had been, bound hand and foot to her and to my reading.

"Poor Susan!" said Kelvin tenderly. "So easy to deceive. It is when you are a child, my dearest, that the most enduring impressions are born within you and are apt to remain with you for the rest of your life."

"I was too ordinary and shallow to resist her, Kelvin. The longer I lived the less I cared for living until you came round the corner of Springfield Town and opened up a new world for me."

"How did we first become friends, Susan? Can you remember that?"

"It was at an unimportant little party," I replied. "You asked me to dance and I was grateful; but afterwards Henrietta said she had commanded you to dance with me, and so the evening was spoiled."

We heard the clock close to White Orchard Manor striking midnight and we knew that it was time to part. Kelvin wrapped my cloak about me and we went slowly from the hut which had now become so dear to me. Gone were the ghosts of Mr. Bemrose and his shameless violence. Gone were the dusty shadows with the lustful spiders and their gruesome meal. There was a new beauty in that ragged, tumble-down ruin which we had not seen before and which we could now look back upon with grateful affection.

When we drew near the house Kelvin took me in his arms and with a sudden swift passion he rained kisses on my face. Again and again his lips sought mine with sudden freehanded desire.

I was struggling with myself to gain control. My dread of passion was almost amounting to terror. All my thoughts became scattered and confused as I remembered things that Henrietta had told me about men, their unscrupulous exploitation of our sex and the cruelty of their approach. Pages and pages of the books I had read waved before my frightened eyes: the edge of men's appetite and their rapacity of love. It seemed all at once I was a little girl again and Mr. Bemrose had hold of me in the wood. I was in Papa's room and he was touching my breasts and saying, "They will become little mountains of joy men will delight in."

I had thought that when I loved, when I really and truly loved, I would lose this sense of fear and ugliness and my soul would at last be free. I had thought the wretched ignorance of real emotion—this not knowing the difference between love and lust—would go from me. Kelvin felt me stiffen in his arms. He was aware of the sudden change in me, the sudden, insane desire that he should let me go. With an oath he thrust me from him and stood towering above me with his face grown white with rage.

"You told me that you loved me," he said fiercely, "when you do not even know the meaning of the word, when your whole body shrinks from me and curls from my embrace. There are tears on your cheeks. Shall I count them for you?

228

Shall I catch them in my hands and wash myself clean in them? You are not a woman, Susan. You are a poor pitiful shadow, a reflection of some other self. Go home, my dear, go home and find out once and for all what ails your heart. Ask yourself this question, 'Am I to marry Kelvin Abigail, or am I to enjoy perpetual virginity?' Until you have found the answer to this do not let me see you again, for I swear to God I am sick and tired of your staring purity."

When I looked up he had gone.

Fool, fool that I had been. So long had I dreamed of loving and being loved and yet when it came I drove it from me. Why was it that to me it had seemed nothing but unmeaning violence?

As I stepped through the iron gates and ran the length of the brick path, my face streaming with tears, Mr. Bemrose moved out from the shadows and confronted me. His injured countenance, with its bruised disfigurement, looked unclean and distorted. The cut on his lip was crusted with blood. He stood looking down at me, barring my way.

"It was my turn to peach and gab this time, Miss Susan," he said slowly. "Her Ladyship is in so ill a humour it would seem she can hardly find voice to scold with; and as for Miss Henrietta, she is frothing and flaring like a heated filly, and there is no knowing what this crabbed vixen may do to you."

"Could you not have held your tongue just for one night?" I replied. "What have you said? What have you done?"

"Nothing, Miss Susan, nothing of importance. But of this much I will warn you. One word to her Ladyship of what happened between us in the hut and both you and Mr. Abigail will suffer for it."

"Has not Mr. Abigail already proved how well he can take care of himself?"

"Against me he cannot, not with the way I work. Underground, Miss Susan, that is the way I go about things. In the bowels of the earth and in the bottomless pit is where I shall find revenge."

"Will you please let me pass, Mr. Bemrose."

"So now it is Miss Hoity-Toity, Miss High and Mighty, is that it?"

"I only know I am no longer afraid of you, that is all."

At this he stepped to one side, my grave tranquillity bewildering him. This was a new Susan Darlington he had not bargained for, and he realized for the first time he no longer disturbed me by his presence. I could feel his baleful gaze following me as I walked with what dignity I could into the house.

The shadow of the too-familiar place fell heavily upon me as I entered the door, and now a vision came before me of a little girl with her lessons in her hand, waiting to go into Mamma's room. I could feel the terror of those early morning rituals and my small knees knocking together and my heart hammering in my ears. For a moment I paused, irresolute and quaking, and then I said to myself, "That was another Susan. I am different," and as I went up the cedar stairway I thought more maturely of my childhood and smiled pityingly back at it, just as one might shrug one's shoulders or put out one's tongue at someone one disrespected. The puny passions, the little scoldings and corrections, seemed so meaningless and unimportant at this moment; all except Henrietta. Looking back to the earliest recollections of my infancy it was always Henrietta who stood out. The hardness of her, with not one single act of kindness to her credit, no service rendered to anyone but herself. Henrietta's course left nothing but a trail of ruthless inhumanity behind it.

I thought of Papa. . . . Dearest Papa with his gay and amiable qualities. Papa wallowing in his good opinion of himself but with such a humour, such a warmhearted disposition, that it did not really matter. His artless vanity beating against the acrimony of Mamma, Mamma who never really understood him.

For so many years I had allowed my soul to be destroyed and my heart half broken. For so long a time I had abused my imagination, making my books and Henrietta's treatment of me a devilish dwelling place from which there was no escape. Then, like the glittering prince of some old-fashioned fairy tale, Kelvin had broken into my kingdom to rescue me.

"I am well and whole again," I said to myself. "I am completely healed. There is nothing anyone can do to me any more now that my heart is mended."

And then I remembered Kelvin's kisses and the way that I had treated him, and all at once the exultation and assurance went out of me. The realization of what I had done stood between me and Kelvin. It was a stubborn fact, not a dream, a tangible substance drawn like a knife between us.

When I reached the top of the stairway Mrs. Trouncer was there to meet me. She looked extremely perturbed and her eyes started out of her head.

"Oh, my dearie," she cried, "wherever have you been, for there's a deal of trouble. Her Ladyship is in a tantrum, Miss Susan, and your sister seems half crazed."

I patted her shoulder and smiled and went slowly towards the door of Mamma's room, with Mrs. Trouncer looking after me with her mouth agape.

"Well," I could hear her say, "if that doesn't take the skin off a snake. What's going on this night?"

And she was still muttering to herself as I opened the door and went in.

I felt like a soft silk pin cushion that was being jabbed by a succession of needles and I became aware that this sensation was caused by the expression in the two pairs of eyes that were directed upon me.

Mamma was seated, as was her wont, beside a tall prim lamp, the wools of her embroidery lying in a splash of colour at her feet. There she was, as I had seen her so many evenings in so many years, work poised in mid-air, her haughty face raised and her gaze most penetratingly fixed upon me. And there was Henrietta pacing the floor, her face so white and her red hair so vivid, it seemed almost as if she were enveloped in flames.

First she came towards me as if she would strike me, her eyes never leaving my face. She surveyed me and scanned and inspected me as if I was some rare specimen she had not beheld until now. The anger of her stare burned into me and flayed me, and the fever of her fury ran over me like scalding rain.

I approached Mamma and sat in the chair that had so evidently been placed for me; and still no one spoke.

"It is late, Mamma," I said at last, "and you should be in bed."

Then Henrietta could control herself no longer.

"A pretty game you have been playing," she screamed. "You, the pious one, the pretentious, mincing little beauty of holiness

232

with your assumption of piety, your sanctimonious saintship, carrying on an illicit love affair as the lowest slut in town. You . . ."

"Henrietta," interrupted Mamma, "will you please leave this to me? There is no use in violent ill nature and abuse. Susan has brought shame upon us and, like any common chambermaid, resorted to the rudest form of courtship, a pursuit most highly unbecoming to our family prestige. I would not have dreamed that any child of mine could so degrade herself, especially Susan, but what is done cannot be undone, and we are head and shoulders in this scandal. I sincerely hope that no one but Mr. Bemrose knows of this, and I think I can rely upon him to guard our honour and protect our name. As for you, Susan, I have not yet made up my mind what is to become of you, but I wish first of all to hear what you yourself have to say about such conduct."

"To what conduct do you refer, Mamma?"

"Hark at the little innocent acting bewilderment," said Henrietta scornfully. "See her wide open eyes of overwhelming wonder. Are you going to permit yourself to be deceived, Mamma, by this play of stupefaction?"

"Be quiet, Henrietta," replied Mamma. "Susan knows perfectly well to what I am alluding."

"Do I, Mamma?"

"What have you to say, child? Must I stay here all night?"

"I have nothing to say, Mamma, since I have done nothing."

"Nothing!"

"You have already heard a story that I have no doubt our dear Mr. Bemrose has told with all the pungent fragrance of a seasoned morsel, so what more is there for me to say?"

"Mr. Bemrose merely informed me of the truth, Susan. He

considered it expedient that I should know what was going on behind my back."

"And what did he say was going on, Mamma?"

"He said that you had made a secret meeting in the hut with Mr. Abigail, that you crept out this evening like any village hussy to see this man."

"Did he say why? Did he say why, Mamma?"

"I did not lower myself by asking him. Was it not enough to know that you had gone there."

"Shall I tell Mamma, Henrietta?" I said clearly. "Shall I reveal your so-called love tale and imaginary wooing? I went with a letter from Henrietta, Mamma, a letter of proposal from Henrietta to the man she said loved her. Over and over again I have been her messenger, and tonight was to have been the last time. She asked Mr. Abigail to marry her because she could not bear this house any longer. She threw herself into his hands rather than continue living here."

"It is a lie," Henrietta's voice rang through the room. "She is lying, Mamma. I swear to God there is no such letter. I tell you it is not true. . . . It is not true."

"Well, Susan," said Mamma continuing her embroidery and looking at it angrily as if the little coloured threads were to blame for her vexation, "are you indeed lying and is this perhaps one of the many scenes you conjure from your books?"

I felt in my cloak where the letter still lay. Triumphantly I drew it forth and flourished it.

"Here is the letter, Mamma. It was never delivered for I found there was no need."

Mamma took it coldly and gave a stricken half-accusing look towards her favourite daughter. Slowly she opened it and gazed

234

at it with open mouth and rounded eyes. It seemed at first that she was spellbound, lost in an overwhelming awe, and then she said in a whisper:

"This is a blank piece of paper, Susan. There is no writing here."

For a moment we all three were silent staring at the sheet of paper which Mamma held up before us, and then Henrietta laughed and it was a most horrible sound to hear.

"Do you not see, Mamma," she cried, "do you not see? Susan invented the letter. It was a clever trick, but not quite clever enough. Can you not see the slyness of Susan, Mamma, and how she is using me to cover her misconduct?"

Mamma pressed her hand to her head. She looked unusually disturbed and her face was flushed.

"I wish someone would tell me what all this is about," she said piteously, "for it seems I have two daughters who are strangers to me, two children I have never really known."

"Mamma, will you listen to me?"

"Yes, Susan, I will listen."

"Early this evening Henrietta sent me with a letter to the hut. Ask Incubus, he knows, for he escorted me. Henrietta said the letter was for Kelvin. But it was not Kelvin Abigail who met me, it was Mr. Bemrose. Family honour, high esteem, he knows nothing of such things. His carnal mind is empty but for one thing, the desire to destroy. This was Henrietta's planning, that I should be alone in the hut with such a man."

"It is a lie," moaned Henrietta, her face distorted with rage. "Do not believe her, Mamma. I tell you it is not true."

"I would be obliged," said Mamma faintly, "if you would send for Mr. Bemrose."

"Mr. Bemrose has retired, Mamma. His accident has considerably upset him."

"And pray, Henrietta," I said quietly, "may I ask what misfortune has befallen Mr. Bemrose?"

"He was out watching for poachers," replied Mamma, "and it seems that he caught his foot in a rabbit snare and fell heavily upon a stone. His face is badly bruised and cut, and he is feeling far from well. Nevertheless, I am obliged to send for him. He has always held our family in great respect and his estimation of us has always been a high one. We have a long line of revered and honourable ancestors lying in our wake, and it is regrettable that Susan of all people should have been the one to break this almost blameless record, blameless indeed but for poor Papa. I think if you had lived more healthily and consumed less ill-favoured literature, Susan, you would not now be involved in this most unsatisfactory business. It is the evil consequence of reading imaginative fiction. You cannot live decently, my dear child, with indecorous books as your companions."

I waited for her to finish what she had to say and then I burst forth vehement and wild with indignation.

"The lying braggart . . . the shuffling hypocrite," I almost sobbed in my endeavour to persuade her. "Out for poachers was he, caught in a rabbit snare! Well, let me tell you this, Mamma —Mr. Bemrose was out for poaching kisses of his own, and he was entangled in a trap of his own making. Send for him, send for him by all means, and then we will see how much of this is true."

All the colour had drained from Mamma's face and I thought for a moment she would swoon, but instead she ordered Henrietta to ring the bell. No sooner was the bell rope in Henrietta's

236

hand than Mrs. Trouncer came tumbling into the room, her cap over one eye and a smear on her face where she had leaned against the woodwork. Mamma glanced at her coldly.

"Listening again," she said. "I might have guessed. Well, since you have heard, what are you waiting for?"

Mrs. Trouncer straightened her cap and smoothed her gown with an air of profound indignation.

"You wish to see Mr. Bemrose?" she asked.

"Is that not what you heard me say?"

"I do not think he will come, my Lady, if you will pardon the expression."

"Mr. Bemrose will do as I command him."

"Very well, my Lady."

Mrs. Trouncer curtseyed to Mamma and, with a strange look at me and a scowl at Henrietta, she vanished from the room. We all three sat in silence, waiting; Mamma slowly and carefully selecting her wools, and Henrietta twisting her handkerchief in her hands and biting her lips with her eyes turned resolutely from mine.

I do not know how much Mrs. Trouncer had revealed to Mr. Bemrose of what she had heard, or how much he sensed from the atmosphere as he quickly entered the room; but there was a look on his broken face that made me shudder, and the happiness, the bright happiness which had brought new life to me seemed suddenly to have lost its radiance. There was about this man such a menace to my love, such a warning of things which he might do, that all at once I was afraid again, not for myself but for Kelvin who was so much part of me.

Mr. Bemrose stood before Mamma with an air of jaded sullenness; his small eyes turned suspiciously from one to the

237

other of us as he waited for Mamma to speak; and she, looking suddenly shriveled and strangely old, seemed in no haste. First she laid down her embroidery, patting the wools and smoothing the surface of it as if the thoroughness of her work concerned her deeply. Her lips moved and she appeared to be groping for words, which was unlike Mamma, and never before had I seen her less voluble. Drawing herself up and taking a deep breath, she stared fully at the man before her.

"I do not suppose you can divine the purport of my sending for you once again," she said. Her voice had thickened and her hands were fumbling in her lap. "But a great many things have been spoken of this night I do not understand. It may be that I do not wish to understand them. I cannot tell, for I do not appear to know myself or any of you any more. It does not seem long ago, Mr. Bemrose, that you came distressfully to me in search of almost any employment I could offer you, and because we had known you for some years I gladly reinstated you in the occupation you once held, believing you would serve me well. In what way have you rewarded me, in what way have you used the trust I placed in you, that is for yourself to answer. I am told, by my daughter Susan that you have deliberately and violently abused that trust. There is nothing uncommon in the lamentable story of the quite ordinary lust of a man like you for those superior to him, but I did not think that I, with my own hand, would open the door to such a circumstance. You are a fool, Mr. Bemrose, a poor misguided imprudent fool. Did you not know that I had such a liking for you? You could have remained in my service to the end. I had even considered altering my Will for the purpose of leaving you a small security. But now, because of your contemptible behavior, you are no longer necessary either to me or my estate. It is your fault and yours alone that matters between us have been obliged to take this turn. Beyond this house you have no prospect. I advise you to leave Wingmeadow and Springfield Town, where tongues wag swiftly and gossips tread the streets. Go to some place where no one knows you and start all over again. Now, if you please, I am tired and sick at heart and I wish to be alone. If you have anything to say in your defence I beg you will be brief, for the hour is late and it is long past my bedtime."

This, for Mamma, was indeed a long oration, and when it was over she sank back in her chair with her eyes closed. Mr. Bemrose seemed of a sudden to have crumbled and grown smaller, as if his outer covering was now too large for its miserable contents.

"I have nothing to say," he muttered, "nothing."

"In that case," she replied, "will you please leave us? Mrs. Trouncer will pay you your salary, and you can pack your things in the morning and leave my service. I cannot find it in me to forgive you, but may God have mercy on your darkened soul."

Mr. Bemrose, who had thought himself so secure within our walls, was once more thrown out into the world again without a character. There would be no use in pleading. He knew Mamma too well for that. He knew her strange and terrible religion, her worship of propriety for which she would have sacrificed herself and her whole family to feed the ego of her stern convention.

He turned towards me a look so venomous and cruel that I could but shrink from him.

"You accursed gibble-gabbler," he shouted. "I have you to blame for this, and if there is a heaven or hell I swear by either of them that all your life you will regret that you could not hold that chattering tongue of yours. I will not say farewell, Miss Susan, for you will see me again and wish to God you had no eyes. You will hear of me again and wish to God you had no ears. You will be sorry for this day's work, Miss Susan, sorry for yourself and sorrier still for Mr. Kelvin Abigail."

Without another word he turned on his heel and went swiftly from the room.

XV

IF YOU LOOK at any village in any country lane or road you will be sure to be struck by its extreme loneliness; that is if the windows are shuttered and the doors closed and the people all out in the fields gathering in the hay and enjoying the sweat of their labours. You will observe how dejected the village seems without its inhabitants, and how each house has the face of a man or a woman who has given up hope. But, as soon as the fields are cleared and the hay ricked and the windows are flung open and the children emerge on their way to school, it is different. When a strip of washing is slung in the back yard the whole aspect changes, and the little village takes its place in the world again; meaning in other words that houses need people in them and people need small domestic undertakings such as washing their clothes and painting their doors and weeding their gardens, to turn their house into a homestead.

Now the summer was waning, the little roads round Wing-meadow lay tired and drowsy from too much sun, and the lane no longer seemed in need of the deep shadows cast from the trees. The garden at White Orchard Manor was still carpeted with colour, and the brown earth was strewn with rose petals as they tumbled from their stems.

There was dust and dryness everywhere. Dust lay upon the cobblestones in Springfield Town and collected in long thin streams along the gutters. Dust was drawn into the throats of the townsfolk so that there was always at this time a great deal of coughing and wheezing to be heard behind the closed doors of houses and shops. Doctor Wiffin would be busy scurrying hither and thither to those who could afford imaginary ills, prescribing gargles and mouth washes to rinse the dryness from their noses and throats and rid his clients of the aftermath of summer.

The Season was once more at an end and the world of fashion on its way to the appointed places of pleasure and of sport. Some went to the Scottish moors for deer-stalking and partridges and game; others drove in coaches to the spas, where they drank the waters and washed the rich food from their livers and the thick bile from their bellies in preparation for the winter's roast beef and crackling pork.

The Abigails had returned to Wingmeadow Lodge, but as Mamma had issued strict orders that Kelvin was not on any account to be admitted to our house, and I was forbidden to walk out without an escort, there was no way of seeing or hearing from my love unless I resorted to the complicity of Mrs. Trouncer.

This should have been the best time of my life, but it was strangely sad.

I had everything before me, yet it was what lay behind me, the cloud of darkness and fear that crept up over the good times ahead. Moreover, Mamma was sick and gravely ailing with a light form of paralysis. Ever since the dismissal of Mr. Bemrose and the scene that had ensued, it seemed she had quite lost her identity. One side of her could walk, but the other only moved with the aid of a stick. She never went beyond the rose garden, and there she would go up and down the brick paths with the stick tapping and her leg dragging, holding herself as erect as she could and never complaining. She still had beauty of a kind, but there was no life in it. A fine clean mask without warmth, and strangely quiet. One side of her brain she could use, but the other was forgotten. One side of her went on giving orders and discharging her duties, whilst the other could not remember what those orders had been. She was alive and yet dead. One side of her active, the other immovable. She could not embroider any more; she merely sat and looked out, puzzled and frowning over the half of her that knew who she was. Yet she still appeared to enjoy the sound of her own voice giving orders, for she clung to the command of the house and to the fact of being mistress of White Orchard Manor. It made her feel important and useful, though, whilst in repose, she had a way of putting her hand to her head as if to brush away some pain or else some thought that lay too heavy upon her brow.

Mr. Bemrose had left, with a great noise of loud talking, dragging of boxes, banging of doors. When Mrs. Trouncer gave him his salary he all but spat on it and said it was little thanks for what he had had to put up with from the Darlingtons. He insisted upon taking the runt back where he had first found him, because he said he would not have any friend of his working for a family such as ours, even if he was a bastard; and Incubus, bewildered by this sudden change in his fortune, asked me if I knew what wrong he had ever done to us.

"I served you well, Miss Susan. I did as I was told. I am happy here. It is a great pity."

"It was not your fault, Incubus," I replied gently. "Mr. Bemrose is a most peculiar man and does not care for happiness."

"Does her Ladyship wish to be rid of me, is that it?"

243

"Her Ladyship does not even know that you are going, Incubus. It is Mr. Bemrose who has his account to settle. He harbours revenge, and malice rankles in his heart. What he cannot have himself he will not let others have. He is ruthless, Incubus, and pitiless, and I am glad, in a way, you will be rid of him."

So the runt returned to the Cattlewigs and the Squirrel Inn, and Mrs. Cattlewig put him to work in the stables and in the little back garden of the house. Whenever we passed she pursed up her lips and tossed her head with a look in her eyes as much as to say, "If Incubus isn't good enough for the likes of you, *you* are not good enough for me."

The next time I met Incubus I asked him if he was happy at the inn and he replied:

"I miss the farm and the rich milk and the smell of newly turned hay, but I reckon it's better to coax a flower to grow than to stuff a pig for the market. Then of course there's always Josephine."

"Josephine?"

"She's Mr. Mortician's mare who lives in the back stable here, as loving a beast, when you know her, as ever you could see. Josephine's not a fast trotter, Miss Susan, but she's got style, and I shouldn't wonder if there was breeding somewhere in that mare the same as there is in me, for she's kind of haughty looking when on the go, as much as to tell you that she's only between the shafts of a cab by misfortune rather than by class."

"You are fond of horses, Incubus?"

"I'm fond of all dumb creatures, Miss Susan," replied the runt with a gleam in his kindly eyes, "for I feel closer to them than to anything else in the world."

244

Henrietta was all milk and honey these days, a strange new mood I found most disquieting. I could not help feeling she was up to something, and I poured out my fears to Mrs. Trouncer who merely laughed and said:

"I wouldn't imagine things if I were you. Just leave well alone until it takes place, and then it will be time to start worrying."

It was a touching thing to see Henrietta so contrite and to hear her say how sorry she was for the things that she had said to me regarding my love for Kelvin. It was a most unusual thing for the proud and overbearing Henrietta to be so humble. I could not help feeling it was but a cloak she was wearing to conceal her real emotion, beneath the folds of which her same offending faults would suddenly emerge.

Day after day I watched her grow paler, and I counted each tear, each sigh of hers, as atonement for my tortured past. Her suffering face and saddened eyes enchanted me. Did she remember, I wondered, how my face had whitened and the way I had looked at her sometimes? Heaven forgive me if I was wrong to feel no mercy for her. I was only human and she had plenty to atone for. I could not forget the part she had made me play, those ventures in the snow, Kelvin's letters which she had made me believe so loving; those hours of agony at Wingmeadow Lodge, the tears and the heartbreak as I heard them whispering behind closed doors. And, last of all, the hut with Mr. Bemrose and his suffocating passion. . . . How could all this, these many years of discord, be accounted for by Henrietta's seeming penitence?

These were my hours of triumph. I no longer concealed myself in lonely places or sat in obscure corners of a crowded

245

room. I was reborn on the ashes of Henrietta's failure. Henrietta's last mischief, so I thought then, had been made.

As the days passed there was little word from Kelvin beyond one lengthy letter couched in the coldest terms, declaring that his intention to marry me remained and that he had informed his mother of the fact. He had no desire, so he said, to decide upon our wedding day until I had, as he expressed it, properly matured.

"I do not wish to be loved with pathetic resignation, dearest Susan," he wrote, "and I am distressed that my passion was so profitless. When I took you in my arms why did you hesitate? Did it occur to you that I might rape you? Had you no more faith in me than that? Of what were you thinking, and how did you feel? Or is it that you have no thoughts, no feeling whatsoever? Are you a phantom, Susan, a creature of gossamer and dreams? Have you no blood in your veins, no soul that can be stirred, no heart that can be made to beat? I thought my kiss would rouse you from your virtuous sleep, but I realize now that I have failed in love."

Again and again I sent Mrs. Trouncer with my pleadings for forgiveness. Again and again I implored him to remember all I had told him of Henrietta's training, of the books I had allowed myself to read and the horror of what had taken place within the hut. Could he not see how I had been almost out of my reason and that therefore my actions had been unaccountable? Would he not find it in him to forgive me?

"Give me one more chance," I begged him. "Let me endeavour to prove my love for you. I am not cold, Kelvin, not really deep down within me. It is that I cannot find expression to my feelings. I have neither words nor actions to convince you."

Upon the receipt of my penitent epistles his letters softened and he wrote to me again.

"All through the days and nights, my well beloved, I have one consolation, and that is the memory of your voice telling me you love me. I did not force this admission from you; you gave it to me of your own free will. What is the barrier between you and me? Is it Henrietta? Is it, Susan? Is it some old abuse of hers that stands between us? When I tried to kiss your unconsenting lips it was as if there was some strange shadow forcing us apart. Perhaps your eyes are too calm and your lips too cold for me. Would to God I could love you less, Susan, but I am defenceless. I swear to you, neither my faith nor my fervour will ever leave me."

"Beautiful they are," said Mrs. Trouncer. "They fair melt in the mind they do. It makes me wish I was young again when Mr. Trouncer was nigh at his best and hadn't taken to the bottle."

"Mrs. Trouncer, you have been reading my letters. Oh, how could you be so mean?"

"Things have been powerful dull since her Ladyship was taken bad and the keyholes have nothing but dust in them. What else can I do to help pass the time in this dismal shadow of a house?"

I received also a letter from Mrs. Abigail expressed in the tenderest terms.

"I consider my son highly honoured by your love for him," she wrote, "and my happiness and gratitude I cannot properly express. I thank God that my dearest Kelvin will have such an excellent wife, and I so exquisite a daughter.

247

Pray tell your dear Mamma, who I am aware has little liking for me, that I shall hope to see her in the near future restored to her good health. This union of our families was what Lord Darlington most fondly wished and may tend to remove or diminish her disapproval of me, and I do most earnestly hope that you, my dearest Susan, will look upon your marriage with the utmost confidence. You have the eternal devotion of my son and can therefore dismiss from your mind any apprehension. I beg you to excuse the shortness of this letter but I was so hurried to inform you of my happiness.

"Your most loving and attached friend, Florence Linton Abigail."

I showed the letter to Henrietta. I did not see the smile curving her deceitful lips. I suppose I was a strangely constituted creature to suppose she could change in such a little while. When I look back upon my conduct then, I have only myself to reproach for the manner in which she duped me and played upon my implicit confidence in her redemption.

Mrs. Abigail had not long been back at Wingmeadow Lodge before she restarted and reformed her little choir. It was such a minor product of her genuinely musical talent, and yet she felt she could not do without us. Moreover, her sons' visits to London had become more frequent as they rose higher in their various professions, and she would have been very much alone if it had not been for those weekly assemblies of the neighbours.

Henrietta came to me with honeyed words, saying that now we were released from our mourning for Papa there was no reason why we should not go.

"After all, we do exert ourselves over Mamma, Susan. We are

never unmindful of her illness. We fulfil our obligations at home and nothing in regard to her comfort is overlooked or neglected. We should be allowed to have our own way in this one thing, do you not think so?"

And then she caressed me and sat with her arms about me, calling me her sweet sister, her dear Susan, and begging for forgiveness. And I, poor fool that I was, poor trusting, boggled fool, believed in her supposed sincerity. All my life I had stood in my own light and taken what was only shadow for substance. Never had I for one moment been truly conversant with the treachery of human thought. I believed Henrietta was reclaimed and conscience-stricken. Her acknowledgment of wrongdoing seemed sincere; her expression of regret, her tenderness, soothed and composd my outraged memories. She threw gold dust in my eyes and blinded me so that I no longer saw how double-faced she was.

I wrote to Kelvin and told him of this heavenly-awakened Henrietta and implored him to be kind to her. "My dearest, she is indeed repentant," I told him. "We are to be so happy, you and I. Would it not be a gracious gesture to forgive her and forget all that has passed?"

Kelvin wrote back to me:

My Dearest Susan,

I might find it in my heart to forgive an injury, but to forget would be contrary to all reason. I will of course be amiable and show your sister courtesy, but more than that I cannot promise.

Believe me always, dearest Susan, your humble and devoted
Kelvin

Henrietta persuaded me that it would be wiser not to inform Mamma that we had made up our minds to return to Wingmeadow Lodge; indeed, she said she saw no reason why we should tell anyone but Mrs. Trouncer, who would be sure to find out for herself anyway. Mamma's confused memory held no knowledge of the choir or her disapproval of it; sometimes she would even forget Papa was dead and send us with some message to his room; and at mealtimes she would fret and fume because he was late as usual, and then, in a flash, she would forget again and not once did she wonder why he never came. All she remembered was that Kelvin and I were in love, and that Mr. Bemrose was no longer in our service. Now and again she would speak of the runt and ask why he was not on the farm, but by the time we had found an answer to this question her mind had wandered off again.

So we arranged to slip from the house on practice days, leaving Mrs. Trouncer in charge of Mamma, nodding and dreaming in her chair.

"If she wakens, poor lady," she said, "I will tell her you are both at the vicarage. It will not anger God to tell lies on her behalf to ease the pained confusion of her mind."

Mrs. Abigail received us with open arms. She was as vivacious as ever and made us feel so welcome we wondered how we had passed these many months without the warmth and fervour of her greeting.

The choir had not altered beyond certain happenings in their private lives. The Misses Tinnerlies' skirts were a little dustier and their laces a little more crumpled and their eyes more strained as if they had been through some privations. It appeared that they had found their lodgers over troublesome and had made up their minds to forego the little money they made from them and become ladies at large, living like little mice in the back part of their house.

"We cannot do much," they said, "for we are very simple ignorant people and our lodgers took advantage of us. Mrs. Lumsden would break her coffee cup so regularly we could not supply her with enough; and Mrs. Dingle was so partial to a pork chop she would even demand one for her breakfast. Their orders were so insulting and exacting that we could not continue with them. If only we had been taught to take care of ourselves, but you see our parents believed we had never really grown up and treated us as children. We were nearly thirty when they died, but we were still little children to them; you know how it is with people who will not permit others to grow up."

The Garmington daughters were thinner-lipped and more short-sighted than ever. They did not seem to care any more what became of them and buried themselves in church-going and charity.

Lady Agatha Swann's sole offspring, on the other hand, was gayer and appreciably more sprightly. She had been told that gentlemen were enticed by constant chatter and an animated smile.

It was only Miss Amelia Pinchbeck who had found herself a suitor, an individual who dealt in second-hand clothes but who defined himself as a Gentleman's Gentleman Tailor. He had, so Miss Amelia informed us, quite an imposing establishment at Windsor, and was specially recommended because the Queen's valets and chambermaids purchased their clothes from him. Part of the shop was hung with samples of ladies' wear, and the other side with gentlemen's coats and cravats. Mr. Mongermart himself was a red-faced bewhiskered salesman who did not work in the store but collected his clients from the houses and taverns which he frequented. He had a manner of bowing and rubbing his hands most obsequiously as he propelled his unhappy purchasers into the store. It gave both Mr. Mongermart and Miss Amelia Pinchbeck the greatest satisfaction to see his name in flamboyant colours above the door. "Although Mr. Mongermart is not exactly in society," said Miss Amelia, bridling and drawing herself up, "he is closer to it than a lot of people. Silks and satins of the nobility pass through his hands and give him an air he would otherwise lack."

Mr. Mongermart prided himself on his judgment of character.

"Precognition, that's what it is," he would tell Miss Amelia Pinchbeck. "It's an inborn knowledge of mankind. You become cognizant and well acquainted with all kinds and conditions of clients through the clothes they wear, and the manner and means whereby they cast them from them."

The Honorable Diana Quirk was most impressed with Miss Amelia's account of her unusual lover and declared she would like to write an article about him and his knowledge of the bartering and exchange of fashionable attire. She had but lately written a treatise upon the suppression of sex and female frustration which the Queen had demanded be withdrawn from publication, with the consequence that the Honorable Diana was under a royal cloud and so regarded in Springfield Town as a woman to be avoided.

Miss Withering, on the other hand, was well looked up to as she continued painting pictures that nobody wanted. She could be seen all through the summer at various corners of the countryside dabbling in colour to her heart's content.

The little Miss Gimp, who was engaged to Phillip, looked more anxious and pathetic than ever, and her turned-up nose more demanding. Phillip, it seemed, was in no haste to be dragged to the altar until he was more certain of his position. People were beginning to say that it might so be that after all she was to be left in the lurch.

Miss Georgina Baffit had had a mishap with her archery and had thereby well-nigh blinded the impoverished and underpaid little man who collected the arrows for her, so the two sisters had retired to croquet to conceal the discomfort of their un-decorated faces.

They were all very pleased and attentive as they chattered together, exchanging these various happenings, and of course exceedingly playful about my engagement to Kelvin Abigail, asking me how, in the name of wonder, I had managed to snatch such an elegant young man from under my sister's nose. I watched Henrietta, but she did not seem in the least put out; neither did she show any sign of the turmoil and rage I after-wards knew had been within her.

Sometimes Kelvin was there, but the choir would so surround and suffocate him with their well-wishing that more often he kept away, yet, whenever he was beside me, I could feel Henri-etta's eyes burning into me. She did not say a word to Kelvin, either for or against our future marriage, so that Kelvin also became reassured and would say:

"You were right about Henrietta, Susan. She could not be more amiable. How little one can judge a character until it has been put to the test."

"She looks very lovely, does she not?" I questioned him wistfully.

"Very lovely."

"Prettier than I am."

"Much, much prettier."

"You are a monster," I teased him, "and I hate you for that!"

But he would merely laugh and we would fall deeper and deeper in love every time that we met.

And then one evening, on returning to the house, we met Mrs. Trouncer at the outer door.

"God's mercy on us," she cried, "I wish I had never lived to see this night. You are to go upstairs at once to her Ladyship, and may the Lord have mercy on your welcome."

When we went into the boudoir we found Mamma standing waiting for us, and she was terrible to behold in her stern rigidness. She was, so it seemed to me, at bay, entrenched in her own mantle of displeasure. She shuffled close to me and looked into my face. She touched me with her hand and her fingers were ice cold. I drew back from her, but she followed me, holding on to my arm, and the sound of that paralyzed foot dragging along the polished floor was worse than any sound I had ever heard.

Her staring eyes gazed wildly into mine. She did not seem to notice Henrietta in the room. Her ice-cold fingers pawed and clawed me, and her lips moved in an effort to form the words.

Then she screamed rather than spoke, a weird hollow sound as if what she was saying was being torn out of her in pain. There was something in her manner, half sane, half inhuman, a travesty of the severe proud woman she had once been.

"You deceiver," she screeched, "you dissembling wretch, to take advantage of the ill my flesh is heir to and to gloat over my decrepit mind. You said to yourself no doubt, 'She is infirm and her wits have gone from her. She will not know that I am at Wingmeadow Lodge.' But you see I do know, Susan. My sanity is not so impaired as you imagined. It seems that after all I have one friend, one human being who will not see me wronged. Do you want to know who that is, Susan? Shall I tell you his name? It is the man I so wrongfully dismissed, owing to your lies; the man I turned twice from my house because of what you told of him. Never again will I listen to you. I will not trust you any more. Everyone is against me, plotting and planning to hurt and injure me, nobody loves me . . . there is hatred in every corner of this place I once called home."

She started to laugh and then to cry, whimpering as any child might do, so that Henrietta went over to her and drew her gently towards her chair.

"No one is trying to hurt you, Mamma, and as for loving you, you have always your Henrietta."

"Henrietta," she replied vaguely, "I seem to know that name. There was a child called Henrietta who used to sit on my lap."

"I am that child, Mamma. I am Henrietta."

But Mamma thrust her away with her stick and turned angrily to me.

"This is the cunning one," she cried, "with her double tongue and feline intrigue. I know the craftiness of her concealment. I know how she accepts my orders. I forbade her to go to Wingmeadow Lodge. I thought she was obedient. I shall send you away, Susan. You must go away, you must never live here any more. I shall send you so far away you will never find this house again. You do not belong here any more. You are no longer my child. All I have left is Henrietta."

She grasped my arm convulsively and her lips moved again, but no sound came from them. Henrietta called out to Mrs.

Trouncer and between us we placed her in her chair, still muttering and moaning and with a thin froth dribbling down her chin. I could not bear to see her so and ran quickly from the room, my heart beating so that I could not breathe. At the foot of the stairs I waited for Henrietta.

"What does she mean?" I whispered. "In Heaven's name what was she trying to tell me?"

"It is pretty evident, my dear Susan, that Mr. Bemrose has once more been to see her."

"You mean, he has told her about us? Everything about us going to Wingmeadow Lodge?"

"Everything about you, Susan. There was nothing about me."

"But you came to Wingmeadow Lodge. It was your idea in the first place. You begged me to go. I would not have dreamed of deceiving Mamma if it had not been for you."

"Mamma is not angered with me, Susan, only with you."

"But why? Why, Henrietta? What have I done that you did not do also? Why am I the one to be blamed?"

Henrietta smiled in her superior way. I could see that her face was flushed.

"Perhaps you were not kind enough to Mr. Bemrose," she replied. "Perhaps if you had been nicer to him he would have been more merciful to you."

"But how did he know about our going to Wingmeadow Lodge? Who could have told him, since no one knew where he was living?"

"There is always somebody who knows everything about everybody," said Henrietta complacently, "and there is no safety to be had, my dear sister, either here or in Springfield Town."

And still I had not the slightest suspicion that Henrietta herself was mixed up in this affair. When I look back at it I often wonder how I could have been so fooled.

As I lay in my room that night all I could hear was Mamma's strange utterance saying, "I am sending you away, Susan. You will never live here any more. I shall send you so far away that you will never find this house again."

I drove my fingers in my ears. I rolled from side to side. I called out to Kelvin and prayed aloud to God. My small bed creaked and the pillows shifted, and then I fell asleep.

My dreams were like a storm that raged round and round and would not settle, dreams of things which seemed to have no end to them. First Mamma, with her mental incoherence, and then Henrietta, bending over me, telling me the meaning of sex. I was being dragged through the woods by Mr. Bemrose, and the runt was running ahead with a little lantern that gave no light. Days and days of suffering crowded in one dream, and then it changed and Mr. Bemrose was a dog with his nose to the ground, seeking me out. I could hear the snufflings and scratchings of the earth, the howling and panting at my heels. I ran and ran, yet seemed not to be moving; and then there was a great noise of stampeding and the rumble of wheels as a coach flashed by with Kelvin leaning from the window. I called out to him to save me, but he did not seem to hear me, and I fell, down . . . down to the foot of a tree where there was a paper parcel, and out of the parcel grinned Incubus, saying, "This is a merry place for love."

When I rose the next morning with aching eyes and the bloom faded from my cheeks I found that my door was locked and that Mamma had given strict orders I was to be kept in my room until she had determined what was to become of me. It was Henrietta who brought me my breakfast on a tray, and I noticed that she had the key of my door dangling on a ribbon attached to her waist. Her eyes were shining and she looked in a way triumphant as she gazed at my melancholy appearance.

"Poor Susan," she said. "I am sorry it has ended in this way."

"What has ended, Henrietta?"

"Kelvin and marriage and all that you had planned."

"But, Henrietta," I said earnestly, "this cannot end what has passed between Kelvin and me. As long as I live I will never give him up."

"Never can be a long time, Susan."

I turned away from her. I could not bear the sight of her smiling, scornful face.

"Mamma has made you my jailor I see. I wonder why she did that?"

"Your jailor. Those are hard words, Susan. I am here to comfort and console you, and to attend to anything you might need. Mamma said she could not trust Mrs. Trouncer and that is why she has given me the key."

I laughed bitterly.

"You comfort me," I replied. "Such felicitation is magnificent. If I am not your prisoner, what else would you call me, Henrietta?"

"Mamma is perturbed and upset, Susan. I think it would be much better if you did not go so much against her. You know her change of mood and how her memory will trick her. Humour her, my dear sister, play with her vagueness, pretend to agree to her wishes."

She lurked and lingered in my attic for a while, surveying

258

my small possessions with a curl of her lips, and gazing contentedly at her own lovely reflection in the mirror.

"I will help you," she said, "if there is need of my help. I will see Kelvin for you and tell him of your plight. Would you like me to give him your love, Susan, and beg him to be patient, or shall I go to Mamma and ask her to set you free?"

My heart was full at her seeming tenderness. I clung to her hand and she, with tears in her eyes, embraced me warmly. Had she not been so excellent an actress I might have seen through this mood of hers. But I saw nothing, God help me, but my own despair and the narrow glimpse of Heaven that she held out to me.

"I did not expect you to be like this, Henrietta," I said gratefully.

"How then did you think I would be?"

"I fancied you would agree with Mamma, that perhaps you were jealous of Kelvin and his love for me."

For a moment her face darkened into a heavy frown, and then she smiled and shrugged and pointed to the tray.

"Now will you take some nourishment," she said, "and rest whilst I am gone."

"You will tell Kelvin that I love him more than life and that I will never, never give him up?"

"Yes, Susan, I will tell him."

"God bless you, Henrietta."

"And God be with you," replied Henrietta. "I wish you joy," and, with a great show of seeing that the door was properly fastened, she was gone.

A week went by and I could scarcely believe I had been imprisoned in my room for so long, although the time had hung like a dead weight on my mind. I saw nothing of Henrietta or Mrs. Trouncer, and my meals were brought to me by one of the unsightly chambermaids who thrust the tray onto my table without a word. The weather outside was grey, and now and again rain slashed against my windows. A faint breeze rose into gusts of fretful wind and I could see the tops of trees bending and hear the faint rustle of the leaves.

Then one evening there was a footstep along the passage, the key turned softly in the lock, the door creaked open and there stood Mrs. Trouncer. She came in with her finger on her lip and stared at me solemnly.

"I appropriated her Ladyship's key whilst she was asleep," she said, "because it is of the utmost importance I should speak to you. Gracious, child, why do you sit here in this miserable manner?"

"What else is there for me to do, Mrs. Trouncer? I have time on my hands to mope."

"You have time on your hands to do some thinking. Have you been thinking, Miss Susan, have you?"

"Of what?"

"Of your position and all that it entails. Of your love and what you are going to do about it. How much do you love this Mr. Abigail?"

"He is my life, Mrs. Trouncer."

"Then, if he is your life, why do you sit here dying?"

"What means of escape have I, answer me that?"

"Where there's a will there's a way, Miss Susan. Do you love him enough to forsake your own family and be with him for the rest of your days? That's a solemn question, my dear, we most of us have to face at one time or another. I remember before I was united asking myself, could I be loving and amiable and faithful and obedient to Mr. Trouncer, and would I perform and keep my vow and covenant?"

"I could do all these things for Kelvin Abigail."

"Could you indeed, Miss Susan? Then I'm mighty glad to hear it, for you may be called upon sooner than you think, and yet, not too soon I trust; there's no fault more fatal, in my opinion, than being in a hurry. Are you afraid of marriage?"

"I was, but not any longer. I am not afraid of anything now."

"'Mystical union,' it says in the prayer book, though where the mystification comes in is more than I can see, for, of all the down-to-earth pastimes, matrimony has it. It's a mortal sin to deny yourself human enjoyment, Miss Susan, providing of course that it is a sense of pleasure. There are them who are not agreeable to snug cuddling and kissing, and who turn and writhe at the thought of plighted love. But you couldn't be of those, Miss Susan, not with his Lordship's blood in your veins, now could you?"

"I think you forget Mamma, Mrs. Trouncer, and her estrangement. There never was much rapture about her love for Papa."

"Unsuited . . . that's what they were. Morally and physically unsuited. I can't say that I got on particularly well with Mr. Trouncer, but he kept me warm in the winter and he stood for security, bad investment though he was. I remember when the parson asked me if there was any known impediment why Mr. Trouncer and I should not be joined together in holy matrimony, I felt inclined to reply, 'There's no just cause against it, your Reverence, but there's a powerful impediment in Mr. Trouncer being a habitual toper.'"

"Nevertheless, you married him?"

"For better and for worse, and worse it turned out to be. There was nothing to thank Mr. Trouncer for, and he had no graces or benefits to bestow upon me. There was too much Lord and Master about him, Miss Susan, for, so to speak, he let the marriage service get away with him and really behaved as if I were his goods and chattels."

"Mrs. Trouncer, why did you ask me how much I loved Mr. Abigail and if I was afraid of marriage?"

"I am very much put out," replied Mrs. Trouncer, "very much put out indeed. There's things going on in this house I don't like the sound or the look of."

"What sort of things?"

"I don't rightly know, Miss Susan, and I can't rightly put my finger on the spot. All I can feel is that Miss Henrietta is at the back of it, of that I am sure."

"Oh, but you are wrong, Mrs. Trouncer," I cried eagerly. "Henrietta has had a change of heart. She has offered to help me, to go and see Kelvin herself and to beg Mamma to set me free. She is as concerned as I am and . . ."

"Is she," replied Mrs. Trouncer bitterly, "is she indeed? Then I suppose it was concern that made her go to Springfield Town and find Mr. Bemrose. I suppose it was her love for you that made her force Mr. Bemrose to inform her Ladyship of your visits to Wingmeadow Lodge. I suppose it was her sisterly devotion that got you locked up here whilst she fawns and dotes upon Mr. Abigail like a love-sick calf."

I covered my ears. I could not bear to listen to her, but Mrs. Trouncer seized my arms and shook me to and fro.

"I heard them," she said, "I heard Miss Henrietta talking to her Ladyship, numb-headed dizzards that we are."

"Are you asking me to believe that my own sister did this to me, that she deliberately set this trap for me, that all the time she has been petting and soothing me she has known in her heart that it is only because of her that I am here?"

"Her heart, Miss Susan? She has no heart. Think how she must have hugged herself as she looked soft-eyed at you, when all the time she had not for one moment's space turned from her dread purpose. With what skill she played you into this trap, how easily she cheated you. How carefully she spread the toils to have you put away."

I stood quivering beneath her words, my blood running cold.

"She said she was going to Wingmeadow Lodge to give Kelvin my dearest love," I said helplessly. "She said she was going to tell him I would never, never give him up."

"Fiddlesticks," replied Mrs. Trouncer grimly. "She has gone no farther than her Ladyship's room, and there they are together at this very moment, planning and plotting, with her filling that Lady's poor demented mind with things you'd be ashamed to listen to. 'Susan is still unrepentant,' she says, 'and will, when set free, no doubt kiss and cuddle in the open roadway. It is the pastime of chambermaids and grooms,' she says, 'and should at all costs be put a stop to. You must send Susan away, Mamma, you must send her a thousand miles from here, where Kelvin will never find her,' and her Ladyship, poor soul, giggles and cackles as if it were the funniest thing she had ever heard, and keeps crying, 'Yes, yes, we will do that, Henrietta, will we not? Fetch me an atlas and let us see where we can send her.' If you are to save your happiness, Miss Susan, you must do something widespread, something extreme. How far would you be prepared to go to attain your heart's desire?"

"I would do anything . . . anything, Mrs. Trouncer. I would even give my life."

Mrs. Trouncer drew out her handkerchief and dabbed at her eyes. She muttered and mopped and snivelled until her nose was as red as a berry.

"That settles it then," she said firmly. "You have made up my mind at last. Miss Susan, would you go so far as to elope?"

"Elope!"

"Don't say it as if I had asked you to cut your own throat, child. What's wrong, may I ask, in running away with the man of your heart? Mr. Abigail *is* the man of your heart, I presume, and your priceless blessing. Well then, go off with him and be done with it. Scamper . . . skedaddle, take to your heels and run."

"But where could I run to, where could I go?"

"God bless my soul, child, there's the whole world ahead of you and yet you ask me where you can go. To Mr. Abigail, of course. You want the man, don't you, though why, in pity's sake, any sensible woman wants to get wed is more than I can fathom unless as a remedy against sin. Take the law into your own hands, Miss Susan, and bind yourself in holy wedlock and then even the devil himself cannot harm you, not even Miss Henrietta."

"But, Mrs. Trouncer, suppose Mr. Abigail does not want to elope?"

"Suppose fiddlesticks, Miss Susan. He's a man and you're a wench, and as pretty a wench, if I may say so, as he's ever likely to bring to bed. Do you think Mr. Trouncer came to me to be wedded? Not he. I just sat myself down on his knee and I said to him, 'You marry me now, you little whipper-snapper, or I'll break your neck with a broom.'"

For a moment I stood and a sudden great joy swept over me, an overwhelming happiness.

"Mrs. Trouncer," I said, whirling her round in my arms, "you are a wonder. You are the nicest, dearest person in all the world. Please tell Mr. Kelvin Abigail with my compliments that to-morrow he wins him a wife. Tell him to meet me at the Squirrel Inn and to have a carriage ready for us to elope in."

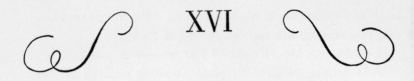

XVI

THAT NIGHT CAME a storm unlike any I had ever known. The wind started whistling and howling, and large clouds were driven savagely across the sky. My little attic roared and rumbled, the door shook, tearing wildly at its fastenings; the carpet belched up at the corners, revealing grey heaps of hidden dust.

At first I was relieved by this strong unfathomable storm with its relentless tumult of sound. Its mighty turbulence fitted into my mood as I tossed from one side of the bed to the other. Its circling energy and the ferment of this squall seemed to race with the thoughts that sped at random through my mind.

Tomorrow was to be my wedding day. No church bells and sweet white robes for me; only a runaway chaise to a distant town, a few spoken words, and I would be Kelvin Abigail's wife.

Everything would be prepared and I was to be at the Squirrel Inn at dawn. It was about a mile and a half from White Orchard Manor, but there was a short cut to it through the forest. From there we would take a carriage through Springfield Town as far as Windsor, and then by coach to London where we would be wed.

Kelvin, it appeared, had been so enraged by what Mrs. Trouncer had told him of my imprisonment that at first he could do nothing but curse and swear with such oaths as were almost unbelievable. He was in so violent a fury that Mrs. Trouncer was afraid that he might choke. "Then he calmed down," she said, "and spoke only of his love for you, Miss Susan, declaring that you were his life and the darling of his heart."

"He said that, Mrs. Trouncer? You are sure he said that?"

"And nothing else," she replied, "nothing else but of you. His love for you raised him to an extravagance of speech that brought tears to my eyes. Of course I didn't understand most of what he was saying, quoting poetry and that, but it was wonderful and highfaluting and made me feel most peculiar."

Needless to say, I did not sleep many hours that night. Long before dawn I was ready, dressed and waiting. Mrs. Trouncer, in a gaudy bedgown and her hair in innumerable paper curlers, let me out of my prison room, and, embracing me, warmly poured blessings on my head.

The storm had not abated, and the trees were bending and swaying beneath its force like faithful vassals bowing before their lord. As I crept through the front door a capful of wind well-nigh tore the cloak from my shoulders. The leaves romped and went headlong down the pathway, a blustering fuss of red and gold, fluttering this way and that in maddened disorder. An extravagant forcible gale, desperate and tameless, lashed at the branches, breaking the smaller ones from their bodies and scattering them into my face.

It was exciting and unappeasable, riding with a high hand before me and along the countryside, and with my head bent I went as swiftly as I could out into the road.

The morning had brought no freshness to my mind, and I was glad of the rain to cool my fevered brow. Grey sky without a glimmer of a break in it stretched to the horizon. It seemed to me to be grey to the very edge of the world. There was mud in the road and along the sides of the slippery ditches as I wound my way through the lane and crossed into the forest. Here was a vast green world all of its own. The small paths, making patterns through it and threading in and out, seemed to lead nowhere except back into the forest again. The moss was like an emerald sponge spurting out water as I trod upon it; and my button boots sank deeper and deeper into the pathway. All I could hear was the roar of the wind and the drip, drip from the trees; all I could see was the soaked ferns, and between the rain-sodden branches these grey skies. All I could think of was that this murky storm had no real right to continue into my wedding day. There should have been a blue covering over my world and the sun glistening and fine weather for the joy that was in my heart.

I cut a sorry figure with the mud edging my petticoats and my little straw bonnet hanging damply to one side. I kept stumbling and tripping over my long skirt, and with the brown case flapping against my legs it was difficult to run. I felt foolish with my scarlet cheeks and panting breath and streaks of dark hair blowing across my mouth. How captivating a bride-to-be. . . . What a dear seductive creature to wind round the heart of a man, I thought to myself as I wallowed on my way.

There were children shouting together, and even in that early hour they chased one another in a glimmer of rain, their heads lowered against the wind as they battled with the storm. But they were laughing and light of limb as they raced through the soaking fields, and I called out to them, "What are you doing there?" but the gale scattered my voice so that it tore past them unheeded, and soon they were out of sight.

The Squirrel Inn was not a lovely inn, for it pressed too hard against the roadside and had only a small garden to it so that whoever went by could be seen from the inside. Neither was it a busy inn; at least not at that time in the morning. The empty road zig-zagged from it to the little village and on towards the high-standing hill to disappear over the top.

Outside the inn there was a small stable where Incubus worked, with just enough room for one horse and chaise. I could hear a noise coming from there as if the runt was already astir.

There was no sign of either Mr. or Mrs. Cattlewig so I lifted the latch and went quietly into the parlour from which led a taproom reeking strongly of stale beer.

As I sat and waited in a corner of the parlour the memory of my home was like a coloured canvas from which only the laughter and the tears stood out in vivid colouring. At this moment it seemed unreal somehow, as if I had only belonged to it many years ago. The garden with its perfume of mown grass, the chains of clematis and roses; Papa swilling from his favourite decanter or playing the little melodies we loved so well. I could hear a voice calling in the cows. I could see Mamma embroidering, her severe face bent over her work; and Henrietta running along the brick paths to the hut, with her red hair gleaming in the sun. Then there seemed to be open spaces in my dreams which I could not fill, spaces that were wide and silent and unshadowed by the footsteps of events, void of emotion, void of thought, in which my body moved through the years taking no account of how they had been passed.

Very soon Mr. Cattlewig came in. He was small and red-faced as if he had been out in all kinds of weather and had warmed himself therefrom with many a tankard of grog. They said of him that he was a man of shrewd perspicacity, a needle-witted man who was a match for anyone. There was a wart on his nose the size of a small egg, and a little tuft of hair grew at the end of his chin. He looked me up and down and then said slowly, "So this is the young lady I was to expect?" as if he had hoped for something infinitely better.

He told me that Mr. Abigail had ordered him to wait until the sun had properly risen, but as there was to be no sun that day he did not know what time that would be.

"I haven't any books you can read," he said, "but you can watch the trees blowing and the leaves flying to help pass the time. Time is a funny thing when you're waiting for it, Miss Susan. It's a lagging, dawdling sloth which never seems to go by."

With this profound statement he started to clear and clean the taproom, emptying the mugs into the sink and sweeping the ashes from the floor. When he came to the spittoons he held them well away from him, mumbling and grumbling at the filth of some of his patrons. Then he returned to the parlour and said suddenly:

"Are you fond of horses?"

I replied that I had not had much experience of them, upon which he shook his head and said that was a pity.

"If you go round to the stables you will find Incubus," he informed me, "and when you have found Incubus you will be sure to find Josephine as well. It is worth your while just casting your eyes upon her, Miss Darlington, I can assure you, for she is a creature who's a character."

I rose obediently, and smoothing my damp hair and rearranging my hat I retired to the stables.

There was an agreeable smell of hay about the place, and the runt was busy cleaning out the stall which was so dark as to prevent me from seeing much of the mare that was standing there. Incubus grinned all over his face when he saw me and seemed not in the least surprised at my presence at such an early hour. He stood beside me with his hand on the rake and peered into the shadowed stall.

"I'm glad you've come to see Josephine," he said, "for she likes to be taken notice of. There's nothing she doesn't know, Miss Susan. It's an entertainment taking care of her, I can assure you. She's as cunning a creature as ever I've seen and not bad looking when you come to think of her age. It's this weather that gets her," he continued, scratching his head thoughtfully, his brow puckered up with worry. "A wet day with a wind like this and she wants to stay home same as we do, and in consequence she kind of goes gloomy on me. You've no idea of the crabbiness of a horse, Miss Susan, when they've got to do something they don't want to. Josephine's got a nasty disposition when she's thwarted and has got to be humoured. If she doesn't come out of her stables kindhearted, I can't get her between the shafts. On a wet windy day such as this she wants coaxing and wheedling to take her mind off the storm as it were. She doesn't rightly care for a breeze; it makes her eyes run at the corners and tangles her mane."

He took the old mare from the stall, leading her gingerly as if she was some sacred emblem. Josephine's hide was dull and mangy looking, and she turned her eyes upon Incubus with sleepy venom for having roused her at this early hour.

"The Lord help us, Miss Susan," said the runt anxiously, "if Josephine is in one of her moods. If she doesn't feel like working she just won't work and that's all there is to it. There's nothing you can do about it if she's made up her mind she won't operate. But, believe me, it's a beautiful sight to see her when she likes the job and the weather's just right for her, with her tail streaming out and her neck arched and a kind of proud way of going that does the heart good. Weddings and funerals are her specialty, so this morning she should be at her best."

If the look of her now was her best, I did not think much of it. As he took the old mare towards the pump, she gave it such a virulent look that he led her back into the yard again.

"She doesn't like the noise of the water belching up," he explained in a whisper. "She's got sensitive ears, she has, and no belief in washing unless she's obliged to, that shows how human she is. When Josephine's set on an idea, Miss Susan, she's not easily nipped. There's no getting away from the fact, she's a creature as knows her own mind, and washing is one of the things she minds most."

"She looks a little sad," I ventured to remark, "do you not think so, Incubus?"

"I was thinking the same, Miss Susan," he replied, "but it's no fault of anyone's but her own. She has no right to have dejection, no right whatsoever to have disgust of life. She's got a good homely stable and she's only had out on an occasion, but she's the best mare in all the district for pulling a long face."

I returned to the parlour to see if Mrs. Cattlewig was awake and there I found the landlord brewing some tea in the kitchen and cutting up slices of bread. Mr. Cattlegwig had trouble because Mrs. Cattlewig was well-nigh bedridden and suffered from varicose veins. As Mr. Cattlewig explained, her veins were of a degenerate nature. They were stretched and dilated out of all proportion, and, although he had refused many months ago

272

to permit her to wear garters and insisted upon her remaining with her feet in an elevated position whenever she sat down, the disease had persisted until her valves had become of no use to her. Yet, in spite of her affliction, Mrs. Cattlewig was of a cheerful disposition, whereas it was Mr. Cattlewig who had the feeling of weight and aching limbs because, as he said, there were too many hours of standing at the bar. He would have welcomed Incubus to help serve if the taproom were full, but the runt was of too low a stature for the customers to know he was there. So Incubus waited upon Mrs. Cattlewig most of the day and played his guitar when she wished to be lulled to sleep.

All the time that Mr. Cattlewig was expatiating upon his good wife I was listening for the sound of Kelvin's footstep or the gallop of a horse. Something had happened. I began to be filled with trepidation and doubt. Perhaps Mamma had discovered my escape? Perhaps Henrietta had once more interfered. Kelvin, I knew, would have been here upon the appointed hour unless something dreadful had occurred.

It was now full daylight and, although the rain had stopped, the gale had, if anything, increased.

The village was astir and Mrs. Cattlewig could be heard calling out for her cup of tea. Mr. Cattlewig bustled about in the kitchen mumbling to himself about the impatience and intolerance of women, and how early visitors, such as I was, upset the whole kettle of fish.

I went outside with my case in my hand to see if there was any sign of Kelvin.

The runt had now harnessed Josephine, who stood with her head on one side and a martyred expression in her eyes. Incubus was brushing the inside of the chaise and hissing between his

273

teeth, but as soon as he saw me he pointed to the mare, shook his head, then shrugged his shoulders as much as to say, "She's not too bad and she's not too good, if you know what I mean."

The wind was still scouring over the yard, and bits of dirt and hay went whirling into the road. Mr. Mortician, the owner of the chaise, had by now emerged and was watching Incubus with his thumbs in his waistcoat and a straw between his lips.

Mr. Mortician was a middle-aged man who never had much to say. He liked his grog now and again and it was only under the influence of this stimulating beverage that he became noisy and loquacious. There was no real reason why Mr. Mortician should smell of saddles and damp hay, since the runt did most of the work; but the fact remained that Mr. Mortician did have the odour of the stables about him, as if he spent the whole of his life surrounded by leather and dung like any ordinary hostler or groom.

He looked at the mare, and the mare gazed back at him with extreme animosity; then she curled her lips, as if the bit in her mouth tasted acid from the polish on it, and whisked her tail so that it spread across the shaft of the chaise where it remained as though she had not the energy to navigate it down again.

I was now in a panic of anxiety and fear. People who were passing had recognized me, and one or two of them had said, "Good morning, Miss Darlington," as if it was the most natural thing in the world for a dishevelled young lady to be unattended at the Squirrel Inn in the early hours of the morning. Mr. Cattle-wig came out onto his doorstep with a slice of bread in his hand and a rasher of bacon across it, munching and chewing with complete disregard of the fact that I had had nothing to eat at all.

"The young gentleman is late," he said with a wink. "We are wondering if he can be coming. There's many a man been known to absquatulate at the last moment, and there is such a thing as being eluded and left."

But, before I could answer him, there was the sound of a galloping horse. Kelvin at last! With a rush of joy to my heart I turned to welcome him. Then that same heart missed a beat and seemed to stop altogether, for as the horse turned the corner I saw that its rider was not Kelvin, but Henrietta.

I wrenched open the door of the chaise and closed myself into it. Had she seen me? I hardly dared take breath as I watched through the small back window to see what occurred.

With a clatter of hoofs Henrietta drew up her horse upon its haunches; her cheeks were flushed and her red hair was wild about her face. Mud had splashed all over her clothes, and her horse was restive with distended nostrils as if she had ridden in haste.

"Where is Miss Susan?" she called out, her voice as sharp as steel. "You mooncalf," indicating the runt with her whip, "tell Miss Susan I wish to see her at once."

Incubus pulled his forelock; he was obsequiously polite.

"Miss Susan is not here, Miss Darlington," he said, "and moreover I have not seen her. I doubt very much if she would come here in this early hour of the morning."

Mr. Mortician removed the straw from his teeth and was about to contradict the runt, for he was righteously indignant at such falsehood being told to a lovely young lady like Miss Henrietta. But Incubus started to bother with Josephine and to make out that she was restive.

"Whoa there!" he said loudly. "What are you fretting and

fuming over just because a horse has come into the yard? She doesn't like strangers, Miss Henrietta," he continued with a twinkle in his kind eyes, "specially horses. She's a confirmed bachelor, is Josephine, and believes in single blessedness."

Henrietta turned her horse round sharply, splattering the mud all over the chaise that Incubus had so carefully cleaned. With her whip lashing her horse's flanks she dashed into the open road again, calling back to the runt that she would look for me in Springfield Town. When she was well out of sight I emerged and stood silently before the two men, my legs trembling and my face as white as a sheet.

"Well," said Mr. Mortician, "if that doesn't beat the yoke from an egg. Why all this flim-flam and misstatement, Miss Susan? Why this trickery and clap-trap? I tell you I do not like it; it goes against my better nature and turns my stomach sour to hear Incubus lie like a conjuror. Never have I seen such goings on as this at the Squirrel Inn."

It seemed only a few moments after the sound of Henrietta's horse had faded into the storm that we heard a noise as if a whole regiment was about to descend upon us; and there, along the road where Henrietta had but lately ridden, with their backs low over their saddles to escape from the wind, came Kelvin and his six brothers.

As soon as they reached us they drew up their horses, and Kelvin leapt from the saddle. His face was drawn and he looked just as he had appeared when I first saw him in the coach and Henrietta had stepped out and stood in his way.

Without so much as a word he seized my hand and dragged me into the chaise.

"Drive," he shouted to Mr. Mortician, "drive like the devil

to Windsor. There is a bag of crowns for you if you get us there in time."

Mr. Mortician nearly swallowed his straw as he scrambled onto the seat of the chaise and Incubus swung himself up beside him. With a crack of his whip and a "Get along there, Josephine, and show them what you can do . . . none of your spleen, mind you, or I'll swop the hide off you," we tore out of the yard with the six Abigails galloping behind us.

"Henrietta knows," I gasped, "she knows about us?"

"She knows everything, God's curse on her," replied Kelvin furiously. "She is like a creature demented. She swears that this marriage cannot possibly take place; that, whatever the cost, this elopement must be stopped. There is a reason, so she says, why you and I can never be man and wife. That is the message Mrs. Trouncer brought to me just as I was mounting my horse. 'You cannot be wed,' she said, 'and Miss Henrietta alone knows the reason!' "

"But we will wed, Kelvin? We will, we will."

"Yes, my beloved, we will."

There was slush and mud everywhere, and as Josephine plodded through it her hoofs squelched and slopped and the wind tore through her mane. I remembered what Incubus had said about her mane and the wind, and I wondered how long she would go on with it. We could hear the Abigail brothers coming along behind us, but the wheels of the chaise were throwing up so much dirt upon the windows, and they were so spattered and smudged with mud that we could hardly see out. The gale was at the height of its fury, and the wind came whistling in at every chink and hole in the chaise. As I clung to Kelvin, some of the lower branches of the trees struck against

277

our carriage, and the leaves raced past us as if on wings. Both Mr. Mortician and the runt were clutching their hats, and it was all they could do to remain in their seats. As for Josephine, her ears were laid back and her head jerked up and down until the foam flew out of her mouth.

As we swung round the corner of the lane into the open road, there was a loud shout behind us and Kelvin and I lowered the window to lean out and see what was amiss.

There, just ahead of us, an immense tree was beginning to fall and I heard Kelvin say, "My God, it will kill us!"

It was a tall ragged oak tree which should have been felled months ago, for it had been struck by lightning on one side, and the other had been ravaged and torn by many a gale such as this.

The runt stood up and roared at Josephine, striking her buttocks with his hat, and Mr. Mortician fell upon her cruelly with reins and whip. Josephine, outraged and indignant, leapt forward straining with all her might, and the six Abigails scattered to either side of us.

The tree first toppled, and then with a cracking and tearing of branches it uprooted and crashed heavily across the road.

It must have missed us by the breadth of a hair because we could feel the chaise quiver as the tall trunk struck the ground. Mr. Mortician pulled Josephine to a standstill and mopped his brow.

"By the mercy of God," he said solemnly, "that's all there is to it. Just by the mercy of God."

Kelvin helped me from the chaise and we stood in a little group, our scared faces looking like blank sheets of paper. We did not speak, we did not feel there was anything we could say, for the fall of the tree was a mighty turning point to all our plans.

"Who would have thought it?" said the runt at last.

"Who would have thought what, Incubus?" asked Kelvin, and the hand that held mine was trembling.

"That a thing like this could happen, Mr. Abigail, just here on this very spot and at this very moment. Why it's almost as if . . ."

"As if what?"

"As if Providence had sent us a warning, Miss Susan, as if somebody was trying to tell us not to go on."

"Oh, stuff and nonsense, fiddlesticks and fads," cried Mr. Mortician. "I don't believe in superstitions and omens and suchlike. I only believe in God and His will. In a forest like this any tree is liable to fall when a storm strikes the belly of it. The fact that it missed us is what is important, and there's nothing queer about the Lord having a hand in our welfare, now is there?"

"I don't rightly know," replied Incubus, "but if there was, Josephine would be the first to take notice. Horses are subject to spooks and apparitions, and she'd be in a sweat. But, you can see for yourselves there's nothing wrong with Josephine, she's not fretting nor fidgeting, nor in any kind of a tantrum. Nevertheless, my opinion is that it's queer about that tree, and it seems to me as if it had been blown down for a purpose, whatever anyone else may say."

It is an unaccountable fact that during long periods of one's life nothing of any particular importance will take place; and then, of a sudden, in a few hours, or a few moments only, an event of such immensity will break upon you that your life is

279

brought to a standstill and must wait, outraged and convulsed, to resume its normal progress.

It may so happen that one's whole existence is broken forcibly apart, and there is nothing left of it but violent disorder.

And so it was with us that morning. The fall of the tree in itself was fearful enough, but there was something more terrifying to come. Something which petrified our souls and stopped our breath and made our blood run cold.

For, suddenly, round the same corner, at a devil's pace with her red hair flying and her whip lashing at her horse, came Henrietta.

We had no time to call out, we could not even move to prevent it. Before we even had time to think . . . it was over.

Henrietta, seeing the tree lying across her path, dragged the reins to try and avoid it. The horse, maddened by fear and the cruel whipping she had inflicted upon it during her ride, crashed headlong into the immense branches. It plunged and reared and slid onto its haunches, and then came down upon the tree with wildly kicking hoofs.

Henrietta was flung from the saddle into the very roots of the giant stem.

It was Kelvin who picked her up from the mud and torn leaves and broken twigs. There was blood all over her lovely face and running from the ends of her hair. The whole roadway was a network of hoof marks and crusts of dirt where the chaise had slithered and drawn up.

Henrietta's horse now stood quietly by with drooping head and sweating flanks, the reins hanging down to the ground. Once or twice it stirred up some earth and snuffed at it as if on the search for a fresh bit of grass. There was a gash on its chest and one of its legs had been badly torn. But this was nothing compared to Henrietta.

Kelvin carried her to the chaise. She was still breathing and we did not know how badly she was hurt. We sat with her across Kelvin's knees and her head on my lap, and I endeavoured to wipe the blood and dirt from her face, and to smooth the red-gold hair from her brow.

We drove to Wingmeadow Lodge whilst Phillip and Silvain galloped ahead to fetch Doctor Wiffin. Gently we carried her upstairs to that same room in which Papa had drawn his last breath, and carefully we laid her on the same bed with its four dark and heavily carved posts.

Henrietta had now recovered consciousness. First of all she gazed fixedly and steadily at me as I stood upon one side of the bed, and then at Kelvin who was on the other side. She turned her head slowly from one to the other; then her lips quivered and parted in the scornful smile which I will always remember so well, and into her large dark eyes there came a look of triumphant exultation.

"I was trying to stop your wedding," she said clearly. "You see, Susan, I was going to have a baby. . . Kelvin Abigail's baby."

And then with a little fluttering smile she was dead.

Kelvin and I stood for a moment, too horror-stricken to move, and then as he tried to come towards me I drew back shuddering from his touch and ran from the room. I ran down the stairs and out of the house, passing Mrs. Abigail who endeavoured to stop me, and along the lane to White Orchard Manor. Up the cedarwood stairway I sped, and along the corridor to my room; and there I flung myself onto the bed and sobbed and sobbed as if my heart would break.

XVII

I was very ill for a while, seeming to have neither pain nor feeling at first, and then only waves of delusions and dreams. Days and nights passed in a state of semi-consciousness wherein I talked wildly and incoherently with my arms waving and my head rolling from side to side. Events became tumbled together; people I had seen, the choir, Incubus, Mr. Bemrose, Papa and Mamma, moved incessantly before my eyes.

I seemed to see Henrietta smoothing her pregnant body and repeating proudly over and over again, "Kelvin Abigail's child . . . Kelvin Abigail's child," and then Kelvin himself standing by her deathbed with a look on his face I could not wipe from my mind. I tried to cry out that it was a lie, but even as I assured myself that Kelvin had been true to me, a great doubt remained in my heart, a weird doubt that came and went, gnawing at my better judgment and arguing with my common sense. Kelvin, to be sure, had once been in love with Henrietta. Had he not told me so himself? Something about "being bewitched" and the "easy road to tread." But I had not believed it. I could not believe that a man like Kelvin could wed one sister as he wooed the other. It was a lie. Henrietta had died with a lie on her lips. There was no animosity more bitter, no revenge so deep as that of a frustrated woman. But, suppose it were true? What then? Kelvin was but human and Henrietta had had all the loveliness that God could provide.

Was it to be wondered at? How could it be condoned? All men were beasts hunting their prey; Henrietta had told me so, she had sunk that thought deep into my brain. It was Henrietta herself who had taught me through the years to see the shadows in Nature, the shadows in Life. Henrietta who had shown me the shadows in the hearts of men.

As the fever left me Mrs. Trouncer broke it to me that when Mamma was informed of her beloved daughter's death she gave one heart-rending scream and went into a coma from which she never recovered, and that Doctor Wiffin had said that only a few months might pass before that poor ravaged soul would be laid to rest. She had nothing to live for now that Henrietta was gone, and there was no more reason for her to combat the confusion in her brain. "She's just letting herself go," said Mrs. Trouncer, "and God knows, no one can blame her." And yet even then, when I thought of Mamma I could not weep for her, and the thought of her lying there left me almost unmoved.

The days went by and still I would not see Kelvin. I wanted to be alone with my mental anguish. I wanted to be given time to think. I wished to be given time to bring myself to pray for Henrietta's final sin.

How she must have hated me. With what unnatural cruelty she had struck at me with the last breath of her body. And now the full force of her revenge had fallen upon me, her last words twisting and writhing in my heart. Unrelenting and remorseless to the end, she had had no charity, no mercy. All she had left to me was this heritage of doubt.

I tried to persuade myself that it was natural that I should wonder, but, was it so natural to believe one word against the

283

man I loved? Had Henrietta still some hold over me? Had she still a cold possession of me, even from the grave?

I was not well enough to go to Henrietta's funeral, but Mrs. Trouncer told me of it, weeping loudly and copiously, not because she had ever had any heart for Henrietta, but because a funeral was a funeral and always left her prostrate with emotion.

"It was a sorrowful affair," she said, "a pitiable affair indeed, for it was likely to be an emptier funeral than his Lordship's. There were not many who would have gone out of their way to see Miss Henrietta, even when she was alive, for as we know, she had not many friends. There were one or two sight-seers who stood round and about the graveyard; the kind of people who go to all burials, Miss Susan. Greedy, gloating folks as have no feelings of their own to devour and so feed upon the thoughts of others. Amongst this host of shabby onlookers was Mr. Bemrose, who stood leaning against a wall. He looked repulsive and was unnatural in his manner, and it did not take me long, my dear, to realize he was drunk. He seemed to be muttering and mumbling like the devil, and he looked like Satan himself with his unshaven chin and dust all over his clothes. He stared wildly before him and kept passing his hand across his forehead as if bewildered. And then he shouted out:

" 'There was a heavy score to pay, Miss Susan. Remember?' And then a little later, 'God's justice will be served one way or another.'

"Those were his very words, Miss Susan, and then he kneeled down by the covered grave and placed one flower upon it. One deep-red rose which he said was the Darlington blood.

"Miss Henrietta was buried side by side with your Papa. The

runt hung unhappily amongst us, and the Misses Tinnerlies were there, standing close to the reverend with their hands clasped and the tears rolling down their faces. I think Miss Henrietta's death, and the manner of it, had shocked the townsfolk and the village, just the same as her life had done. But, grave or no grave, she will not rest, poor soul. Her spirit will wander through the world searching for forgiveness, for retraction of all the things she has ever said to you, Miss Susan. That's what she'll be asking for, to let bygones be bygones. Doomed to a hell upon earth is that poor soul, and a long weary journey through Eternity."

"Oh, Mrs. Trouncer, do not say such a thing. I forgive her, I really and truly forgive her and bear her no ill will."

"You may not, Miss Susan, but there are others that do. Mr. Abigail, for instance, has no real cause to weep for her."

"What do you know about Mr. Abigail, Mrs. Trouncer?"

"Nothing, Miss Susan. Nothing, except what people are saying."

"And what are people saying?"

"Only that Miss Henrietta had a crow to pluck, and left you with a wound she would keep green to the end."

"And you believe this?"

Mrs. Trouncer shrugged her shoulders.

"Maybe I do, and maybe I don't," she replied, "but since you've been ill you've done a mountain of talking, Miss Susan. I kept the door closed, nobody heard . . . nobody knows what I know. But one thing I'd like to remind you of, I'd like you to bear in mind. For what purpose are men and women brought into the world? Not only to eat and drink and sleep and wake again, but to love one another. You hear what I say, Miss

285

Susan? To love one another, and there's nothing more to it than that."

As soon as Doctor Wiffin permitted me to do so, I went to see Mamma. She lay as if in a deep sleep, with a flushed face and breathing heavily. It seemed strange to see her so utterly helpless and with such a complete loss of power. One side of her face was slightly affected, twisting and destroying the beauty of it.

A strange woman sat beside her who rose when we entered and stood rigidly close to her patient as if to defend her. This woman was a highly skilled nurse, so Doctor Wiffin told me, who had come all the way from London and whose name was Mrs. Large.

Mrs. Large was lean and middle-aged, and her pinched face emerged from behind immense spectacles. She seemed to be drawing herself up from an extraordinary quantity of white aprons and flounces, and there was a sniff on her face as if from a perpetual cold, or a prolonged gesture of contempt.

The good doctor presented me as the daughter of the house, and Mrs. Large curtseyed reluctantly, so unwillingly in fact, that I felt her knees might snap in two; and when I timidly asked her how she thought Mamma's health had improved, she replied:

"It never can and never will. It's just a question of sooner or later."

"Is there anything I can do, Mrs. Large?"

"Nothing that I cannot," replied the nurse with a twitch of her nose as much as to say, "Have you not done enough already?" and I realized that she probably held me responsible for Mamma's condition and condemned me as heartless and cruel.

"Her Ladyship is well taken care of," she continued. "She has what she should have, and what she doesn't have she doesn't know. That's how it is, Miss Darlington, and that's how it will be until she passes on."

She edged me towards the door whilst Doctor Wiffin inspected the bottles on the table beside the bed as if he had never seen them before and had not himself prescribed them. When we were both out of the room he apologised profusely for the nurse's ill manners.

"She suffers from acute aggravation," he said. "It is her nerves, Miss Susan. She is a good woman but a worrier."

"She does not seem to be much concerned about poor Mamma," I replied.

"No," said Doctor Wiffin sadly, "it is more about herself. She has nothing to hope for and it has soured her disposition. She has a damp on her spirits, Miss Susan, and she is sick at heart; but she is excellent at her work, and that, after all, is the reason of her presence here."

I felt it would have been far better to have hired a nurse less capable than Mrs. Large, and when I asked Mrs. Trouncer what she thought of the newcomer she replied:

"Nurse Large is an abomination, and the sooner she is out of here the better. She eats her meals as if there were maggots in them, and every vegetable she consumes has to be brought to her room and washed before her eyes. You'd think we lived in a pigsty, Miss Susan, by the way she carries on."

The following day I went to the churchyard to see Henrietta's grave, but I could not stay there long for the memories it brought me and the sadness of its setting.

The dew upon the grass was like a moist grey veil, and in the centre of the grave lay the withered rose that Mr. Bemrose had placed there. I thought to myself, how happy Papa must be to have his darling lying so close to him, and if he knew what had been her last act upon earth. I remembered what he had once said to me regarding sin.

"It is so easy to be wicked, Susan, for the devil himself will strew the path with honeyed words and passionate desire. To keep within the bounds of high esteem, to accept convention and bow down to God's good will, does not of necessity mean that you are nearer Heaven than I am. If you can confront sin and emerge from it in a good state, then indeed you are an angel beyond praise."

When I returned to the house I was told that Mr. Abigail was in the library. My heart stood still. I wanted to go to him and yet I would not. I went instead to my room and locked the door.

But Kelvin Abigail was not a man to be split upon a rock. Very soon I heard his footstep upon the stairs, then along the corridor, and finally there was a thunderous blow upon my door. I let him strike it, though each blow made me shiver and recoil. I had not made up my mind what I would say to him. What indeed could I say? And so, I would not let him in.

He thumped and clouted the woodwork, and then he started to push upon the lock.

"If you do not open up, Susan," he shouted, "I will break

down the door. I will beat and kick it down, even if it raises all hell in the doing."

Trembling in every limb I slipped back the bolt, and he came striding in with a face so dark and frowning I scarcely knew him. He went over to the window, then turned to look at me.

"So this is love," he said contemptuously. "A fine upright and honest pledge it has proved to be. Such fairness, Susan, such singleness of heart. I must congratulate you upon your scrupulous fidelity."

"Kelvin! . . . listen to me. I implore you to listen to what I have to say."

"Words, Susan. Of what use are they between us now? I have no faith. I shall not believe one single word you utter; for I find you are no longer to be depended upon. You have had time, Susan, to perfect your answers; you have doubtless already perfected the tone of your defence. I do not wish to hear your ingenious and high-principled excuses; your moral turpitude. Your shuffling perfidy has been enough. Love," he laughed bitterly, his dark eyes flashing his contempt of me. "Such an honourable deal. So incorruptible. God in Heaven, Susan, what kind of a woman are you?"

"I have been ill, Kelvin, I . . ."

"*You* have been ill? Do you think I am unscathed and hearty as a buck? Do you believe I have not suffered as well? It is not your body that is sick, it is your soul, my dear, it is your heart and your mind. You believe what Henrietta said is true . . . you actually believe this thing of me and that Henrietta's child was mine. I hoped for everything from you, Susan, but I asked too much. There was only one thing I could have sworn upon and that was your entire faith in me."

289

"But I have faith, Kelvin, I have indeed."

"Indeed," he repeated, with raised and incredulous eyebrows. "And I suppose you have love for me as well? You only thought you loved me, Susan, but I doubt if I have ever really touched your heart."

He went from the room as quickly as he had entered it and left me overcome with grief.

The following morning I sent a message to him by Mrs. Trouncer to meet me in the hut upon the hill. I implored him, even if it was for the last time, to hear what I had to say.

Mrs. Trouncer, grumbling and scolding, told me I had only brought this upon myself and was getting what she considered I so rightfully deserved.

"It's Miss Henrietta's word against his," she said, "and you are still so weighed upon and spellbound, you no longer know right from wrong or love from hate. Whatever I may have thought of Mr. Trouncer, and mark you that wasn't much, I believed what he said was God's truth and nothing else. If it's once in your head that a man's lying there's no more living with him. You've just got to believe him or go. There's no other way to it."

When I went into the hut Kelvin was already there, and at the sight of my tear-stained face and trembling lips he held out his arms to me. I ran to him, clinging to him as if I would never let him go.

"Oh, Kelvin, my dearest, dearest love, forgive me," I sobbed. "Nothing in this world matters but you. It was not that I believed this thing of you, not really, but I could not conceive Henrietta dying with this lie on her lips. How could she, Kelvin? How could she hope to rest in peace? How can she atone?"

"God help her, she will atone," replied Kelvin. And then we spoke of nothing but our love, and his kisses rained upon my face.

"No drawing back now, my beloved," he said. "No regrets. This is for ever, Susan."

"For ever, my dearest," I replied.

"The completeness of my love for you was so overwhelming," he whispered, "so terrifying, Susan, when I was alone and you and White Orchard Manor gone as I thought, for ever, I could not believe it. I remembered everything you had ever said to me, remembered it until every word was part of me. I searched my soul to ask myself why, why in God's name had I parted from you, when everything inside of me was crying out for you. The vision of you would not fade. I could see it in the daytime and at night, and in the clear solitary clouds on the horizon. I could see it in the eyes of a stranger and in the smile of a friend. Everything in my life reminded me of you."

We did not hear the door of the hut softly open, and Heaven alone knows how long Mr. Bemrose had been standing there before he spoke.

"As pretty a picture as ever I have seen," he sneered, "a sight to fill the eyes and glut the stomach. Pure love. A gentleman's love for a lady. A nauseating, vomiting passion that makes me want to disgorge."

Mr. Bemrose was drunk. He was befuddled and top-heavy, and there was upon his pale face a bibulous and sottish leer as he swayed upon his feet.

Kelvin placed me against the wall of the hut and went a little forward to meet him.

"Come," he said quietly, "had you not better go home?"

"And where, may I ask, might that be," replied Mr. Bemrose, "whose home can I go to? Since I was turned out into the street I have no home. Who wants me? . . . Do you want me, Miss Susan? I asked you once, remember?"

"Why did you come up here," said Kelvin, "and what do you want?"

"There is a little matter I wish to discuss," replied Mr. Bemrose, "a matter that has been conveniently overlooked. You see it was not one life that was destroyed, Mr. Abigail, but two. Do you not think there was something queer about Miss Henrietta's death, something that could be searched and pried and sifted until a reason was found for it, dark enough to be the truth?"

"Miss Henrietta's death was an accident, she . . ."

"An accident, you say, with all of you there and never a word of warning? What kind of an accident would you call that, Mr. Abigail? You, all of you, had eyes and ears in your heads, yet not one of you warned her, not one of you stood between her and the tree."

"Are you trying to insinuate. . ."

"I am not trying to insinuate anything, Mr. Abigail, I am merely making a statement. A man may make a statement, may he not, without interruption?"

Kelvin's face was flushed and I could see that he was controlling himself with the greatest effort.

"Come, Susan," he said, "let us be gone out of here. This man is insane and does not know what he is saying."

Mr. Bemrose laughed and swayed, his hands waving wildly before him.

"I am sane enough," he shouted, "but I admit I am not sober. Who would be if they had a conscience inside them? I am a mongrel outcast I know, but I still have a conscience. Now Miss Henrietta had none. She was no paragon, no saint was that young lady. She put the saddle on the wrong horse when she bribed me to wreak her revenge. She lied and cheated to settle her account. I know, Mr. Abigail, for I was her lover. She took me to her bosom in her rigorous revenge. Do you blame me for making the most of this mopsy for a few silver coins? Besides, her planning suited me. I had my own bone to pick. I had a little account to settle with Miss Susan. I am as dissolute and mean a man as she was wench. We were a bawdy pair, Miss Henrietta and I, as we played our last card, and by the look of things now, we lost the trick. Miss Henrietta was going to have a baby all right, but it was not your baby, Mr. Abigail . . . it was *mine*."

Kelvin stepped towards the madman. God knows if he meant to strike him, for his fists were tightly clenched. Mr. Bemrose must have thought he meant to, for he drew a knife from his pocket with a blade in it that sprung from the handle. At once he rushed at Kelvin who did no more than raise his arm in defence and step to one side.

Mr. Bemrose staggered. He tried to draw back, but instead he overbalanced and fell with a crash onto his back. It happened so quickly. It was all over in a flash of a moment, for, as Mr. Bemrose fell, the back of his head struck against the iron fireplace, and when Kelvin went over to raise him, he found that he was dead.

Quietly and in silence Kelvin took me home, and then he went back to Wingmeadow Lodge, saddled his horse and rode in to Springfield Town to report what had occurred to the police.

The police notified Mr. Snitcher, the local coroner, who promptly arranged for an inquest.

Nobody in the village seemed surprised at first to hear that Mr. Bemrose was dead. They took it for granted that a man who drank as much as he did might well have an accident. But after a while the gossips and the scandalmongers took a hand, and during those three days between the accident and the inquest tongues wagged and all manner of tales circulated throughout the town.

There are always people who prefer to believe the worst and very few who are willing to admit the best, and it was these who did most of the talking. Mr. Abigail had every reason to hate Mr. Bemrose, so they said, and there were rumours of a previous quarrel that had remained like an open sore between the two men. Why had they been at the hut together? they asked one another, and for what reason had they met there?

Kelvin had been quite honest in his confession to the police and admitted that I also had been with them, but he had taken care to avoid mentioning this fact to anyone else. Nevertheless the news leaked out, as such news will, for nothing ever could be kept secret in Springfield Town, and on the day before the inquest the words, "Miss Susan," were thrown in to add relish to the gossip-pot. They stirred this extra titbit and made much of it, delighted to find that it was the little lady of White Orchard Manor who might prove to be the root of the whole evil.

Even the Misses Tinnerlies were curious, like two small birds coming on some unusual worm to pick at. Of course the members of the choir did not seriously believe there was anything wrong, but, after all, they knew how hot-tempered dear Mr. Abigail was, and it did seem such an unhappy coincidence that there was nobody who knew anything about the affair excepting Miss Susan, to whom, after all, he was betrothed.

No wonder, then, that a large crowd was waiting outside the town hall on the morning of the inquest, for such a thing as this had seldom happened in Springfield. The doors of the building opened a quarter of an hour before the inquest was due to commence, and there was a heated and undignified scramble for the thirty-odd seats allotted to the public. Those present seemed to be of two minds about the case: a minority, including the Abigails and a few of the choir, who were in sympathy with me; and those whom I could feel were bitterly against me. Kelvin and I sat upon an improvised bench which consisted of a stretch of thin wood between two chairs. As we waited, the eyes of everyone in that room seemed turned upon us. Then there was a scraping of boots and a rustle of skirts as the Springfield Town coroner entered and the company rose to their feet.

Mr. Edward Snitcher, the coroner, was a crotchety, pompous little man who seemed always to be in a pottering hurry. He had, moreover, the most extraordinary habit of picking his ears with the end of his pen. Across the round paunch of his belly lay a heavy gold watch chain, and his eyes protruded and bulged from his face as if he were perpetually startled by the revelations of his witnesses. He was, by profession, a medical practitioner of quite exceptional ability, and our good Doctor Wiffin looked upon him with awe and admiration, calling upon him in cases when he, poor soul, was at his wit's end. An unprepossessing little man to hold such an important position in the town, he was nevertheless entirely relied upon by all who knew him as a man likely to give an honest verdict.

When everyone had been reseated Mr. Snitcher called upon the jury to take their places so that they could be sworn in. This was a somewhat lengthy and tedious ceremony during which the coroner seemed unable to conceal his indifference. He leaned his elbow on the table and surveyed us as if we were so many specimens in a museum, and once or twice yawned between intervals of picking his ears.

Most of the jury, seven men in all, I knew by sight, though only a few of them was I actually acquainted with. At the end of the line I suddenly noticed the red- and moon-faced man who had been at the fair and called himself the Lord of Hosts. His name was Mr. Hoberdine, and without the influence of liquor he had the heart-sinking expression of one who has nothing but withered hopes. To look at him now further depressed my spirits, for I could not believe any living thing could appear so mopish unless from a perpetual chop-fallen view of human existence.

Mr. Couchmarrow, on the other hand, was a blaze of geniality. He was the owner of the largest pharmacy in the town, and I could not help feeling that nothing but death would strike that rollicking grin from his face. He had a manner of rubbing his hands together and exuding such waggish merriment that he jarred upon the nerves of Mr. Hobberdine who disliked him intensely.

Mr. Locket Barr, the schoolmaster, was there with his long grey beard and his expression of a ruminating goat; and there was Mr. Salt, the local draper, and one or two others whose names I had heard but could not place. When they had all sworn themselves in, Mr. Snitcher then called upon the witnesses and questioned them closely.

First, the local police sergeant who, like so many policemen, recited his evidence as if he had learned it by heart, and rather unwillingly. He told briefly how Kelvin had reported the accident and then made arrangements for the body to be removed to the police mortuary.

Next to come forward was Doctor Wiffin, who told in somewhat technical language how he had examined the body. Mr. Snitcher asked him what he considered had been the cause of his death and Doctor Wiffin replied that it was undoubtedly from the one wound at the back of his head.

"Was there any sign of a blow on the face or any other part of the body?"

"No, sir," replied Doctor Wiffin emphatically, and then sat down.

Then came Kelvin, and I do not think I had ever seen him look more handsome. Mr. Snitcher asked him to relate to them what exactly had taken place in the hut, and very simply and clearly Kelvin told his story. When, unavoidably, he mentioned that I had been with him, I could feel the eyes of the scandal-mongers burning through me. I could feel them piercing me like gimlets, and their hostility enveloped the room.

Kelvin told how he and I had been estranged for a while and how we had arranged to meet at the hut in order to amend our differences.

"A lovers' quarrel, I presume," said Mr. Snitcher, with a flicker of amusement in his protruding eyes.

"Yes, Sir," replied Kelvin, "a lovers' quarrel." But he omitted to mention that the cause of the dissension had been on account of Henrietta's unborn child.

He described the sudden entrance of Mr. Bemrose and his unfortunate condition, and when he came to the drawing of

297

the knife a shiver of exultation went through the inquisitive crowd. So, there had been a fight after all, and it was evident now that there was more in this affair than met the eye!

In spite of further careful and crafty questioning on the part of Mr. Snitcher, Kelvin was not trapped into admitting that he had made any further move than to step out of the way of this infuriated man. He said that he had neither struck Mr. Bemrose, nor even threatened him that he would do so.

"Then why should he suddenly draw this knife?" enquired Mr. Snitcher.

Kelvin replied curtly that the gentleman in question had been swill-soaked and bosky with liquor.

This, as far as Mr. Snitcher was concerned, seemed a somewhat unsatisfactory explanation, and even the jury raised their eyebrows in censor so that when, at last, I rose to take Kelvin's place I could not help feeling that things were going badly for him.

Whereas, hitherto, I had been seated with my back to the "audience," I now found myself facing them and their appetite for unclean information. Some were looking sideways at one another, licking their lips and nudging each other in their obvious enjoyment, whilst others kept their eyes lowered and appeared genuinely uncomfortable at my discomfiture.

Mr. Snitcher asked me to tell my story, and then leaned back, busying himself with the exploitation of the pen within his ear.

I told him that everything had taken place just as Kelvin had described it, and I could distinctly hear a few titters from the "audience," who had made up their minds that it was only natural that I should, of course, defend my lover. Mr. Snitcher

298

said, with a twitch on his face that was half sneer, half smirk, that it was *my* evidence they now required and not Mr. Abigail's, and would I kindly explain the situation in my own words.

Quietly I told my story, but several times Mr. Snitcher was obliged to ask me to raise my voice, and there was one impudent cry of "Speak up," from the back of the room.

The whole time during my giving of evidence I was becoming increasingly conscious of the presence of those among the onlookers who were filled with hostility and violently bearing me malice. I could not help feeling that *they* were the jury and that Kelvin and I were in the prisoner's box before them. I began to stammer and hesitate for words and in a flutter of fear I revealed the fact that Kelvin had at one moment advanced upon Mr. Bemrose with clenched fists. There was a murmur of "ah's" and "oh's," and a great shuffling of triumphant feet as Mr. Snitcher whipped up my remark and laid firm hold of it. Here was something new, something that Mr. Abigail had said nothing about. Mr. Snitcher leaned forward and wagged his finger at me, questioning me and spinning my mind round like a top. Deeper and deeper I fell into the skilful trickery, the net that this designing coroner was throwing, and I could feel him drawing Kelvin into it with me, when quite suddenly there was a violent commotion outside the door and a storm of high-raised voices. The door was wrenched open and Mrs. Trouncer entered, dragging the runt by the hand. She came up to the bench and confronted Mr. Snitcher, with the runt standing humbly by her side.

"I claim your attention," she said, "and to be given the permission to speak."

"Who is this woman?" demanded Mr. Snitcher angrily. "Is there anyone here who is acquainted with her?"

"Her name is Mrs. Trouncer," I replied, "and she comes from my home. She has been with us as long as I can remember."

"And this?" pointing to the runt. "What, may I enquire, is this?"

"He is my friend and his name is Incubus."

"Mister or Master Incubus?" asked Mr. Snitcher, with a wink of his bulbous eye.

"It is neither," replied the runt, "but just plain Incubus, and very plain at that, Sir."

"If I might be so bold as to interrupt," said Mrs. Trouncer, "there is something I would like to say."

"You may proceed," replied Mr. Snitcher pompously, folding his arms and leaning back stiffly in his chair.

"Suppose," said Mrs. Trouncer, "there were things you considered you ought to know and things you believed you *could* know if you went about doing other things? What would you do?"

She gazed with indescribable ferocity at the faces before her. She rested her hands on her hips and looked them up and down, inspecting each one narrowly and with the utmost displeasure. As nobody seemed inclined to reply she continued.

"There is only one thing to do, and that is to listen and look. That's a reasonable deduction. Listen and look. In short, bend your eye to the keyhole and your ear to the door. This practice I have resorted to all my life and with the most remarkable results, I can assure you."

"Has this any bearing on the case, Mrs. . . ."

"Trouncer, Mrs. Trouncer, and if it please your Honour, it

has everything to do with everything. Life is a series of incidents, ladies and gentlemen, and fate and divine providence have their part to play, but you will agree that neither fate nor providence can listen and look as I can. There's an art in telling a story, and I'm praying to God I've got it. It's like opening a bag of tricks, you mustn't let anyone find out the contrivance of it. Keep them guessing, so to speak, and dangle the pith of the narrative in front of their noses. Spin a yarn like a web and then pop it out at them when they least expect it. It's a knack, ladies and gentlemen, and if you know a hawk from a handsaw it's an ingenuity only Satan himself gave to humans."

"We are not here to listen to an edifying discourse upon the science of living, Mrs. Trouncer," said the coroner, "and you would oblige us by keeping to the point. We have already been too long upon this case, and an enquiry such as this is not usually accompanied by such volubility. All we desire is a plain statement and a straight answer, if you will oblige."

"Sir," replied Mrs. Trouncer, "it is difficult to give a straight answer to a crooked question, however obliging one may be." And then she took out an immense handkerchief and started to weep.

"Come, come, Ma'am," said Mr. Snitcher impatiently, "kindly restrain your feelings. Tears will not help. Bless me, this is no time for compassion or grief."

"And I say it is," replied Mrs. Trouncer, "for if it had not been for the fact of my listening and looking, Mr. Abigail there might be now on his way to prison. Permit me, ladies and gentlemen, to present Incubus, the hinge, so to speak, of the door of this evidence. Incubus, tell your tale, have no fear and speak loudly so that all these carrion crows may hear you."

The runt stood before Mr. Snitcher, who stared at him with the most profound amazement.

"Can it be possible," he said, "that you know something of this case?"

"I know it all," replied the runt, "for I was there."

"You were where?"

"Close to the hut where this accident took place."

"Accident, my good fellow, are you sure of that?"

"Accident, Sir, and nothing else. As I was saying, close to the hut there is a large piece of wasteland where many of the village folk throw out their unwanted pots and pans and rags of clothing. It is a place I frequently visit in the hopes that there may be a shred of something handy for my welfare. On this particular day I went to the wasteland and stayed there for a while, kicking the rubble and lifting up various objects which I considered might be of use."

"Yes, yes, please continue. We are not interested in your life story, Mr. . . er . . . Incubus."

"I agree, Sir, but it so happens that the future of Mr. Abigail is concerned with it. I therefore take it, it is your duty to listen to my story, however tedious it may be. I stopped upon this piece of land to look about me, bone and rag picking, as you might say. There were bits of ironwork and rusty nails and one or two broken brooms and cracked earthenware half filled with rain. Children's socks with the heels out of them, and gentlemen's waistcoats stained with rum."

Mr. Snitcher clicked his tongue impatiently, his face was becoming red.

"Really, I cannot see what bearing this wardrobe has upon the case," he snapped.

"Wait until he comes to the point," replied Mrs. Trouncer, "and lets the pith out of the bag. Give him his tongue, Mr. Snitcher, Sir, if you please."

"One of the waistcoats had a button attached to it," continued the runt, not in the least perturbed, "an ornamental button of which I am particularly fond. I was about to snap it off with my teeth when I heard voices raised loudly in dispute."

"Voices from the hut?"

"Yes, your Honour, from the hut."

"Would you kindly tell us, as briefly as possible, what happened after that?"

"After chewing off the button and placing it in my pocket, I proceeded quietly to the hut. On account of my stature I could not be seen above the ferns. I looked through a large crack in the woodwork and I saw Miss Susan standing by the window with her face as white as a sheet. Mr. Bemrose and Mr. Abigail were facing one another. Mr. Bemrose was exceedingly drunk and was swaying from side to side; it was a wonder to me that he could even stand on his feet. I heard Mr. Abigail say to him, 'Had you not better go home?' and Mr. Bemrose retorted about having no home and nobody wanting him and that he had been turned out into the street. Then Mr. Abigail asked him what he wanted and why he had followed them to the hut, and Mr. Bemrose started abusing Miss Henrietta."

"In what way was he abusing her? Can you not repeat to us some of this conversation?"

Kelvin stood up.

"Is this necessary?" he enquired.

"If we can do without it, we will," replied Mr. Snitcher. "Please continue."

303

"Mr. Abigail took a lot from Mr. Bemrose, in my opinion he took more than enough. All he said was that Mr. Bemrose must be insane and did not know what he was speaking, but Mr. Bemrose shouted that he was sane enough but not sober. At the end of it all, Mr. Bemrose drew a knife from his pocket and fell upon Mr. Abigail, who did no more than raise his arm and step to one side. Mr. Bemrose staggered and fell with his head on the iron fireplace. I saw Mr. Abigail lift him up and it seemed to me he was dead."

There was silence for several moments, during which Mr. Snitcher scribbled notes on a piece of paper. Finally he put down his pen and looked steadily at the runt.

"If you knew all this, why have you waited so long to come forward? Surely you realized the importance of what you had witnessed?"

Mrs. Trouncer stood up, settling her bonnet and blowing her nose.

"It's like this, your Honour," she replied, "Incubus has a thing about the law."

"What sort of a thing?"

"It's 'noxious to him, Sir, that's what it is, and on account of him being as he is, he's kind of sensitive, if you know what I mean."

Mr. Snitcher nodded and then, looking down at his notes, proceeded to sum up the case. In this he was about as tedious and long-winded as a man could be, continually repeating himself as if he had suddenly become aware that he was the centre of attention and was making the most of it. Long before he had finished, the jury had begun to fidget and fume and cough behind their hands, and when he finally ordered them to retire to consider their verdict there was an unseemly and undignified scuttle of confusion. They were out of the room for so short a time that it seemed as if the foreman of the jury had re-entered it before the last one had actually made his exit.

After the foreman had returned a verdict of "Death by Misadventure," all eyes were directed upon Mr. Snitcher, who looked down modestly like a child who had suddenly been called upon to recite. Slowly he folded the papers he held and thrust them into a large leather case, and then he raised his head and smiled.

"Well, ladies and gentlemen," he said genially, "there seems nothing else we can do but adjourn, and may I be the first to congratulate you, Mr. Abigail, on this satisfactory conclusion."

When I went to bed that night I asked Mrs. Trouncer how she had discovered that Incubus had gone up to the hut.

"It seems that he talks in his sleep," she replied, "so I got permission from Mrs. Cattlewig to go up to the inn and listen. For three nights I waited outside his door, but never a word. So what did I do? I bought a bit of meat so tough that even a dog wouldn't touch it, and cooked him as heavy a roast as ever I've seen on a spit. That did it, Miss Susan. He spilled the whole story and a good deal else besides, but that's neither here nor there; I had got what I wanted."

"Mrs. Trouncer," I said happily, "you are an irreclaimable old sinner, but I love you nevertheless."

"Thank you, Miss Susan," she replied, and she went back to her room with the tears pouring down her face.

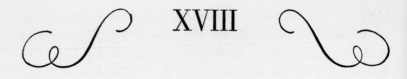

XVIII

I WAS SITTING on the window ledge, laughing and singing to myself; the same window ledge where I had wept so many years ago when my heart was breaking.

I had good reason to be happy, for gladness had come back to me, the world was full and I was no longer sick and faint with the fear of it.

Outside my window was a lovely morning. A summer morning, drowsily blue. Everything was silent but for the birds. The trees hung down branches heavy with green leaves, and there were wild flowers and foxgloves in the hedges. It was my wedding day and God had given me sunshine and laid a gold carpet at my feet.

Mamma had passed quietly away and lay side by side with Papa. What she had never been able to do in life had happened in death, and she was close to him now for ever and ever.

White Orchard Manor was mine, and Kelvin and I planned to live there for the rest of our lives. He loved the gracious residence as much as I did. He loved the tall gables, and the castle tower with the little attics, and the immense trees like sentinels protecting the manor from the road.

Nothing was to be altered, the roses swinging upon iron chains, the wide herbaceous borders lining the brick paths, and the large weeping willow in the middle of the lawn which Papa had so aptly named Victoria; all would remain as it had been.

Only the hut had been redecorated and turned into a place where we could sit in comfort and see the countryside unfold before us, for, in spite of its shadows and the streaks of fear that lay among them, the hut had been a good friend to us and our affection for it was deep. So we had large windows made to lighten it, and we built a verandah, and we had the roof re-threaded with pale thatch.

Romantically, we had planned to elope. There was no reason for this beyond the fact that we wished it to be so. Rushing hither and thither I packed the same things in the same case; a sad collection of belongings simple and unlovely was my trousseau.

Mrs. Abigail had purchased me a new dress for the occasion, a white muslin with billowing soft skirts, and there was a little straw bonnet to go with it with a bunch of flowers on either side.

It was not, of course, a secret or runaway marriage, for the whole village seemed to know of it almost as soon as the idea entered our minds; so, as I went through the deep forest, I was no longer alone but accompanied by a group of school children strewing flowers all the way.

The air was filled with memories and shadows of things which had been; but they held themselves respectfully in the background and did not intrude upon my happiness. Far away was the sound of a church bell, which had nothing to do with our wedding but was ringing just the same.

When I reached the Squirrel Inn Kelvin was there to meet me. Dark haired and dark eyed, with passion in his face like a gathering storm on a clear day, he took my hand and smiled, and quite suddenly I seemed to walk into his heart and rest there.

"Are you happy, Susan?" he asked.

"Very, very happy, my beloved," I replied, "for am I not marrying the man I have wanted for so long?"

There was a crowd round the doorway of the inn, the choral society, the Abigails and a few neighbours from out of town. Mrs. Trouncer was dressed in a brocade gown which had not seen the light of day since her own wedding. It gave her a queer feeling, so she said, and reminded her of things best left forgotten. It was a gay and merry crowd, and they had all united there in mutual goodwill; even Mr. Snitcher had come from beyond Springfield for no other purpose than to see the fun.

The Abigails stood in a group round their tall and gracious mother. A family to be proud of, one that had never brought trouble or disgrace into her life, and I prayed to God that if ever I was blessed with sons I could have them be as they were.

Silvain Abigail was handsomer and more winning than he had ever been. He was still the wild one of the family, a gay, changeable gambler and still undecided as to what he was going to do. A young gentleman of the moment most elegantly dressed and, so it was said, a frequenter of almost every betting house in the town.

"Alas, my dear," Mrs. Abigail would say wistfully, "I wonder what will become of you when I am gone, for I am the only protector you have, Silvain, from your headstrong escapades."

There was still a certain gravity about Henry, an exactness which seemed to have set its mark upon him. Indeed both in pleasure and in his profession he worked with severe precision and conformed to every rule of this mid-Victorian era. He was a well-grounded solid citizen, an excellent lawyer and unimpeachable friend. Henry could always be relied upon to tell the whole truth and nothing but the truth. Life was one straight road to him, easy to follow because he knew the shadows and the substance of it. He simply could not understand Silvain with his wild waywardness and would remark coldly of him:

"My dear brother is a ticket-of-leave man with no idea on what journey he is travelling."

Shelly was the obscure one, the one whom nobody really knew. On account of his hurried speech and unobtrusiveness he did not mix well with company and lived a life of his own; where, exactly no one quite knew. He was the least good-looking of them all, being pale and loose-skinned, with wide protruding eyes. I suppose in a family of this size there was sure to be one who did not seem to belong in their midst.

Geoffrey had grown into a careworn oppressed-looking man with withered hopes. He had become an artist of no great standing, and dabbled and daubed in a little studio quite close to London's embankment.

"I do a lot in a little way," he said, "but I am no phenomenon. No colours can paint my thoughts or tone my moods; I am, in effect, as I always was, a failure."

Roger had married a London parson's daughter and set up a small medical practice on the outskirts of the town. He was a man of learning, high-browed and intelligent with sterling qualities no doubt, but dull. His wife was a shallow soft-faced woman who was also dull and foolishly inept. She doted upon Roger who seemed to her to be the god of gynaecology without whom no woman could give birth. The suburb where they lived was in her eyes the haven of all healing, and no one was really well unless they had drained to the dregs of Roger's doses and sovereign cures. He had married not so much from desire but because his patients demanded it of him, for it embarrassed them to have a bachelor probing at their ailments. Roger's brothers said of him that he was infinitely more skilful than poor Doctor

Wiffin, which, when you came to think of it, was not saying very much.

Phillip was the genial one, with such a generous nature that people took advantage of him. Mrs. Abigail had given him a farm. Just a small neck of land upon the shoulders of a hill. There he and Incubus would discuss loam and mould and sub-soil, whilst little Miss Gimp to whom he was still engaged would go sniffing round this resourceful property with the smell of cow dung and pigsties in her turned-up nose and a hearty dislike of the whole affair. Her soul was half in the city and half with Phillip, and she was to marry him at the end of the year for better or for worse. When she looked at the hogs and the cattle and the heavy ploughing to be done, she thought it was for worse, but when she gazed into Phillip's warm, kindhearted face, she knew it was for better.

"He treats me well and gives me great comfort," she said fondly, "even if I am no more to him than a chicken or a calf."

The dear, dear Abigails, how much they had meant to me, and I often wondered what my life would have been had they never come to Wingmeadow Lodge.

Mr. and Mrs. Cattlewig had set up a table in the parlour with wine and wedding cake. Even the choral society were merry, their voices happy and their faces wreathed in smiles. Mr. Cattlewig had a white bow in his buttonhole and his wart seemed very prominent upon his nose, whilst Mrs. Cattlewig moved gingerly in a pair of high elastic socks to ease the aching of her varicose veins. The runt was scurrying in and out with glasses and mugs of ale; he was in a new suit with his eyes all aglow and a grin on his face which would not come off.

Fowls scuffled round and about the yard, and somewhere a dog was barking. Kelvin was joking with the ladies and was the life and soul of this strange party. The tittering and talking was tumultuous, everyone was laughing heartily as people do at weddings for no particular reason at all. There was a flushed and boisterous group about the wedding cake, and even the Misses Tinnerlies were dressed up in their best. Their best consisted of what most other women would have considered their worst, with faded silk gowns and dusty moth-eaten bonnets. But this was of no concern to the Misses Tinnerlies who were only too glad to be at the wedding at all.

Mr. Snitcher, no longer judicial or pompous, was thumping Kelvin on the back.

"My boy," he said jovially, "when we get to know one another better I would deem it an honour to have you call me Ted."

"Ted it is now, Sir," replied Kelvin shaking him warmly by the hand.

"This all reminds me of Mr. Trouncer," said Mrs. Trouncer dabbing at her eyes. "The best day we had together should have been our wedding day. Abstemious he was and as sober as a sheep, he wouldn't even drink a drop of water for the fear that it might rouse the grog in him. 'I'll go to the altar undefiled if it costs me my life,' he declared. But his good resolutions went to the wind because I myself was somewhat the worse for wear."

"Not drunk, Mrs. Trouncer?"

"As a fish, Mr. Snitcher."

"Well, well, well," said Mr. Snitcher looking at her curiously. "Whoever would have thought it."

"Obstreperous, that's what I was," continued Mrs. Trouncer, "tweaking the ear of the reverend's good wife herself. By the time I had sobered, so to speak, it was too late, Mr. Trouncer had taken to the bottle."

"A sad story, Mrs. Trouncer, a very sad story indeed if I might say so."

"But one that many a female could tell of a wedding," replied Mrs. Trouncer. "It's the nerves that does it, of having to conjecture what comes after."

Tears poured from her and lodged in a drip at the end of her nose. A trivial occurrence to everyone but myself who knew it so well. It gave me a warm and friendly feeling, this drip of Mrs. Trouncer's; it belonged to me. These people belonged to me, they were the background to my world. Each one of them stepped out of some memory, and each and every one of them had had a part to play throughout the years.

"Incubus," said Mr. Cattlewig, seeing that something was amiss, "fill everyone's glass, for there is to be a toast."

The glasses were charged and they all stood up and turned towards me. Mrs. Abigail raised her arm.

"To the bride," she said.

"And to the groom," said Miss Amelia Pinchbeck archly.

There were to be no speeches, but Mrs. Abigail looked across at me and smiled.

"Bless you, dear Susan," she said fervently, "for the blessed person you are."

"Amen," murmured Mrs. Trouncer, and they all echoed after her, "Amen."

Then Mrs. Abigail turned her head towards Kelvin and the tears fell from her eyes.

"May you enjoy all the happiness you deserve, my dearest son," she said, "and God be with you."

There was a gust of applause and everybody embraced everybody else, some laughing and some weeping. Then amidst more clapping of hands the cake was cut, and Mr. Snitcher took a small slice and wrapping it in paper thrust it into his pocket.

"To sleep on," he said with a prodigious wink, "and to dream of the future Mrs. Snitcher."

The little Misses Tinnerlies also took slices and furtively slipped them into their handkerchiefs.

"Perhaps," they sighed, "you never can tell, can you?" and they smiled at one another as if a new hope had been born in them.

After this it was time for us to take our leave, and with many a handshake and kisses and pattings on the back, we escaped into the stable yard. Josephine was outside already harnessed to the open chaise, and if ever it was possible for a mare to chuckle she was certainly doing so now.

"The old girl is really roused," said Incubus proudly. "It takes a wedding such as this to shake her out of her miseries."

"Dear Incubus . . . Dear Josephine," I cried happily. "How much I love you . . . I love everyone today."

"And so you should, my dear," replied Mr. Mortician gallantly, for he had partaken quite freely of the wine. "I am sure I am right in saying that everyone here loves you."

Kelvin assisted me into the chaise, Mr. Mortician climbed laboriously into his seat and Incubus swung himself up beside him. With a crack of the whip and a cheer from those left behind us, we turned away from the inn into the road.

I leaned back in the chaise to look at Kelvin, to feast my eyes upon the man I loved so well.

"We will never be apart again," I said. "It is you and I now, my dearest dear. The world has stepped aside for us."

Softly he kissed me.

"Just you and I, beloved Susan," he whispered. "Today is our world, we have it all."

And so, as my story ends, my life really only began on that glorious drive to Windsor. We did not go down the road where the tree had fallen but skirted round Wingmeadow Lane with the village behind us.

It was market day in Springfield Town and everyone had driven their cattle to the sale. I saw the boy with his goats walking down the cobblestone street, grown wiser by now and not so wound up with anxiety. There were women with baskets of flowers which Kelvin purchased and dropped into my lap. I longed to call out to them that it was my wedding day, and tell them how happy I was.

We descended High Standing Hill very gingerly and at the slowest of paces for, as Mr. Mortician pointed out, Josephine took an extremely poor view of the shafts digging into her sides, and the loose harness, and the chaise seeming to roll upon her heels. But when we were on the level road again she arched her neck and pricked up her ears and went off at a gallop.

"She's all right now," said Mr. Mortician. "She's in the mood again," and so he laid down his whip and had time to gaze about him and discuss with the runt the condition of the fields, and the hopes of the farmers, and how rain was much needed to feed the crops.

There was a slight wind over the countryside; a cool wind laden with the perfume of meadowsweet and roses, and there was a shimmer of sunshine upon the long white road to Windsor.

Incubus tuned up his little guitar and started to sing.

314